Behind Heaven's Veil,
Part One:
Emergence

Michelle Brown

"Greater love has no one than this, that someone lay down his life for his friends." – John 15:13 ESV

First printing, January 2018

ISBN-13: 978-1976205828
ISBN-10: 1976205824

The characters and events in this book are fictitious. Any similarities to real people are coincidences.

michellebrownauthor@gmail.com

www.facebook.com/MichelleBrownAuthor

www.BehindHeavensVeil.wordpress.com

This book is dedicated to:

my Lord, Who saved my life and gave me one worth living.

my husband, who edited every draft.

my daughters, who taught me a mother's heart.

the many police officers who took me under their wings.

Prologue

The assassin holds the blade against my throat. In seconds that feel like hours, I accept God's will: I'm going to die.

Jesus, please be with Peter. Help him. Heal him. Give his next life meaning. Thank You for the time You gave us.

Chapter One

A dozen tormented women stand before me. Their faces have been cut off. One in particular stands out: She's wearing a red coat while the others are black and white, even their hair.

They fall dead, but my eyes can't leave the last girl in line as her body collapses to the ground, limp and lifeless. Her red coat turns to blood.

Heavy rainfall.

A dark sea, waves crashing and carrying a coffin that sinks in the water, a boulder of burden.

Jesus calms the storm of sorrow that drowns me and He parts the waters. Still tsunamis grow hundreds of feet high as I point to freedom. Masses of people—hundreds, maybe thousands—race through the harrowing tunnel, the herds clamoring in hope and desperation. I can't see their faces as they run away from an evil administration coming from behind me, chasing them. This entity is a government, racing for their targets with spears and bows and arrows. They think I'm one of them, but I'm one of the people they're chasing, one of the citizens they hate.

Upright in bed, everything's moving fast: My chest. My heart. My hands as they race over my biceps, sticky with sweat and tense with stress.

I rip away the covers, heated and moist with perspiration, and wrench off my tank.

A storm is coming.

Father?

Chapter Two

Kaitlyn
Sunday, February 19, 2040
11:48 A.M.

"... It was beautiful and sunny this morning. As you can see in the background, the sky is blackened with smoke and ash." The reporter steps aside and there are people in orange vests digging through a collapsed, smoldering building. "People inside Harvest View Church were holding their Sunday morning service when the explosion happened."

"Mom! Dad!" I shout.

"Few survivors are expected. This is the fifteenth attack on a religious building since the year started two months ago ..."

"What is it, Sweetheart?" Mom hollers from a distant room.

"Our church blew up!" I scream through my stuffy nose and sore throat, the reason we weren't in that building this morning.

Yvonne, sick as well, sits beside me on my bed as we watch the broadcast. She's six. How much does she understand? Does she know the dead bodies are our friends?

"What?" Mom runs into my room with Dad on her heels. Her hands cover her mouth when she sees the SpectScreen, but she makes no noise. I've never seen her this scared. Dad nudges past her, his white face reddening with anger.

Their reactions are bigger than mine. Do they understand more than

I do, like how I see more than Vonnie?

Dad doesn't make a sound as he listens to the reporter. He's always quiet, but this time it's scary. Mom mutters a question, but Dad raises a finger to silence her without taking his eyes off the display. He never treats her this way. He always lets her speak.

"Most of you will recall that another church was bombed last week, taking the lives of one hundred and three Christians. Another ninety-eight were killed the week before that, when gunmen opened fire during service. Both of those attacks happened here in the nation's capital, as this bombing has.

"Attacks on religious individuals have been increasing rapidly nationwide for the last two years, since the Government's Security sector announced Christian extremists were responsible for terrorist attacks that ended thousands of lives in bombings, shootings, and transportation crashes. Security warns that assaults on Believers will increase as vigilantes grow in number. In defense of peace, they are killing Christians before they have a chance to strike. The Government is cautioning civilians to avoid members of religious communities, since none can be trusted. Security believes most of them are armed terrorists."

Workers sort through rubble. Small robots with cameras enter the debris. Bigger robots enter the ruins and return with corpses in their claws.

I focus on Mom. A pretty dress flows over her wide hips and a white sweater hugs her full chest, her black hair barely touching her shoulders. She's normally peppy, and bright clothes add to her personality, but even cheerful colors can't take away this sadness. She eases onto the foot of my bed. I don't think she's breathing.

Dad stands tall beside her, his jaw set and his face hard. The white mole on his left cheek is the only part of him that doesn't change. His shoulders rise with tension. Is this what he would look like in a fight?

Vonnie's nose is red and puffy. Her raven hair is shiny with grease and locked in clumps from the sweat of the fever we can't break. We both need baths but don't have energy. She stares at the screen hypnotized. She doesn't blink. Doesn't swallow. Doesn't move. Is she scared? It's hard to tell because she's a quiet person like Dad. Part of me wonders if I should take her somewhere else so she doesn't see any more of this, but the news catches my attention again, warns me that as terrible as this is, the worst is yet to come.

"Arms have been illegal since the fall of the United States. Security has informed us that terrorists and vigilantes are supplying themselves through the Black Market. Officials are doing all they can to contain the violence, but it's impossible to eradicate underground suppliers.

"We'll be back within the hour with updates on the latest massacre. With CATO News, I'm Alexis Peneda."

The air in the room is heavy as the broadcast changes to mindless programming, what Vonnie and I wanted to watch to forget our colds.

Dad yanks the remote off my bed and shuts down the SpectScreen. His head and shoulders slump forward, like he's trapped under a heavy weight. Mom is slouched on my bed. She isn't moving. I've known Vonnie her whole life, but she's hard to read. An event this powerful should draw out a frown or cocked brow, but she reveals nothing. Maybe it's because of the cold medicine she took an hour ago.

We could've died this morning. If Vonnie and I weren't sick, all four of us would've been in that building. We'd be dead. Did any of our church friends stay home? Did any of them survive? For the first time, I'm thankful for the flu.

Could I be right? It's hard to accept that a cold is why I'm alive. To believe that we made it, but maybe no one else in our church did.

I catch up with the reporter's comment that the Government says Christians are bad people, that we are responsible for the attacks that happened a couple of years ago. We give people money, clothes, and food, even if they don't believe in God. We do favors for others and help them. Why would we hurt anyone? The Government was blaming us before, but now it feels more real. People are murdering Believers and the Government isn't helping.

I don't understand, but Mom and Dad remember several acts of terrorism. Maybe they can explain.

"Dad, what happened?"

"A storm is coming. Get ready." He leaves without giving me or Vonnie a hug or a kiss on the head, very unusual for him. The look on his face . . . He's broken. He ignores Mom as well. Void of a protector, the room turns icy in his absence.

Chapter Three

Victim One
Wednesday, August 26, 2040
8:52 P.M.

Is that the man who asked me out last week? He's coming straight at me, Lord.

I search to and fro, over both shoulders, around corners. Surrounded by blackness, the dark divided by street lamps, the sidewalk is deserted, save for the man rushing toward me. Hands in pockets, his gaze is locked on me as he scarpers through shadows. Nobody drives by, but a few empty cars are parked at the curbs.

Stay calm. This could be a coincidence.

Keep moving. Don't make eye contact.

The black-haired man walks faster and swerves toward me, grabbing my arms.

I pull away, but his grasp tightens and he covers my mouth.

"Don't scream." As his hand comes off my lips, his expression warns against fighting or yelling for help. There is no one around to aid me if I did. Businesses line the road, their windows dark for the night. My apartment building is a block away; the residents inside wouldn't hear me. Even if they did, they couldn't respond in time.

My captor's light blue, almost translucent, eyes are unmistakable. He is the same man.

His grip jerks me, crushing my flesh.

"Why'd you choose Isaiah? Why'd you say no to me, Amy?"

"How do you know my name?"

"All I wanted was a date. I'm better-looking than Isaiah. I'm smarter. Richer."

"You don't love God."

His eyes flicker with hatred. "How would you know? You never asked."

He twists my arm. Shooting pain radiates through my shoulder, but I mask it with clenched teeth.

"God warned me against you the first time we met. If you loved Him, you wouldn't hurt me." Grind my teeth again.

His other hand drifts into a pocket and re-emerges, his thumb pressing on a handle. A razor pops out.

Unblinking, a meek gasp of air is my sole reaction.

"In the car." He motions a half-block away.

His fist presses against my back, hiding the blade. Surveillance is everywhere, but it is dark. Will someone see us? Will the police catch him?

Lord, send someone to stop him.

"Listen—"

"Don't talk."

A hard shove makes me stumble. I regain my balance, only to trip over a stone.

"Watch where you're going," the monster growls in a whisper.

His hand leaves my back with a click. His touch returns. No longer a fist, but an open palm flush against my tailbone as he opens his door.

His ride is red. Who kidnaps somebody in a flashy car?

A shove forces me in the front seat. He slams the door, sits behind the wheel, and drives. Holding the headrest, I face the back of the car. My bedroom window grows and shrinks as we pass it by.

I commune with the Holy Spirit. There are no words; it's a back and forth of emotions with God. I give Him my weaknesses and fears; He replaces them with His strength and courage.

The man pulls into a clearing in a wooded area and slides out of his car, slinking to my side. He opens the door and yanks me toward him, my feet barely keeping me balanced. Terror coats my arms and legs in goose bumps, the cool air sending chills down my spine.

"Let's go."

He guides me from behind into thick trees. Pushes me to the ground. Flips me on my back and hovers over me on all fours. Pulls out his blade. Snaps it open. Staring past him, I focus on the stars. I can't begin to count them, and I marvel that God has named each one.

"God doesn't love you."

The Lord's Spirit softens me as the blade meets my skin. His force is a sudden power, a calm thunder shuddering through my soul. The strength I need in the moment of my death.

My hand wraps around his wrist. With the slightest pressure, I lower his arm and bring the blade off my face. Blood trickles down my cheek.

"You have freewill, the power of choice, the only authority anyone has. You've already decided to kill me."

He brings the razor toward my jaw, but a commanding energy divides us, stilling his hand and moving my lips. Like Daniel in the lions' den, an invisible shield protects me from the man who's waiting to tear apart my flesh.

"But before you do, God wants you to know that He has revealed Himself to you, and He has seen you reject Him. It's not too late to come to Him and know a greater love than you ever have. You have never been alone, and that should both comfort and frighten you. God allowed your wealth and power, and He gave you your beauty, your intelligence, your perceived perfection. He has seen you abuse it all. He is watching you now."

The spell is broken and the blade digs into my flesh.

"You cannot create. You can only destroy."

Another sting in my cheek.

"But nothing you destroy can ruin God's plan."

He backhands my face. My blood coats his hand, almost softening the blow.

"You've locked yourself in hell. Break down the door by asking the

Messiah into your heart."

The hole in my cheek drains blood into my mouth.

"Proof of His existence is everywhere. Open your eyes before you're blind."

He stabs my forehead.

Chapter Four

Peter
Saturday, July 25, 2042
12:36 P.M.

"Mom. Dad. I've been praying about this for a long time. It might shock you—it did me—but I'm certain this is what God wants."

My parents, sitting on the couch to my left, focus on me. Dad's face is calm, contrasting with his stunning green eyes. Mom leans against the armrest, her fingers in her caramel-blond hair graying with age. She's not as frantic as she was in my younger years, but when she does panic it's obvious. Prone to impatience, she's watching me with raised brows.

"He wants me to be a cop."

Sitting on the other side of Mom, Dad beams with pride. He opens his mouth, but Mom speaks first.

"I've got a bad feeling about this, Peter."

Dad gapes at her, the overhead light bouncing off his lemon-yellow hair. "You've got a bad feeling about our son obeying God?"

She turns her attention to Dad. I've witnessed their expressions dozens of times when they've negotiated on various topics.

But there's no compromising with God: We either listen to Him or we don't. I am the only person who decides if I'll follow His will, and I've already committed myself to Him. Dad's defending my choice; I pray Mom accepts this isn't a bargain.

"Of course I want Peter to obey God, but this has to be a mistake. Why would the Lord want Peter protecting this nation? Religion will be illegal soon. He'll be expected to defend immorality. He'll be corrupted or killed."

Dad's rough hand, callused from decades of installing and repairing floors, slides over Mom's lap, his fingers wrapping around hers. "He won't be alone. God is with him."

"You think God would place him with the enemy?"

"He's placed His children with His enemies before."

"When?"

"Moses was raised by Pharaoh's daughter, who knew he was a Hebrew when she adopted him."

My lips part in shock, but I close my mouth before anyone notices. I've told no one about the dream I had two years ago. I can still play it in my mind: the waters parting, the people fleeing, the government pursuing.

"Joseph was sold to slave traders and became a ruler."

Dad must have several examples, because he's counting them on his fingers. Mom notices and, irritated, shuts her eyes.

"There was Esther, who became queen and risked her life to save her people. Then there's—"

Her hand rises. "Okay."

His face hovers inches from hers. She doesn't open her lids as her fingers rustle through her hairline, a habit she resorts to when she's troubled.

"All of them trusted God, even in times of anxiety and doubt. Peter trusts God, too. I can't guarantee our son won't be hurt or . . . killed." His voice cracks, but faintly enough that I might be the only one who noticed. "But God has already prepared for what Peter's future holds. I'm not surprised He's calling our son to this. He follows the Lord, and he's earned God's trust and favor.

"Our job thus far has been molding Peter into the man God wants him to be. Now we encourage him as he leaves home and steps into God's will, and we pray daily for his safety. If every Christian refused to serve God in the Government, how much faster would the corruption grow?"

Dad stares at Mom with a reassuring visage that she can't see behind closed lids as she admits the truth. I invisibly commune with God, recalling the months I spent in prayer over this. Even after my confirmation, unanswered questions remained. I thank the Lord again for giving me amazing parents: I've learned a lot from them, but today I'm grateful for my father, who hears about my calling and has all the answers—despite the fact his only child will be in harm's way.

He wraps his arm around Mom, his thick knuckles arching over her shoulder. He rests his head on hers, bringing his mouth close to her ear. "Know what else they had in common? They delivered His people in times of danger. God is working through our son to accomplish something great, Dianne. Wait."

Mom, her elbow on the armrest and hand on her forehead, rocks her face back and forth in reluctant acceptance.

"Well, you can sit there and worry if you want." He pats her knee, suddenly jovial. "But I'm rejoicing that we did an extraordinary job raising our son and God sees him as a deliverer."

Dad rises and comes toward me with an outstretched hand and a broad smile, an uncommon display of emotion. I stand, placing my palm against his. He pulls me in for a hug and a pat on the back.

"I'm proud of you, Son." He steps back with a grin. "Be safe and stand firm with God. His deliverers are always met with adversity. Hard times are coming."

No evidence of my dream exists outside of my mind; I haven't written or talked about it. I was skeptical that my dream and calling were connected, but hearing my dad speak this truth despite not knowing about my vision that itched with prophecy, I wonder again if the two are connected.

"I look forward to hearing about your calls. You'll have good ones, and you'll have scary ones."

"If this is what God wants, I support you." Mom's voice lacks enthusiasm. "But something is going to rip your heart out, Peter, and I'll be here for you." Small tears collect in her ducts, but if I didn't know her well I wouldn't notice them.

I wrap my arms around her thinning frame. "I know, Mom. I know."

She grips my shirt as if she'll never hold me again. "You bury me; I don't bury you. Okay?"

"Okay," I whisper, her tears saturating my shirt.

"Stay safe, Son. I can't lose my heart."

My gut sinks, imagining the pain she'll endure if I end my final shift in a casket. I remember the coffin on the water, the anguish I felt as it floated on the sea of sorrow. "I love you."

"I love you, too, Peter."

Chapter Five

Victim Two
Saturday, October 11, 2042
11:01 P.M.

"It's hard to believe a guy as good-looking as you isn't taken."

The man with light blue eyes grins at me over the candles burning on the table, though his smile is restrained. He's enigmatic; I can't help but sense he's hiding something, but I keep pushing the feelings at bay. He seems like a nice enough guy. Polite, cordial, punctual, and attractive. Maybe I'm not used to his reserved nature. He's been a gentleman through the entire date: opened every door, pulled out my seat, paid for our meals, even politely reminded the server to refill my soda when she forgot.

"You're quite good-looking yourself."

Unsure what to do, I tuck my hair behind my ear to keep one hand busy. I never realize how still my hands are until I'm nervous.

"Was dinner to your liking?"

"Yes. Thank you." I rub my belly, feeling distended though it appears flat. "I'm ready to go home."

"Let's go then."

He stands beside me and sticks out his elbow. Light shines in his black hair, every strand gelled in place. His skin is unblemished and supple, his scent intoxicating. I wrap my arm around his, admiring his strength as I rise.

As he leads me to his car, I peek at the handsome man I'm arm in arm with. I might have a boyfriend. I turn my grin away and keep most of my joy contained, not wanting my eagerness to scare him off.

In the glow of street lamps, I see couples holding hands as they laugh and enjoy each other. I used to be jealous of them, impatient for a man of my own. I gave my envy to God.

Until two days ago, when I accepted this man's dinner offer without praying about it.

"I like you, Marie. I can see this working out."

I can't shake this horrible hunch in my gut; it's been building the whole night. I made a mistake saying yes to him. Despite that I didn't seek God first, He warned me to cancel. I ignored Him; I didn't want to hurt my date's feelings, and I'm tired of being alone. This man said he's a Christian. I didn't see the harm.

But God told me I have no place with him. Tonight is all there will be. In an effort not to offend this man, I have affronted my God. Every giggle, every smile, every act of flirtation grieves his Spirit more.

My head hangs. *I'm sorry I went outside of Your will, Father. I won't go out with him again.*

"Something wrong?"

I glimpse at him before gazing at more couples laughing on their Saturday night dates. I'm not one of them.

"No."

He shrugs as he escorts me to the passenger's side and opens the door. As he helps me in, he peeps in the backseat and nods.

Twisting my torso to see what's behind me, a rope tightens around my throat until I can't breathe. Can't scream. I tug at the cord. When my efforts fail, my energy comes out in kicks.

The man presses my legs against the leather seat. "Stay quiet."

Nodding against the wire, I give him whatever he wants to stay alive. This man is not a Christian. He's a liar.

He strolls around the car and settles himself behind the wheel. The expression on his face, the way he walks, even the rhythm of his breathing has changed. Everything about him is dark, even his light eyes.

Searching the shadows for some sign of help, I accept God is the only One Who can save me.

Please, God!

I sinned going on this date against His wishes, but do I deserve what's coming?

He drives somewhere secluded and comes to a stop. The cord loosens. I lean forward, but the rope snaps my neck against the seat, the impact burning torn muscles. Eyes closed, I stay flush with the headrest, trying to soothe my predator's impatience until the police arrive. With our nation's surveillance, officers have to be en route.

Abba. Abba. Abba.

My eyes open. Surrounded by blackness, disgust slithers across me like a serpent's skin. Thick trees encompass us, reflecting the headlights and the dim hue of the night sky. There is no one to save me.

The monster stares at me in my peripheral, making no motion. I don't look at him, hoping I'll live longer if I avoid him. That's when I hear the click and the cord falls.

Swallowing hard, my head coils slowly to the side. Half his face blazes in the aqua-hued lights of his dash controls. He smiles, his one visible eye burning with exhilarant hatred. My focus locks on the razor floating in front of his chin.

I scream.

The lights go out.

Blind, a heavy weight presses on my lap as legs straddle my sides. A slap in the cheek. The sting increases and fades to a dull burn. The sensation's familiar, similar to when I've nicked myself shaving, but magnified by a thousand. Warm liquid drips down my jaw, a mixture of tears and blood.

"God doesn't love you."

Is he right? Are You allowing this because I disobeyed You?

Another sting in my temple.

My vision adjusted to darkness, horror glows in the moonlight: The blue-eyed man sitting on my lap. My blood on the blade, burning in the glimmer of stars.

God's Spirit takes control, His courage comforting me as my face is torn off, slice by slice.

My Father showers me with His love as terror shakes my body. He fills me with strength I've never felt as pain scorches through me, blood souring my mouth.

El Shaddai wraps His Spirit around mine, holding me as my body shuts down and prepares for death.

I wince with another sting and stop feeling. Blood gushes down my jaw as he yanks out the blade.

He slices my cheek with a snarl. "God isn't saving you."

"There are two deaths; you can only kill me once. Remember He'll forgive you if you truly repent, but you will die twice without His salvation."

I smack blood in my mouth, push it through my lips, let it flow down my chin. He right hooks me. Filled with God's Spirit, I'm immune to pain as a bone cracks in the impact.

Watching my blood splatter, I wonder how Jesus felt when he was tortured for me, when His blood spilled at His lashing. Was Christ frightened? This Force I taste, this Spirit causing me to feel compassion for the man murdering me, is this what Christ felt? Did this Spirit move Him to show mercy for those who harmed Him? Is this why New Testament martyrs prophesied that they would feel joy when they were executed for Christ? Because they knew their bodies would never feel stronger than when they were dying for Jesus? Because they'd be alive with God's Spirit, filled with His fortitude? Jesus said whoever relinquishes their life for Him will find it. The Spirit flooding through me grants me power. In the hour of my death, I have never felt more alive.

"Deny God, and I'll let you live."

"I love Jesus."

"Say you fear my power, and you'll see tomorrow."

"I will see tomorrow because I fear God."

He stabs my forehead.

Chapter Six

Peter
Tuesday, May 19, 2043
10:29 P.M.

My belt and gear collapse on the desk as I slump into my chair. Exhausted, I scratch my head, glad this shift is over halfway finished. I open a drawer and grab a SimLink—a hand-held, satellite-operated computer that enables communications and regulates most aspects of life, including media, entertainment, and calendars. Nearly every citizen owns one, but those enlisted for Security personnel are more advanced: Depending on the clearance level of the official logging in, they can access the System to search citizens' financial, tax, education, employment, medical, criminal, and traffic records. See who's connected to whom and how they're related. With every camera in the world accessible, complete with facial and gait recognition, the Government can track anyone, anywhere. Learn their routines. Spy on them. The Government has these mobile computers littered throughout their property, and they supply police officers with SimLinks in their desks, uniforms, and squad cars.

With the press of a button, two holographic screens pop out of shatterproof glass, glowing purple at the borders. A blank screen waits for my command as the control panel hovers parallel to the ground. Swiping left, I tap on the icon displaying my Security login and enter clearance codes to catch up on today's caseload.

Law enforcement wears on me. Months into my job, it's astounding how much I've seen. Neglected children. Beaten families. Sex-trafficked women. Overdosed teenagers. A man murdered in a gang initiation. Officers who served fifty years ago encountered these cases on rarer occasions, but these crimes become more common as society grows increasingly depraved. I'm thankful I moved into my own place before I graduated academy; it's nice to have a quiet home where I can rest in solitude and process my thoughts after a dark day.

It's harder to trust others, especially those I don't know. Behind ordinary doors live extraordinary evils. Tracking down and arresting criminals takes from my own sense of innocence; it astonishes me how much law enforcement forces me to rely on God more than I ever have before. When I started this work, I thought I would grow closer to God by standing for the law, but now I see I'm drawing closer to Him because I could lose sight of His morals if all I cared about were the laws of men.

In the last few months, I've met twenty-year cops. Viewing them through God's eyes, I see glimpses of who they were before they joined the force. Now joy is harder to come by. Most cope through humor, but a few relieve stress through addictions. Seeing wickedness, and being responsible for ending it, forces every officer to change. I am a different man than I was a year ago. I can no longer hide behind the idyllic walls of my former life.

Dad's right about meeting adversity; every deliverer in Scripture endured calamity. Those calls were heart-wrenching and I'll never get used to them, but if they aren't the danger I'm meant to deliver people from, then they're practice. Moses spent forty years in the desert before he was ready to re-enter Egypt and rescue God's people. I'm sure much transpired in those four decades to prepare him for his mission. If these horrendous calls are my preparation, I cringe to think what the hardship might be. Will it be those faceless women I saw three years ago?

Evil is everywhere, and it's nothing new: Terrorism grew more violent during the first decades of the twenty-first century, and the

United States passed harsher laws to combat evil. Security turned stricter at public venues, and police became stronger nationwide. Laws tightened as terrorism escalated, until the Government announced the end of the United States. They could no longer trust their people; they never know who's a terrorist or an innocent civilian. Even today's blameless citizens could be tomorrow's threat.

With the constitution out of the way, privacy and warrants exterminated, New America was free to impose the fiercest surveillance system ever developed and monitor every citizen. The Government placed their capital, Imperia, at the southern-most point of the mainland, where their close proximity to the equator granted them firmer control over satellites, rockets, and missiles.

It was believed that uniting state, county, and city justice systems into one entity and combining all intelligence under one umbrella would make the nation stronger. Massive terrorist attacks wouldn't happen. The new Government merged all military and law enforcement agencies together and called it Security; the network encompasses city beat cops like me to the highest officials working various criminal investigations: sex offenses, terrorism, child crimes, gangs, drug rings, serial killings, and technical and financial crimes. There are over thirty classifications, and they overlap on many cases. Security works with allies worldwide to protect our nation's interests. In New America, everyone is guilty until proven innocent.

Five years ago, an array of terrorist attacks crippled the nation, destroying thousands of families in less than a week. The Government pointed the finger at Christians and claimed we were responsible for the havoc and were the latest terrorist threat to New America.

Violence had been mainstream for so long that citizens viewed the latest acts of carnage while drinking their coffee before heading to work, but the attacks that Christians supposedly engineered were bloodier and more extreme than normal shootings and explosions. They were massacres, taking thousands of lives. Rounds were fired at games, shopping centers, and parks. Bombs took out bridges and detonated in cars. Hacked aircrafts crashed into malls. Trains soared off their tracks. Stoplights were seized, and millions of wrecks occurred when every traffic light in the nation went green.

People lost their sense of safety in travelling. If they made it to their destination, would a bus or plane find them? A shooter? A bomb?

Christians have been daily targets of hate crimes since. Before becoming a cop, I watched the news, witnessed the aftermath that unfolded every time a church was bombed or a congregation was slaughtered by an armed madman. Now I respond to several calls a week for brothers and sisters in Christ needing protection. Sometimes the leads are idle threats; other times they're fulfilled promises: Christian charities have exploded, break-ins have resulted in the torture of Believers, and parishioners have been massacred during worship services. The hardest part is that every time I think I've seen it all, I confront something worse.

Those who aren't hateful of Christians are at least growing suspicious of us. Even Christians are wondering about one another, but we're not behind the terrorism; no faithful Christian I know would do that. Maybe someone's framing us, like a religious extremist group is using us as cover.

Regardless, fear has flooded the streets since those attacks. People dreaded dying in explosions, public shootings, or collapsing bridges. Some were so frightened to leave their homes they lost their jobs.

Wanting to end religious-backed terrorism, vigilantes swarmed the Black Market for guns and ammo, made their own bombs, and armed themselves with knives. They've been killing Christians since. They consider it patriotism, believing they're protecting their country from the next brand of terrorism.

Christians are afraid to share their faith, terrified anyone could kill them: family, friends, even former congregation members. It won't be long until religion's illegal.

I'm still reconciling that God called me to work for the Government, and in law enforcement of all things. Despite my dream and an assurance of Christ's hand over me, I'm scared. Will I someday have to arrest another Believer or announce my faith and die? It's easier to pray for help than to be the help. Maybe I'm wrong. About the dream. About my calling.

But God must've placed me here: It was supernatural that the Government hired me—an obvious, church-going, God-fearing man—when they suspect we're terrorists.

I flick through my SimLink's screens, entering information, closing files, and transmitting records to courts and superiors as I mentally talk with God.

Father, I don't understand what I'm doing here. Am I searching for girls with no faces? Are there other Believers who need help? What's Your plan? I see it all from the wrong end.

God nudges me with His answer, but it doesn't make sense.

I'll be an Exodus?

An incoming call covers the screen as it chimes and flashes, interrupting my prayer.

"Officer Tryndale."

A man with blond hair and a white mole on his left cheek stares at me. "Hi. I'm Stanley Reed, calling with New American Securities. We're investigating the disappearance of our client's employee, Melissa Black."

I minimize his image to a small box in the bottom corner and log into the System's citizen registry. "What's her ID number?"

"542981-0302."

My SimLink glows and dims as it loads Ms. Black's profile.

"She hasn't been at work in two days, and there's no one to check on her. She doesn't have any family or friends within four hundred miles; she's only been here a couple of months."

System Error

"Her boss doesn't think Ms. Black is the type to abandon her job. Also, the owner claims she thought she saw Ms. Black in the parking lot Sunday morning before her shift was supposed to start, but she didn't make it into the bakery.

"The employer contacted us to investigate the situation, including the possibility that Ms. Black was up to something, but the owner suspects she was kidnapped.

"I'm inclined to agree. My company installed their equipment and monitors its surveillance. All day Sunday, the day Ms. Black vanished, our cameras in their parking lot are blacked out. At midnight Monday morning, they're working again. My crew called me in to check it out, and I can say with certainty that our hardware and software haven't experienced any issues. This glitch has to be connected to Ms. Black's disappearance."

I try pulling her up for yesterday and today; I receive more system error messages. This isn't right: If she left home or used her SimLink, I should be able to find her. Even if she didn't leave her residence or use her SimLink, there shouldn't be an error message. I've never seen one in previous missing person cases.

"Is there any evidence she arrived at the bakery? Was her car there?"

"No. Ms. Black always walks."

"How certain is the employer that she saw Ms. Black?"

"Fairly positive. She said she could've sworn she saw her standing next to a car and talking to the driver, but her view wasn't the best. You may want to speak with the bakery staff yourself."

"I will," I state, balking at the system error message. "Give me a few and I'll call you back."

He hangs up and I dig further.

Ms. Black's a gymnast. Twenty-one years old. Works part-time in an old-fashioned bakery. Everything seems normal until she disappears from the System late Saturday night. She's last seen on camera entering her residence, followed by activity on her SimLink. After midnight, nothing. Searching for her in the System results in a system error message. Using surveillance feeds and records in the System, I investigate everyone she knows: family, friends, former classmates, and ex-boyfriends—all of whom live far away. I examine her co-workers and fellow gymnasts. I scrutinize the woman who reported her disappearance to Mr. Reed, and I inspect him, too. It's a common ploy for felons to report their own crimes, believing it will make them less of a suspect.

Everyone is clean, including Mr. Reed and the bakery employees. Every person has an alibi, and no one has a motive for abducting her. Rifling through neighboring surveillance, I study cars and pedestrians that passed by the bakery on Sunday, but nothing stands out.

I search for other people who disappeared without explanation. It takes time to weed through everyone who's missing from Imperia, but there are others who have vanished with error messages identical to Ms. Black's: Amy Pikes. Marie Tinsel. Betsy Martin. Are they the women from my dream?

My gut sinks; I'm on the trail of a serial kidnapper.

Lord, which girl is the woman in red? What does she represent?

Maybe she has yet to come.

If the number of women in my dream was prophetic, the hunt will be long. Twelve died, and so far there are only four.

Lord, where do I start?

His Spirit warns me to keep Mr. Reed away from this.

He answers my call quickly.

"Hi, Mr. Reed. Officer Tryndale here."

"Did you find anything?"

"You said the cameras on your end went black?"

"Yeah."

"You didn't see any computer coding? Messages? Anything?"

"No," he shrugs. "Just blackness."

"Okay. I appreciate you contacting me, but I need you to steer clear of this. It's a high-level investigation. I'll work with the bakery from this point, and give me your word you'll drop it."

"Sure." His voice falls. "Is there anything else I can do to help?"

"Just stay far away from it. I'll contact you if I need assistance. If you do your own investigation, I'll be paying you a visit."

"No." His brows press together, as if he's offended that I'd doubt his compliance. That's the assurance I wanted. "I won't. You have my word."

"Good. Thank you for reporting Ms. Black. I got it from here."

We disconnect and I survey the evidence.

Victims are between nineteen and thirty-nine when they're captured. Each of them attended a different church, and their faith cannot be a coincidence since churchgoers are rare these days. These women didn't have any family or close friends nearby. There was no one to search for them. They hadn't built relationships at their churches, either because they went unnoticed or hadn't attended long enough to forge bonds. If not for Ms. Black's work ethic, she probably wouldn't have been reported, either.

While the women have different appearances, they're all beautiful. They're in the System leading ordinary lives until they vanish, and all that remains is the black screen reading "System Error" in white letters. We can't find other missing persons after they disappear because there's no documented activity, but they don't have error messages attached to their profiles. Somebody tampered with these women's records.

The attacks are sporadic; I can't identify a pattern that will indicate who the kidnapper will snatch next or when or where they will strike. I'll have to research each victim and everyone they know. Identify potential witnesses. Visit the victims' frequented locations and where they were last seen. Follow paths they likely travelled on the days they were abducted.

Two points are certain: First, the perp is in Imperia. Second, they possess high authority—or someone powerful is protecting them—if they're choosing Christians with no close contacts, removing them from the System, and leaving behind error messages. This can't be a hacker; the System contains the thickest walls of encryption imaginable. It's so self-protective that when someone tries breaking into it, it locks their device and sends orders for the cyber attacker's arrest or execution, depending on how big of a threat they are.

It might be difficult to find the perp, but I must stop them before they take another life.

Police work is where the prophecy begins.

Father, like in the dream, part the waters. Help me free the women.

Every life counts. The clock is ticking.

Chapter Seven

Victim Five
Tuesday, November 8, 2044
9:56 P.M.

I've been in front of the snack machine for so long I'm fixed on my reflection, not the food. Spacey from the longest English test I've ever endured, my weakness shows: My loose copper hair is tossed to the side in knots, bags devour my lids, and every muscle is limp. I need a snack with lots of sugar. Buy two and save one for later.

Every thought feels choppy, disjointed. Flickering lights grate on my last nerve; I must be desperate for food and rest if something that stupid is annoying me.

"That was horrid."

Someone sounding equally fatigued materializes beside me. I didn't hear him approach, but the college is quiet and built to insulate against noise. The feature comes in handy during tests, though sometimes it's so silent it's hard to fight sleep. Grogginess takes over as questions blur in front of me.

The gorgeous man has soft, clean-shaven skin. He's strong, but his build is subtle, a trait I admire in a man. His eyes are a startling shade of blue, almost see-through, contrasting with his black hair.

I glance at my wedding rings. Why am I wearing them? I left my husband two months ago after he had another close call. He used to tell me when temptation struck, but last September I overheard his inappropriate conversation with another woman and left. He told me he hadn't been unfaithful—yet—but he's flirted with so many women I told him I was through and packed my bags.

David knows that if he seeks help and puts his life together, I'll come back. But I'm not placing my future on hold while I wait for him to change, a possibility that may never happen. So I moved five hundred miles away to Imperia and enrolled in college for a fresh start. Part of me wants to hurt him back. Rip his heart open like he ripped mine.

He messaged me last night; he's sorry and he's gone through hours of counseling as well as acquiring help from our pastor. He loves me and wants me home. Is that enough? But he cheated on me in his heart. I'm within my rights to have a new man, and this guy looks good.

God's Spirit rumbles through my heart, quaking my soul like the ground before a volcano's eruption. He cautions me against acting on this impulse, but I shut Him out and focus on the handsome man.

"Longest exam ever," he sighs.

"You, too?"

His smile lights a fire inside of me. "What class were you in?"

My breath sputters; I'm so centered on his beauty I'm forgetting about air. "English. You?"

"Anthropology."

"That's my major."

Though it's a field most find boring, he doesn't seem surprised. "Can you tutor me? I need to get my grades up."

"Sure. I'll give you my number."

I recall the better times I shared with David: Sight-seeing around the nation. Ice fishing up north. Hiking a mountain. Kayaking a raging river, laughing as we made it to shore and realizing we almost didn't survive the crash. I swallow my love for my husband, quell it with God's Spirit as He warns me I'm heading into danger.

The handsome man wraps his fingers around mine. Gawking at our clasped grip, I grow feverish with desire. I remember, and promptly forget, the times David held me. The moment we shared at the altar, hand in hand.

He licks his lips, one corner tucked upward, as our eyes meet. He pulls me through a short corridor and into an empty study room, locking the door behind us. Energy floods through me, drowning my guilt as his strong arms draw me closer.

Weak in his iron grasp, I'm shocked when my voice roars out of me: "*Stop!*" Awakened with God's power, I shove him with a strength I don't possess; I notice my action as he gains his balance against the door, his chest and arms flexed in his tight, short-sleeved shirt.

"What's wrong?" He isn't alarmed. His calming smile matches his suave countenance, as if he'll talk me into this.

Fixed on the tempter, all I see is Christ on the cross. He died for what my husband did, and He died for what I have done. I forgive my husband. I'll pray about whether I should return to him, about whether he's changed. I'll pray that he forgives me, too. Love covers a multitude of sins, bears all things, and endures all things. I love David.

"I'm married."

"No one has to know." His words flow out sweet as honey, but reek of hell. He travels a couple of steps closer, smirking. The stench of his perversion floats through the air and makes me sick.

I'm sorry, Lord. Please forgive me.

"I'll know."

My hand twists the knob. The door opens a crack and he pushes it closed, his body uncomfortably close to mine.

"Where are you going?"

Eyes burning with scorn, I stare him down. "Home. To my husband."

"But didn't he cheat on you?"

My heart stops as I discern he's more than a tempter: He's a hunter.

"How do you know that?"

"I have my ways."

"Then you should also know he stopped himself, so he didn't really cheat." How could he know from five hundred miles away?

"But the pain is just as strong either way, right?" Still barricading my escape, he brushes his other hand across my cheek. I squirm away, but he blocks me with a raised knee.

Father, help!

His lips trace my earlobe as he whispers: "I can make you feel good. Your relationship with David is over. He'll never change—you know that. It will never be the same. I'm a better man. I can make you feel the greatest pleasure you'll ever know. Don't you want to feel real pleasure? Just once? It can be our secret."

He kisses my ear, his lips gravitating toward my neck as my temper flares.

"There are no secrets from God. Now let me go."

I pull the knob. He lowers his knee and yanks my hand off the lever, anchoring my wrists to the wall. He leans his body against mine, his mouth descending for a kiss. My knee swings between his legs and crushes his groin.

"*Let me go! Now!*" I hope my shriek hurt his ears as much as my knee hurt his core.

Torso hunched from the blow, he straightens his spine as he cranes his face toward mine. I gasp when I see his ice blue eyes are on fire. He looks older, darker—as if his true soul has been exposed.

He growls like a rabid wolf, baring his fangs as he backhands me. I crash to the ground, the hard floor bringing my momentum to an abrupt halt. Farther from the door and further from freedom, my eyes creep against the headache of my concussion to see his hand dart in and out of his pants pocket. A blade pops out with the press of a button.

I scream, unsure if it's a delayed reaction from his strike or fear of his razor.

He grabs my hair. "You're quiet or you're dead. To the back parking lot. Now."

Lifting me by the scalp, he places the blade against my back and shoves me out the door.

Chapter Eight

Peter
Monday, February 13, 2045
1:11 A.M.

Due to a string of robberies and break-ins, I've been lapping the city's business district, watching for suspicious activity. On rare occasions, I catch a criminal in the act. Like the teenager who punched his grandma on the sidewalk. I witnessed it as I drove around a corner. Exited my car and gave chase when he ran. He spun around with a knife and I stunned him. He lay on his back, covered in sweat and vomit, whimpering until medics arrived. I transported him to jail after they assessed him.

Some calls are entertaining, like the woman who reported smelling a drug lab in her apartment building. We arrived and discovered the fumes were from bathroom cleaner she had forgotten she'd used.

But despite the job's funny moments, police work is far from easy. It's one of the hardest careers. It's a lifestyle I can't shut off. Even when I'm off-duty, I find myself searching for what civilians don't notice or won't approach: A busted side door. A suspicious package. Somebody lurking in a closed business or an abandoned house. An addict shooting up. My rule of thumb in life: If I look twice, there's a reason.

City lights glare on my windshield and reflect off puddles bouncing in the night's downpour. Almost every window is black, the businesses closed while people are at home resting. Rain pounds the car's roof; crisp air filters through the cracked window, droplets trickling through and chilling my arm.

I reflect on my first days as a cop, how everyone told me they worried about me. Family. Friends. Buddies at church. Though I understood their apprehension, I didn't share their anxiety. Everyone dies someday. I'm more afraid of dying a slow death, bedridden with some painful disease eating away at my body. I'd rather go down saving someone.

I comfort those who care about me by explaining I'm armed and well-trained. Somebody has to do this job to keep them safe. I have days of self-doubt and shifts when I make bad choices and wonder if I'm meant to do this. I comfort myself by remembering that my Creator led me to this profession. He knows me better than I know myself; if He says I can do this job, I can.

Only those who love me are able to let go and support me in my decision to do what God's asking: Be a cop. Put myself on the line to save others. God guides me through every dangerous situation.

Security had me shadow a cop for a few days to ensure I knew what I was signing up for. He warned me at the end: "Think hard before you take this job. It's one of the few careers where sometimes your only goal is to make it home alive."

I didn't have to think long; God told me to do this, and He paved the way.

I'm not sure why I don't respond how most would to the dangers of law enforcement, but I suspect it has to do with my dream. God's granting me courage. He's molding me into the cop He wants to rescue the girls.

But fear is no stranger. It sneaks up on me in dangerous situations; sometimes it drowns me. All officers feel afraid now and then. We're fortunate if we can describe the horrors we witness to those we love most, and words still fail, but I've never felt safer than when I'm following God, wherever He leads. In this case, donning the uniform.

My cruiser hugs a corner as my mind drifts to the missing girls. I've been hunting for them for two years, waiting for the sea to part so I can point to freedom. I spend most of my time off-duty chipping away on leads, free of the distractions and interruptions that come with work. My biggest issue is civilians seeing my uniform and approaching me for help or with questions. Sometimes they want to chat, as if I don't have priorities. Consequently, I prefer wearing civvies, but interviews are more successful when I dress the part.

The cases that happened before I joined the force are so cold they're frozen, and my search for Ms. Black didn't prove fruitful. I need fresh evidence, but I'll only find it if I catch the perp in the act or right after a kidnapping.

It's old-fashioned, but a map of Imperia hangs in my home office. Even if no one knew the girls well enough to report their disappearances, I figured people had to notice when they stopped showing up for school, work, or church. I found classmates, co-workers, and parishioners who recognized their pictures. Their memories were fuzzy, but I obtained a few details. They might be unreliable, but it's a starting point. I stuck tacks on the map marking the victims' last known locations, attaching them with strings to their photos and notes with their names and other vital information.

The points are few and scrambled. With no rhyme or reason, I can't determine a method or pattern. System error messages begin on various days, making me think they're nabbed at different points through the week. Sometimes they're abducted months apart, sometimes years. They're diverse races and builds. The common denominator: They're gorgeous Christian women with no one nearby to notice when they're missing, but I'll need more than that to figure out who the perp is or whom they'll steal next.

I want to believe the girls are holed up somewhere, maybe trapped in slavery or locked in a basement, but alive. My gut tells me they've been killed. Every girl is six feet under or out to sea.

Out to sea. All the women falling dead. The coffin sinking in the sea of sorrow.

The anguish of the stormy waters in my dream returns, the turmoil impossible to express in words.

Three months ago I pinned another tack on the map: Desiree Swanson. That was when my investigation took a twist. The System's automated dispatch reported her to me—and *only* me—but didn't list the source. Who declared her missing? The System won't even reveal if she was reported by an anonymous tipster.

Mrs. Swanson moved to Imperia in September and vanished six weeks later. She had no local friends or family. Her husband lives five hundred miles away; his transgressions were the reason she moved here. I contacted him, but he had nothing new to share. At least he was forthcoming about his infidelities. I can trust he's honest, at least to a point. He claimed he still loves her, and his tears seemed genuine. I can't imagine what it would feel like to lose your wife to this monster, not knowing what she experienced in her final moments. What she felt. Thought. Suffered. Begged for.

This victim was twenty-four years old and studying anthropology. Like the four before her, she disappeared from the System on the day of the attack. I spent my days off pursuing her, and my quest turned stranger: Her car was nowhere to be found. It wasn't at her school or home, and the System couldn't find it on any cameras or pinpoint its tracker. Did the perp tamper with surveillance feeds? The tracking system?

A search inside Mrs. Swanson's home came back empty. I visited the places she did in the weeks before she was captured, and I traced routes she likely would've travelled from home to school, but to no avail. Teachers said she arrived to class and left as usual, but when I logged into the System, a black screen beeped and read "System Error." I logged into the university feeds and saw blackness. The school said their surveillance system had a glitch, and their recordings from that day had vanished. Wanting to protect staff and students, I didn't tell them the truth.

Supposing the perp might've known Mrs. Swanson, I re-explored every aspect of her life and scrutinized every person, including those far away. No one had motive to harm her, and everyone who is linked to her has an alibi in the System. I suspected her husband; perhaps he wanted out of the marriage? I dug on him as deep as I could, and nothing contradicted my instincts: He's clean. I researched the women he'd flirted with in case one of them knocked her off, but they're innocent. Most thought he was single. Last time I checked, he has assumed his wife is dead. He is grieving and has no females in his life now.

I've done all I can. I hope she's not dead yet, that I'll stumble upon her and return her to someone who loves her.

Who is the perp? Too many Government Officials have access to the System. An official bent on hiding crime wouldn't need long to learn how to manipulate the System. Only an official could, given the strength of the System's automated protection. Maybe the person possesses the resources to debase or bribe someone else in power to control the System for them. A criminal could be threatening, blackmailing, or exploiting an official. The possibilities are overwhelming. I have to believe every clue is driving me closer to solving the mystery, bringing the criminal to justice, and saving the ladies of the future. It will happen someday: God assured me I would be an Exodus. Seconds later, I received the call that led me to the missing women, and my doubt about why He directed me to this profession lifted. He must have me here to rescue them.

My concentration breaks when the SimLink on my dash makes a noise I've never heard before. There, in the strangest font, is an address.

4290 E. DOCK WAY

That's around the corner. Is the perp there? Goosebumps prickle my spine as the screen flickers and turns black.

Crawling around the bend, I pray for God's protection as shrieks pierce through my window. Somebody in the distance forces a girl into a car's backseat and sprints behind the wheel.

My foot smashes the accelerator as the driver bolts. I pull up the System's surveillance feeds of the street as I race down the lane, my eyes shifting between the SimLink's holographic display and the road ahead. If they are the perp, they haven't deleted her yet. The System shows her profile: *Valirie Adams. D.O.B. March 11, 2022. Citizen ID number: 789124-8880. Residence: 2140 W. Stratemore Avenue.*

Speeding after them, I study footage of the attack that happened seconds ago, recording it for evidence I can analyze later. Are the waters parting?

Rain and darkness make the picture hazy, but I watch the vehicle stop beside her as she strolls along the sidewalk. She shakes her head at the driver and scurries away. They move closer and park. She screams and runs. He exits his vehicle and races after her. The System labels him as an unidentifiable citizen, a listing I've never seen, but I can see enough of the attacker's form to conclude he's male. He's fast and bear hugs her from behind. She kicks and flails when he muffles her mouth, gripping her to his chest as he carries her to his car. He opens the door and shoves her in the backseat. She's screeching and fighting as he shuts the door. He rushes to the driver's seat as my headlights slink over them. It's too dark to read a plate or distinguish the make or model. I don't recognize the brake lights; they must be custom. The System can't identify the car or locate a tracker inside of it. It can't—or won't—follow it.

His car is impossibly fast, leaving my cruiser in the dust. With my pedal flushed against the floorboard, his taillights wane smaller until they disappear.

I come to a split in the road, slowing as I wonder which way he went. Are there abandoned buildings nearby? An empty field? A river? The ocean? Where is he taking her?

There are too many options in three directions. I don't request backup; if he is the perp, I have to suspect any officer could be his reinforcement. After a few minutes of creeping and rifling through traffic cams, the System emits its familiar, obnoxious noise and displays two words driving me crazy:

System Error

My fist pounds the wheel when the System goes blank. Valirie was erased, and my recording is gone with her.

Chapter Nine

Peter
Saturday, March 18, 2045
11:19 P.M.

Flames reach into the black sky, a three-foot-tall brick wall surrounding the blaze. It burns fifteen feet wide. Three feet long. A conveyer belt extends twenty feet from the fire, protecting the crowd from the heat.

On one side, the side I stand on, is power and pride. But I belong on the other, filled with oppression and fear.

This is the Burning. Since Muslims have taken countless lives in terrorist acts and Christians were supposedly behind the chaos that happened seven years ago, the Government is declaring every faith illegal, claiming religion is the source of extremism. Atheism and science are all that remains. With the abolishment of dogma, vigilantes are expected to stop using violence to prevent future radicalism.

Citizens woke in the middle of last night to screeching sirens as armored tanks, military jets, and drones traveled over every street in the nation, announcing the end of religious freedom. SimLinks and SpectScreens blared warning sirens, the ordinance written on their displays. Now Security is conducting bonfires in every city, and the Government has mandated that disciples of every creed bring their sacred materials and surrender them for destruction. The Government has deleted all religious digital media.

Thousands of blazes torch the land: Those who despise God ravish the country, burning churches and looting religious charities. Thus far, two arsons have started wildfires growing across the Southeast and West Coast. I wonder what our nation looks like from God's view.

Hundreds of Believers are lined up, approaching the fire in pairs. Some hold hands. A few wear masks to protect against respiratory issues, and many sob as they clutch their Bibles and spiritual texts for the final time. Papers, notes, and bookmarks poke through the edges, containing secrets, anxieties, problems, and promises of each Believer's life. My teeth grind as hundreds of Believers of various beliefs—two at a time—throw their cherished keepsakes on the belt and their hope along with them. They cry out as their mementos drop into the blaze.

I should be on that side, but there's a bigger picture. God's called me to be an Exodus. Like Moses, I'm a stranger in a strange land. It feels wrong not speaking up, but I'm staying for God. It's for the victims of the past and the missing ladies of the future that I stay quiet, remain on the force, stand in front of this fire. I am the person who will take down the perp. I'm not sure who sent me the address when Ms. Adams was kidnapped. Maybe the perp was baiting me, or perhaps someone on the inside was tipping me off. Either way, the dream showed me pointing masses of people to safety. God will lead me there.

To my left and right, two hundred feet away, police barricade the perimeter as haters of God celebrate the occasion, yelling obscenities and throwing rocks at tormented Believers. Some have snuck Molotov cocktails into other burn sites, though not here. Intoxicated women dance on the shoulders of strong men. People get high while others curse God, stomping on Bibles and throwing the demolished heaps of paper at the foot of the blaze.

Hands on my belt and face calloused, I stand with the police, forming a line behind the fire. The officers wear sneers smoldering like evil in the darkness, same as the blaze devouring the physical remnants of God's existence. They drink and laugh and jeer with contempt, mocking Believers who shed tears of sorrow as they say goodbye to their gods and pray their forfeitures into the flames. Officers spit in the fire, reveling even more.

God, this feels wrong. Am I sinning, standing on the enemy's side doing nothing? I want to change sides.

Maybe I'm risking my salvation to save the girls.

What am I supposed to do, Jesus? I can't deny You; I'll never lose my trust in You. Please, tell me what to do. Order me to change sides. Command me to suffer the persecution my brothers and sisters face.

God is silent. My guilt gives way to anger that boils within. I fight to contain it beneath the surface.

Stay neutral. You still have your faith, Peter. Not every Christian is giving in and giving up. God wants you to be a soldier in His army; He's chosen you to serve in Security. The Burning doesn't mean everyone's losing their conviction. It doesn't mean all of humanity is evil.

A pair of Muslim women approach the inferno, removing their headdresses and tossing them onto the belt; their raven hair shines in the fire's unnerving glow. Flames dance as they consume the fabric that had protected their modesty. One woman cowers with humiliation as she exposes herself to the world. Full of shame, as if she feels naked. The other is confident, prideful to reveal her beauty to the world. Perhaps she's pleased to be equal with men, no longer held back by worshippers of a false god. That was the Government's second reason for illegalizing doctrine: Morality infringes on equality.

No officers have asked if I'm a Christian. They assume I'm like them, despite how different I am. But I'll keep choosing God. That is my freewill. If they inquire, I'll say the truth; Christ is my salvation. They might figure it out: Actions speak louder than words.

The ruler of this world can threaten me with death; I will not abandon my Bible, my hope, or my God.

Ceramics bust, the sound sending daggers through the souls of Believers. They mourn as flames consume their belongings and the Government steals their faith. Glass breaks. Paper incinerates. Gold and silver soften. Their remains tinge the air I breathe, and it smells like defeat.

Chapter Ten

Kaitlyn
Sunday, March 19, 2045
2:03 A.M.

Dad is pacing the house, snatching one Christian artifact after another and cramming them in boxes.

He closes one container and carries it to the dining room, setting it on top of the others, all of them full. He hasn't looked this grim since we lost our church.

It's a scary day for New America: Faith is illegal. Punishable by death.

Almost twenty-four hours ago, we heard the yelp of sirens. We walked to the street, where armored tanks crept past and military jets and drones hovered miles overhead. We heard the announcement, witnessed the horror on our neighbors' faces that mirrored our own, and went back inside; our SimLinks were blasting militaristic alarms, the Government's warning repeated on their screens.

Mom was shocked, Vonnie was frightened, and Dad was angry. We stayed home and eventually succumbed to sleep, only to be wakened hours ago by the smell of burning Bibles, books, and decorations from the bonfire down the road.

We followed the smoke outside, its stench searing our nostrils, eyes, and throats as a strange glow flickered in the sky. Haunting laughter of

God's enemies echoed down the eerie, dark avenue as we journeyed to the end of our driveway. Believers cried as they shuffled away from the fire empty-handed. Pedestrians stumbled by in drunken stupors, tripping over a man shooting up on the sidewalk. We tried remaining calm as Dad rushed us inside and barricaded our doors, his eyes wide and jaw set. Yvonne hid in her closet and Mom shook on the couch while Dad started packing every object that could betray us. He's been stuffing boxes at a frantic pace since.

No one knows yet, but I was expecting this. The night before the proclamation, God told me freedom of religion was over—then He asked me to work in Security's counter-terrorism sector. He warned me that the Government will brand all religion as terrorism, but He will guard me from pursuing people of faith.

He gave me a promise: If I enlist in Security, He will work through me to save someone close. I don't know who it will be, but rescuing them will fulfill the yearning to shield others from evil that has lived in my heart since my church family was slaughtered.

My father panicking, my mom and sister too stunned to speak, I know none of them are prepared to hear my destiny. I'll tell them when God says they're ready.

God, please give Dad courage. Don't let him fall down that black hole again.

He strides through the living room and up three steps, pausing on the landing.

My heart falls as he reaches for the canvases that Mom decorated when Vonnie was a baby. She painted four smaller canvases in our favorite colors and wrote Bible verses prophesying over each of us. In the center hangs a big, gold canvas with our family creed. They greet me every morning as I come down the stairs, remind me of the person I want to be, and I'll miss them.

Dad grabs his first. I don't think he sees the irony: His prophecy was that he would be our defender, and that he would rest in God's supernatural safety. He piles the canvases in his arms and totes them to an empty box a few feet away from me.

He saunters to the living room. I stop breathing as he stands on the couch, removing the large wooden cross hanging between two glass panes.

"What are you doing?"

"Protecting us." He doesn't turn toward me, doesn't give an expression, doesn't seem to notice much of what or who is around him.

My palms flip up. "From what?"

"The Government." He carries the crucifix past me and sets it on the boxes next to the table.

I can only pray that he's hiding our belongings, not destroying them.

"We're not supposed to fear anyone but God."

Dad's anger is more intense than I expected. "I'm not losing you! I'm not losing Vonnie! I'm not losing Lorraine!" He points at us one by one, his reddened face contrasting with his yellow hair.

Our wills battle through locked gazes as Mom and Vonnie stare from the side.

"Dad, I love you. I don't want to lose you, either. But protection is never gained through cowardice. If you need help, God will provide. Where's your faith?"

His eyes fall to the side as he takes a breath.

"We have to follow Him and stick together this time. We can't retreat into bubbles of fear like we did when we lost our church. The Government can make it illegal to believe in God, but He's still here. They can kill us, but they can't kill Him. Last time they tried, He rose again—"

"I'm not losing you!" He yells, pausing to steady his voice. "Decorations don't make us Christians; it's the belief in our hearts."

"That's true, but you're packing them out of fear. If the Burning hadn't happened—"

"There might be raids, Kaitlyn! The Government could kick down our door any minute, tear this place inside out, and shoot us if they find one thing. One thing!" He shoves his index finger in my face, the air rumbling with his shouts.

He treads closer, hand outstretched. "It's time you stopped wearing that cross."

I clutch the gold pendant to my chest. "No. M—"

"Kaitlyn—"

"Mom gave it to me to remember Jesus and the importance of keeping my body holy for God and waiting for marriage. My relationship with God hasn't changed, and I refuse to allow the Government to dictate how I express my faith. I'm not quitting. God's out there, and so is the man He made for me. A man after His heart."

"If one person sees it on you—"

"I'll hide it under my shirt, but I'm not getting rid of it."

"Kaitlyn," Dad's voice booms as he takes another step forward.

"Listen," I whisper, rubbing his arms. "I don't think we've argued like this before, but if you make me choose between you and God, I choose God. I trust Him with my life."

"You're being naïve."

"Faith is simple."

Blank of emotion, he shakes his head.

"Sometimes believing and trusting is hard, but it's simple. I'd rather wait on God than spend the rest of my life regretting that I didn't."

Dad's torso sinks, his head hanging as he collapses on a chair. He rests his forehead on his arms folded over the table, his arched back rising and caving. Mom, Vonnie, and I totter toward him, but I have a hard time registering what I'm witnessing: Dad's crying.

I deny it as long as I can, until shudders ripple through his strong body and he groans in sorrow: "I can't watch you guys die!"

We lean over him, wrapping him in our embrace as he trembles.

"I'll die for God, but I can't lose any of you."

His tears hit the table.

Chapter Eleven

Victim Eight
Monday, June 18, 2046
11:09 A.M.

Lord, I need this job. I've been cleaning houses my whole life for next to nothing and I've barely scraped by. This opening pays as much as Government work. Please, Jesus, grant me this one favor.

The white house is mounted in front of the morning sky, a beautiful yet rare tinge of pink and blue. Brown trim and roofing are scarcely visible in the brightness surrounding it. Taking this job would mean leaving my sister. I impulsively flew to Imperia, telling her I wanted a chance for a job that paid what I was worth. If I'm hired, I'm staying here. Hillary can either join me or stay where she is. She's angry, but I need a new life.

I swallow my nerves and cross the street.

God's Spirit warns me to stop; His presence is a flicker flashing into a flood, paralyzing me in the empty road.

Standing on the dividing lines, I peer left and right.

Jesus, I lost my job last week and spent most of my savings on this trip. How will I eat?

His voice, so quiet it's easy not to hear in the clamor of the busy world, reminds me not to worry about what I'll eat, drink, or wear. He loves me more than the birds, and He provides for them. He'll take care of me, too.

I trust You, Lord.

Turning my back on the residence that's offering a huge salary is painful, but my Lord is worth more than the finest gold. In an act of faith, I journey back to my rental car. The sun's radiance bounces off the sea green door, blinding me as I grasp the handle.

"Excuse me."

I twirl around and face the man who possesses the sweet voice, soft and smooth as velvet.

His hair is black as night, seemingly absorbing the morning rays. His eyes are shocking, a shade of blue so light I can almost see into him.

"You look like the girl we were going to interview. You're at the right place."

"How did you know what I looked like?"

"There was a photo in your portfolio."

I rub my forehead, wiping away embarrassment. Tiny slip-ups that normally wouldn't bother me become atrocities when I'm in need.

"Do you want to come inside and talk?"

God told me not to enter, and He must have a good reason. This guy is beautiful; if I spend hours a day with him in his home, I might fall into temptation.

"No. Thank you. I changed my mind." My door pops open as I pull the handle.

"We baked cinnamon rolls for you."

Cinnamon rolls? My tongue digs the remains of my morning donut from between my teeth, maple sweetness dissolving on my taste buds and awakening my desire for sweets.

Good pay. Cinnamon rolls. This guy must like me if he ran out here to avoid missing me. Maybe this was a test, similar to when Abraham took Isaac up the mountain. Once God saw I was willing to sacrifice the position, He sent the homeowner to stop me as He sent His angel to stop Abraham.

Pain tugs at my heart like an anchor tied to my soul. I'm misusing Scripture and abusing God's holy words. He wants me out of here. No negotiating.

"No. Thank you."

God tells me to hurry into the car and lock it, so I do. I mentally slap my forehead as the blue-eyed man reaches through the open window with a quizzical look. He brushes his fingertips over my forearm, and his touch is soothing. A wave of comfort washes away my panic.

"Is something wrong? I was looking forward to meeting you. Your experience is impressive. You're the only person we're interviewing."

I squint in the sun rising over his shoulder. "Really?"

"Yeah. I already decided to hire you if we get along. But my roommate." He sighs and rolls his eyes. "He wants me to interview you first. I bought the cinnamon rolls to soften him up."

He chuckles, and I catch myself laughing, too.

"Do you like cinnamon rolls?"

I smile with the fantasy of satisfying my sweet tooth.

"Please, come inside and have a couple. If you don't want the job, there's no obligation. But it does pay well. A person of your pedigree and experience deserves this money."

He's right. I've earned this. I've been scrubbing toilets and tubs for over a decade, and for what? It's time I tasted the fruits of my labor. With this much money, I can help others who are poor.

"Alright."

The corners of his lips spread to his ears as I exit the vehicle. His teeth are perfect. He leads me across the street, and I'm breaking into a sweat as the day's humidity builds. I blow out a deep breath, thankful for the respite I'll soon receive.

He pushes the door open and the refreshing smell of cinnamon sweeps over me. I savor the aroma as I follow him into the serene living room, where the air is cool and clean. Pillows rest on couches. Artwork hangs on walls. Plush carpet gives way beneath my feet. Sunlight illuminates rooms.

A man with light brown, shoulder-length hair waits on the larger couch facing the front window. I sit on the loveseat opposing him as the guy who greeted me vanishes into another room; its yellow light makes me assume it's the kitchen. Disgust rushes through me as I notice the roommate's evil expression. He's tall, halfway between lanky and well-built, but strong enough to overpower me.

I rub my neck, feeling fidgety with the need to escape. But running away might hurt the nice guy's feelings. If they offer me the job, I can speak with him alone and find a way to clean while his roommate's gone.

The blue-eyed man peeks around the corner with a glowing smile. "What would you like to drink?"

"Tea, please."

He darts out of sight and re-emerges with a large platter of rolls and three mugs of tea. Two cups are a creamy, off-white color; the other is blue. He hands me the mismatched serving and saunters back to the kitchen, returning with a stack of small plates. He gives me one; I set my tea on the table before placing a treat on the dish and taking a nibble.

"So," the blue-eyed man sits on the couch next to his roommate, reclining with a sigh as he hoists his mug to his mouth. "What got you into cleaning homes?"

It's difficult to speak; I first have to break my gaze off the roommate's penetrating glare.

"It was easy money when I started living on my own."

The blue-eyed man chuckles. "The promise that we can be anything when we grow up is quite the lie, isn't it?"

My head tilts at the insult. "What do you mean?"

"We're told as children we can do anything we want, but a quadriplegic can't walk on the moon."

I set the plate on my lap, grabbing my drink and sipping the warm liquid, minty and well-sweetened. "We can do anything we're meant to do."

If believing in God wasn't illegal, I'd explain how He knows the choices every individual will make, sees everyone's fate, understands how we're all intertwined—and He doesn't allow any circumstance to prevent someone from doing what He's designed them to do.

"Fair enough."

The creepy roommate's stare has intensified; he is the danger God was protecting me from. I should walk away from my disobedience.

"Thank you for your time and hospitality. I don't think this will work out." I take another sip of tea. As I lower my cup, my hand feels heavy, then my whole body thickens like a rock. My vision blurs, and the roommate's grinning at me. He grows two faces . . . three . . . They dance like a kaleidoscope.

I rub away perspiration, but for every drop of sweat I remove, three more bleed out of my pores.

Ceramics clank as I set my dessert and tea on the table. I stand, intending to hide inside my vehicle. The heat will be blistering, but I can send for the police.

Barely able to keep my balance, I fight to extend my foot a few inches.

Darkness surrounds me as I collapse.

Chapter Twelve

This is failure: There's no closure and the perp's still out there, stealing women. Contacting remote, sometimes estranged, relatives and notifying them that their loved one has vanished.

Every time I can't find a girl, the earth swallows another body. Three years, no solid leads. Will the waters ever part?

How much longer, Father? This is—

I choose my next words with care.

Forgive my impatience. I need Your wisdom. Please help me save these ladies. Give me strength to tell another person she likely won't see her loved one again.

God led the Hebrews out of Egypt by a pillar. It changed from a cloud during the day to fire at night; He never took it away so the Hebrews would always recognize their path. No doubt they stopped for rest—they were human—but they must've kept their breaks short. God is available to us twenty-four-seven. To have the closest possible walk with Him, we have to diligently seek Him. In addition to travelling at a constant pace, healthy Hebrews carried the sick. Parents shouldered their children. Their freedom came at great cost to their bodies. Likewise, I work hard with every opportunity—day and night—to bring the women of Imperia to safety.

The mission is taxing, and every girl since Mrs. Swanson has been reported to me alone—and I am never given the source of the information.

Another female went missing on Monday: Trinity Lee. Thirty-one years old. I spoke with her sister who said she flew here for an interview for a good-paying housecleaning position, but Hillary doesn't know where it was, other than at a house located somewhere within Imperia.

Like the victims before her, Ms. Lee's footprint in the System disappeared the day she did. System error messages beep at me every time I peek at surveillance feeds.

Ms. Lee lived hundreds of miles away and had no residence or vehicle in Imperia. Her flight arrived in the early morning on the day she was taken, so she likely hadn't rented a hotel room; I couldn't find one in the System, nor did I find a rental car. With the odds against me, I attempted to find a lead through someone she knew. They all live far away, but I examined everyone in Ms. Lee's circle. Everyone was clean. Her sister was the closest person to her, so I followed her in the System for weeks leading up to the abduction and the day after. Analyzed her financial records. Read and listened to all her communications. She isn't involved, and no one in her circle has links to Imperia.

I've scoured every housecleaning ad posted in the last two months. Crossed off ones that didn't match—openings filled over two weeks before Ms. Lee disappeared, positions that paid too little for Ms. Lee to consider—and investigated the remaining leads. Made inquiries at homes and businesses that had interviewed cleaners. Combed through every homeowner and exec who had posted an ad. All of them were clean, honest people. Full of alibis, absent of motives.

How do I find Ms. Lee, Father? How do I find any of them?

I tried, again, to establish a pattern. The closest I've come to catching the perp was when he took Ms. Adams and I was there immediately afterward. Time was short—he deleted her fast—but Ms. Adams and I had hope for a few fleeting moments. If I can detect a pattern and be there in time, I can end this hunt.

Ms. Adams was yanked off a sidewalk; were they all nabbed dramatically? If so, why haven't witnesses stepped forward? The perp must've sent the address, and he made Ms. Adams' kidnapping obvious because he was expecting me. He's allowing me to search the System for him.

The only common denominators I can spot are the victims' beauty, faith, and isolation, but striking women are everywhere, and it's difficult to count how many girls are Christians now that religion is illegal. I'd have to sift through millions of women between nineteen and thirty-nine who are in Imperia, highlight the most beautiful of them, and cross-reference which of them are solitary and used to attend church. There could be thousands, especially if the perp imports another woman from out of town, like he did Ms. Lee. I can't protect them all. How can I predict whom he'll choose next?

Though still in uniform, I'm without my patrol vehicle; only K-9 officers are allowed to keep their units off-duty. Instead, I sit in my truck, lacking the protection of bullet resistant glass but regaining elevation. I can see more of my surroundings from this height. I wonder how much I miss in the police car, my view blocked by fences, signs, shrubs, and other vehicles.

Rubbing the bridge of my nose, I'm exhausted from a long night of patrol and atrocious calls. Some nights are slow and give me a good chance to catch up on reports from wild shifts, the kind that send me into prayer and keep me talking with God for days or even weeks. Like last night. Domestic violence—a woman's eyeball nearly popped out of its socket. Bomb threat—a false alarm and easy arrest. Knife fight—claimed one life. The killer and victim were young: seventeen and sixteen years old. As the sun peeks over the horizon, I'm glad that shift is over.

Watching dawn break, I pointlessly try to relax as I sit idle on the side of the road. The day has barely begun, but it looks like it'll be another warm day. Birds chirp as if it's peaceful. It's not. Not for Ms. Lee or her sister or me.

I ready myself to call Hillary, but nothing can fully prepare me.

A small voice whispers that it's not too late to skip out and avoid this awkward, painful moment.

My human nature breeds selfishness, and I hate it. I aspire to live for Christ, not myself, yet my hands ache to grab the wheel and drive home. Shrugging off the cowardice, I force myself to grab my SimLink. Fatigue is weakening my grip; I haven't slept or eaten in over twenty-four hours. I started Monday night with a notice that Ms. Lee was missing, and I've spent every free second searching for her. I wipe tiredness from my eyes in an effort to appear strong.

I smooth down my uniform and make the call. It's early, but Hillary's expecting me.

An unnatural blonde, over an inch of her light brown roots have grown out. Her hair's tangled. One eye winces closed as she focuses on me. She hasn't been sleeping long: Her lids are red and puffy from grieving.

Clutching her blue satin robe tighter, her face falls.

"Hillary, I have bad news."

"No! No!" She covers her nose and mouth as tears well in her ducts. "You found her?"

"No. That's the problem. The trail went cold."

"Then you haven't searched hard enough! If you haven't found her, she's still out there!" She points to her window, her eyes widening with rage. The finger of her balled fist turns to me. "You're not done!"

She drops her hand, irritated and desperate for the response she desires.

"You're right; I'm not done, but there isn't much else I can do."

"Yes, there is!"

Father, please give me patience.

The Lord infuses me with a wave of peace. "I've dug through surveillance, gone through every ad, followed every lead. Unless you have more information, all I can do now is keep my eyes open."

She shakes her head and cries. Helplessness cripples me as her tears fall. She has to feel powerless; her only choice is to trust me, a complete stranger. Maybe she pleads with God, if she believes in Him. I hold a sneaking suspicion that most people pray when tragedy hits, even atheists. Calamity reminds us how frail and human we are, and we instinctively reach out for something bigger and stronger.

"I'm sorry for your loss. If you think of anything else, contact me."

Her teeth draw blood from her bottom lip as tears gush down. She hangs up, her sobs echoing in my ears moments longer.

I lean back on the headrest, unsure of what else to do. I need help, and there's no one I can trust. The perp is a tracker. He stalks his prey, and he's gathered that I'm searching for him and his victims. He might know I'm a Christian, too. For some reason, he hasn't taken action against me yet, but he will if I threaten his cover by asking for support.

He could be anybody: A co-worker. A high-ranking official. An out-sourced Government contractor. Someone I walk by every day. He could be a person I haven't met. Anyone could be his accomplice. I trust no one.

But putting my life on the line is worth it to save the women. Like my father said, God's deliverers endure hardship. Joseph, Moses, and Esther faced death, but under God's protection they survived and saved His people. God has called me to a great service, and losing my life is part of the risk.

God, I can't do this on my own. I trust You; You gave me the dream before the first woman was taken. You've placed me here, but I can't solve this without Your wisdom. I am blind: I can't identify when he'll strike again, and I can't see whom he'll hurt next. But You, God, You know it all. I'm not sure why You're allowing this, but I trust You. Give me sight. Give me a helper.

Chapter Thirteen

Peter
Thursday, February 14, 2047
1:16 P.M.

Today's been a good day. Not many stressful calls, and I'm spending the next couple of hours at a university educating future Security Officials and giving interviews.

Sun peeks through sparse trees and shines on grassy knolls as I park my cruiser in the lot. I approach the brick building, and my uniform attracts the usual attention. A group of girls stands on the lawn, leaning their faces together and giggling at me.

The entrance slides open at my approach. Daylight floods through vast windows, brightening the lobby as I step inside. Guys passing by do a double take as I enter the elevator.

When the doors part, I saunter down the hall until I find the right classroom. I've never done this, but other officers told me this teacher loves hosting cops. I'm eager to set a good example for future law enforcement.

A weight falls on me as I walk in the room; I skim over the students and notice *her*. A beautiful blonde in the front row. Button nose. Heart-shaped lips. Hot pink shirt, black skirt and heels. My heart is pulled to her like gravity. I freeze for a few seconds, watching her read. Her legs, shimmering in nylons, are crossed at her ankles and tucked under her chair. Her knees wobble side to side, the weight of her legs teetering back and forth on her tiptoes pressed against the carpet. Her rosy cheek is balled over the fist holding the weight of her head. A tiny tendril of yellow hair hangs outside her messy bun; the lock billows in her breath.

I try taking my eyes off her, but I can't. She's different from other girls. Modestly dressed, the hem of her skirt touches the bottom of her knees. Her clothes are flattering but not tight. She emits a sense of well-placed confidence. She seems pure, trustworthy.

"Officer Tryndale, the floor is yours."

I thank the teacher, but I can hardly speak. I can't miss what's happening: The cute girl is looking at me for the first time.

Her expression changes as our eyes lock. She wears her emotions, and I recognize every transient feeling washing over her because I felt them, too: The shallow breathing of awe, and the mouth hanging partway open in gratitude to God. The lightheaded, floating sensation of love—no longer belonging to the world as an individual, but finding a more complete definition in another soul created by the Lord.

I've never felt this way before. I smile at her, and her mouth turns upward as she bites her lower lip.

Lord, is she the one I've been waiting for?

A deep breath gives me the will to break my gaze away.

After introducing myself, I give the class a basic idea of what police do. The job is about protecting and serving. We do more than issue citations, hunt terrorists, and arrest criminals; we help stranded individuals, find missing persons, break up fights, and protect people and property.

Don't look at the blonde. You can't be distracted in front of forty people.

"How often do you deal with terrorism?" A guy in the back asks.

"Security catches at least one terrorist daily. I deal with terrorism about once a week, but some weeks are busier than others."

"So the Christians didn't stop?"

It's difficult to contain my knee-jerk reaction. We aren't the problem, and our God is the cure. Believers are framed for crimes they don't commit, put on trial for what others have done, and—in some instances—killed in someone else's stead.

The blonde cringes with the same emotions I feel, a mixture of hurt and sadness. Maybe what's different about her is that she's a Christian, too? Meeting other followers of Christ is rare. It's hard to say how many there are, considering the consequence of faith is a potential death sentence.

"Terrorists will never stop. We take one down, two more rise."

That much is true. While it's noble and necessary to thwart them, it's naïve to believe we'll eradicate extremism. But I won't argue Christianity's merits with this guy, even if I wasn't in front of a crowd. He's convinced of the Government's claims, and he'll report anyone he suspects is a Believer. God tells me when to share my faith, and He isn't giving me the urge.

"How effective is surveillance in protecting the nation?" Another student inquires.

"It's powerful, but we have to be careful we don't take things out of context. We'll never see every aspect of someone's life, so we have to keep in mind there are numerous explanations for everything we witness. We don't make judgments based on one or two occurrences; we search for sound, consistent patterns. I will never abuse my authority. I don't snoop in anyone's life unless necessary, and I only dig as deep as needed."

The blonde catches my attention again. I gather the strength to keep myself neutral in spite of the energy burning in her eyes. I don't need four dozen people thinking the cop is crushing on a girl in the front row.

God, this woman is beautiful. I don't like jumping to conclusions, but watching her is like beholding my destiny. My heart's growing and making room for her. She feels like my future wife, the future mother of my children. The person I can grow old with.

I see pretty girls every day, and I've felt attracted to a few. But none compares to her. She's the first person to strike me to the core, like I need her.

More questions come, and I answer them while obsessively thinking about her. When class ends, I announce that I'm staying to meet one-on-one with anyone who's interested. I hope she doesn't leave without seeing me.

Ten students flock to line. The blonde resumes reading at her desk. She rises as I help the last person, clasping her hands behind her back as she waits behind him. He leaves, and the blonde and I are alone with the teacher who's in the opposite corner, sitting at her desk and out of earshot.

"Hi." I reach out and introduce myself, a formality I didn't give previous students. "I'm Peter—Officer Tryndale."

About a foot shorter than I, she extends her hand and steps toward me, but stumbles over her own feet.

"Whoa!"

Leaning left, my arm wraps around her. Tiny fingers clutch the loose folds of my uniform sleeve. I notice how light she is as I help her regain her balance.

She giggles off her embarrassment and sticks out her hand like nothing happened. Her eyes are an elegant shade of milky brown, and she's so radiant that experiencing her presence is a blessing, even if these moments are all I'll have.

"Kaitlyn."

I smile as she slips a lock of hair behind her ear. I met her seconds ago, and already there's nothing I won't do for her.

My attention makes her anxious. Every thought, every emotion, is written on her face.

Our hands meet, and hers is fragile in my strong grasp. She doesn't let go when I do.

I grin at her fingers wrapped around my hand. "Ummm . . ."

"Oh!" She pulls away, leaving my palm moist with her perspiration as she wipes her hand on her skirt.

I stifle another laugh. Her clumsiness and nervousness make her cuter. I think I love her, or could easily. She is so different than I, yet it feels like we're cut from the same mold—as if she's the other half to balance me out.

"What can I do for you, Miss . . .?"

"Reed. But, please, call me Kaitlyn."

"Kaitlyn." The sweet taste of her name broadens my smile as I say it for the first time.

She beams, tucking the stray lock of hair behind her ear again. It must be her nervous tic. "I was wondering if I can shadow an officer? It will make my future job easier."

"Sure. We can schedule a ride-along."

Silence lingers as I imagine having her, full of beauty and dignity, at my side for an entire shift.

Her lower lip hangs. "We?"

"Mm-hmm." The corners of my mouth still hovering at my ears, I place my hands on my belt. "So when are you joining Security?"

"In a couple of years, after I graduate."

"We could use someone like you on our team."

A coy smile crosses her face, her weight shifting. She laughs softly, her breath blowing her loose tresses.

Maybe the teacher's not as far away as I thought, or perhaps body language is giving us away, because she's peeping over Kaitlyn's shoulder with a perceptive grin. When our eyes meet, she snickers and leaves the room, giving Kaitlyn and me privacy.

Kaitlyn rocks to her other foot, glancing away with a bashful expression as she sweeps her hair back.

Excitement pulses through me as I admire her pink cheeks, smooth skin, perfect lips, the delicate curve of her jaw giving way to her tender throat, and streaks of light shining like gold in her hair. My heart is racing and pounding in my chest. Standing in her presence, I'm more alive than ever. I can't let this woman go.

She clears her throat, like she's about to speak, but doesn't. It's only to break the newest awkward silence. She doesn't want to leave me, either, but doesn't know what to say or do next. She watches the floor. Hesitating.

"Kaitlyn?"

Her wide eyes dart up to mine. It's then I realize my voice changed. I'm not talking like a cop anymore; my voice carries the same tenderness it held when I said her name for the first time.

My heart beats faster. She's the first girl I've met who's honorable enough to consider trusting. "Would you like to go out tomorrow? Coffee, maybe?"

Her face lengthens with shock. She reminds me of a child waking to a table topped with presents. "With you?"

"Yeah. That's the idea."

Her eyes grow so big I think she'll lose her balance; she grins and makes a noise, but I can't make it out.

"Yes?" I confirm, squinting with confusion but balancing it with a smile.

"Yes!" She gushes, like she's been holding her breath. Her lips part into a magnificent beam revealing perfect teeth. "Yes, I'd like that. A lot, actually." She closes her eyes and shakes her head as she remembers something. "But I want you to meet my dad first."

She must be a Christian. How many girls her age screen dates through their fathers?

"Sure. Can you give me his number?"

She pops with overwhelming surprise as her happiness returns, smoothing over her shock. She steps back to her desk, pulling pen and paper out of her black purse.

Kaitlyn's spirit is so captivating my heart grows more. She glows as her pen glides along the paper; she lifts it away, double-checking what she wrote before handing it to me with the widest smile she's worn yet.

I peek at the note. Her handwriting is smooth and feminine, but not quite cursive.

"I gave you my number, too, but Dad will be upset if you don't call him first."

"Rightfully so. I'll contact him as soon as I have a chance. I'm off work at five as long as no calls delay me." The corners of my lips rise higher, and her grin grows brighter, too.

We can't take our eyes off each other. She's so beautiful it will hurt to leave.

She points over her shoulder. "I, ummm . . . I have another class to get to if I'm going to graduate." Her knees buckle, expressing her necessity to leave. But the way she straightens her spine and peers at me through her lashes, I can tell she wants to stay with me.

I remember work. I'm on Security's time, so I can't spend my day staring at her. "Yeah. I have patrol, but I'll see you tomorrow?"

She nods eagerly, her beam almost blinding. I follow her to her next class. Even the way she walks is stunning. Everything about her is beautiful.

Today is the first day of the rest of my life.

Chapter Fourteen

Peter
Thursday, February 14, 2047
5:58 P.M.

I stop on the porch for a quick prayer. I've mediated hostage negotiations with more ease than this. I shouldn't be nervous: My intentions with Kaitlyn are godly. There's no reason to fear Mr. Reed; I'll take good care of his daughter. Maybe I'm anxious because I hope they're Christians, yet I'm standing on their porch in my police uniform because he asked me to arrive at six, leaving me with no time to change.

Or maybe it's because we've met before, and I'm not sure how he'll react.

My finger presses the button, chiming the bell inside. A broad-shouldered male about my height answers. He's dressed in a burgundy, buttoned-down top tucked into dark blue jeans, a black belt hugging his waist. I recognize his swept-back yellow hair and the white mole on his left cheek: He's the man who called four years ago to report Melissa Black missing.

Mr. Reed balks.

"Peter?"

I stick out my hand. "Yes, Sir."

He searches me head to toe. "You're a cop?" Fear trickles through his voice. He seems like a law-abiding citizen. If he's afraid, and he doesn't recall our conversation, it strengthens my suspicion that they're Christians.

"Yes, Sir. But I'm one of the good guys." I hope he breaks my code.

Brows pressed over the bridge of his nose, his head rises and drops. He peers at the hand I haven't lowered, shaking it before pulling the door open. "Come in."

I enter the foyer and spot a pair of lime green sneakers resting on the granite tile. The laces are tied and the soles are starting to peel off. They're small, maybe Kaitlyn's?

"Don't bother," he interrupts when I bend over to untie my laces. "Those boots are a pain."

"You've worn them?"

"No, but I had a buddy that did."

Mr. Reed leads me past a staircase to our left and into his living room, motioning toward a recliner in front of his fireplace. I take my seat facing the adjoining dining room while he sits on the couch to my right. Vast windows, separated by a three-foot wall, stand behind him. The Reeds have no SpectScreens. Most Believers, I included, threw them out after the Burning, afraid the technology might betray them to the Government. It's further evidence that they might be Christians, but many people don't have SpectScreens because it's more convenient to enjoy entertainment on SimLinks.

My vision shifts around the living and dining areas, searching for more clues. Their surroundings appear ordinary: a large clock, two black hands ticking over a white marble background. A tall plant sitting in the back corner of their dining room. A box of tissues resting on the coffee table. Blankets folded over the couch. Then I notice a blemish on the wall behind Mr. Reed. It's vague—only a keen eye would catch it—but from my angle, a patchy silhouette of a large cross is visible. They must've had a crucifix hanging between the windows for years, took it down after the Burning, and the grime around it left a minute stain.

"So you want to date my daughter?"

"Yes, Sir."

I don't think he remembers me. It's possible he calls the police so often we all look alike, but I could never forget the person who led me to the trail of missing women. In a city of eleven million people, what are the odds his daughter would be the first woman I'd want to date?

He crosses his wrists over his knees, his sharp focus narrowing on me.

I appreciate that he's shielding his daughter. I see too many dads who don't care about their children at any age. What would Kaitlyn be like if her father didn't guard her? Would she be kind? Alive? Being police, I know the difference a protective parent makes in a child's life.

Mr. Reed studies me for seconds that feel like eons.

"Call me Stanley. What are your intentions?" Though his scrutiny is polite, he's not smiling.

"I've never dated anyone, so it's difficult to answer your question. I thought I would start with taking her to coffee and learning about her."

His chin juts forward. "How old are you?"

"Twenty-three."

The tables have turned: Four years ago, I was the one in authority, commanding him to leave Ms. Black alone. Now he's in charge, deciding whether I'm safe for his daughter.

He reaches behind his head as he reclines in the leather giving way beneath his weight. His brows bunch into a knob. "And you've never gone on a date?"

"No."

"Hmm. Why not?"

"I've been waiting for someone special. Kaitlyn is the first lady I've asked out."

He grins with restraint as I call his daughter a lady, though I said it out of respect and not to win over her father.

Silence lingers as we stare at each other. He analyzes me with a small smile while I gawk idly. Normally, I'm fine with quiet, but all I can do is wonder what he wants me to say next.

A short woman enters. Her onyx hair touches her shoulders. A dark skirt lightened with a floral pattern flows from her hips; a loose white shirt falls around her torso. She must be Kaitlyn's mother, but I am going on assumption: Kaitlyn is undeniably Stanley's daughter, but her similarities with this woman are few.

She sits next to Stanley with a cup in her hand, raising it to her lips and slurping its contents. She doesn't seem alarmed that a cop is sitting in her living room.

"Well, Lorraine, Peter here is a twenty-three-year-old cop who's never dated before and wants to take our Kaitlyn out to coffee tomorrow. What do you think?"

She grins at Stanley and me as she lowers her drink to her lap. "Well, I like the boy. But it's up to you, Dear."

His hands rustle through his hair. "I like him, too." Our eyes lock, and his expression is stern. "But there are rules."

"Absolutely."

"If you break them, you're answering to me. A badge and gun won't stop me from defending my daughter."

"Good. My feelings for Kaitlyn are noble. Hold me accountable. If I overstep my bounds, let me know. I'll make it right."

He squints with confusion, as if I'm too good to be true.

"May I make the first rule?"

His perplexity grows.

"I vowed long ago to wait for marriage."

He sinks deeper into his couch, stunned either with my forwardness or that he's met a man who's not having sex.

"Kaitlyn is safe with me. I will protect her from every threat."

Stanley's hands are stuck in his hair, his eyes wide. Lorraine's frozen with her mug halfway to her mouth, her lips parted about an inch. I think they're forgetting to breathe.

Silence continues for a while, but I'm no longer uncomfortable: I've said what I needed to say and my intentions are clear.

Stanley leans forward, clasping his hands with a smile. "Well, I'm sold." He watches his wife. "Lorraine?"

She sets her drink on her lap, licking her lips as she finishes swallowing a sip. "I like him even more." She takes another mouthful.

I blow out a silent sigh of relief when he steps toward me with an outstretched hand. "Have her home by six tomorrow evening."

Standing and shaking his hand, I agree. "Not a problem, Sir—"

"Stanley."

"Stanley." I repeat, my voice changing awkwardly with the lack of formality. "I start a shift at five tomorrow, so I'll have her home by four-thirty."

He pats me on the shoulder with a grin. "Sounds good."

Following him back to the foyer, he scrutinizes me with a tilted gaze. "I can't help but think you look familiar. Have we met?"

"Yep. You contacted me once."

He waves a pointed finger. "The girl at the bakery . . . Melissa Black."

"Mm-hmm."

"Boy," he smirks, patting my shoulder with a shrug. "The tables sure turned, huh?"

"I was thinking that." I chuckle, hoping the reminder won't prompt him to ask questions. I checked on him for a while after our initial encounter, and he kept his word—he never searched for Ms. Black or more information. I'm thankful he obeyed. Given the authority the perp has shown, his life could've been in danger. I'm glad I listened to God: When He told me to protect him, He was commanding me to protect Kaitlyn's father.

"If you don't mind me asking, what happened to her?"

"I can't comment on open investigations."

He slumps forward, so slight it's barely noticeable, and cringes. "Sorry."

"Are those Kaitlyn's?" I point to the green, worn-out shoes.

"Yep." His barreled chest rises and caves with a sigh. "She needs a new pair."

"When's her birthday?"

He gives me a knowing smile, his emerald eyes shining brighter. "Next month."

Chapter Fifteen

Peter
Friday, February 15, 2047
11:19 A.M.

Spoons clang against ceramic mugs as Kaitlyn and I stir our coffee, the steam rising between our faces. The aroma of pastries mixes in the air as patrons hustle by the doors on the opposite side of the coffee shop; the nearest person is over thirty feet away. We sit in opposing booths, taking turns stealing affectionate glances at each other. Neither of us says a word. I can't speak because my entire being is caught up in one thought: *She's beautiful.* More than in my memories of yesterday.

Our tension is uneasy. Her mouth moves, like she wants to say something but can't. I'm content with the quiet: I adore her beauty as she glows in the sunlight trickling through the windows, the stunning yellow brilliance striking off her golden hair.

Her blond tresses are tied back again. She is gorgeous, and I'm glad her face isn't hidden behind her hair. Her baby pink top adds color to the dull, wooden diner.

"Do you like pink?"

"It's okay." She rests on the tabletop with her jaw in her palm. "Why?"

"You were wearing a pink shirt yesterday, and you're wearing another today."

She glimpses down on it with a sigh. "They were gifts. My grandma and cousins send me pink clothes. I wear them to be respectful, but then people see me in them and assume I like the color and buy me more. Then my extended family sees me in other pink stuff and keeps thinking I love the color and gives me even more. No one stops to ask what my favorite color is. Maybe it's because I'm a girl. I guess my DNA is crossed, but I don't care for pink. Somehow, though, Vonnie doesn't have this problem, and she barely talks." Her eyes widen into a cute almond shape as she raises her hand with irritation.

"Your DNA?" I chuckle. "What's your favorite color?"

"Bright lime green. I wear running shoes in that color for my best workouts."

"You're a runner?" I expected as much, considering the state of her shoes.

She nods with a smile. "There's nothing quite like breaking in a new pair of sneakers. I run on a treadmill in my bedroom every day."

"In your bedroom?" I inquire, my head tilted. Their living room was spacious.

"Mm-hmm." She brings her cup to her lips. "I'm the only one who uses it, and Mom was sick of moving it to vacuum."

The corners of my lips pull into a smile as I imagine her mother's frustration.

"There's also a track near my parent's house that I like to use."

"What got you into running?"

Her lips curve into a small smile. "I joined the running team in sixth grade. I realized how great it felt, and now I'm addicted to the runner's high. Do you run? Since you're a cop?"

I sip my coffee and set it down. "I train to be fast. Makes me better at my job."

Another chasm of silence falls between us. I stare at her, darting my eyes away when she catches me.

She's modest. Kind. Attractive. Honorable. She has to be for me to consider telling her about my faith. Then there's the cross-shaped stain on their wall and how protective her father is of her, both clues hinting toward faith in Christ. She was quick to stash her SimLink in my truck while I concealed mine along with my body camera. We gave each other knowing glances as we noticed we were both leaving behind anything with a microphone. She has to be a Christian. Why else would she hide her SimLink?

This coffee shop is secure. It's old-fashioned and utilizes minimal technology. They don't have ordering screens in their tables like most eateries; selections are chosen with a clerk at the counter. I picked the booth in the farthest back corner, and I perused the area for microphones. Kaitlyn squinted curiously as I searched under tables and cushions, raking through every crevice for possible listening devices. She didn't ask what I was doing; I have a hunch she knew. An employee looked at me funny as I flipped cushions, but she won't ask questions because I'm in uniform.

God, am I supposed to tell Kaitlyn I believe in You? Can I trust her?

He's giving me an unmistakable urge to share my faith; it's a joyful weight tugging at my heart. While declaration carries risk, it's a chance I have to take. I'm the cop; she'll never tell me first if she's a Christian. We've been tiptoeing around something big, and I think it's our faith.

Studying my badge with a sense of irony, I lift my eyes to hers and lean over the table with a whisper. "I'm a Christian."

Time moves slower as she hesitates. Her eyes widen before she sighs, her face almost falling in her coffee.

Silence.

"Are you?"

Her smile meets mine. The tension has vanished. We breathe with ease, no longer restraining the air with our dread. We slump forward as our muscles relax, our expressions lightening. We're free to be ourselves.

"That's a relief."

Her head bounces in agreement, her hair dancing with the motion.

"Did you go to church?"

Her face falls. "Yeah. We went to Harvest View."

"Is that one of the churches that—"

"Blew up." She swallows audibly, her lips tightening as she hides the pain. "Seven years ago."

With a sinking heart, I push aside my coffee. "I'm sorry."

I remember watching the wreckage on the news and praying for the people who'd died and those who'd lost loved ones. The blast happened hours after my prophetic dream, which I can't tell her about because it will lead to my quest for the missing women.

"Me, too. I wasn't quite thirteen when it happened. Vonnie, my little sister, was six. We'd stayed home that day because we were sick. Dad called the pastor; they were close friends. He prayed with Dad and died hours later. The flu saved our lives." She wraps her arms together and cradles herself. Focusing on the window next to our booth, her eyes wane into the recesses of her memory.

"I'll never forget the footage: Smoke. Ash. Rubble. Robots pulling out bodies and workers searching for survivors. There weren't any. Seeing remains covered in soot, dirt, and blood. Bones and muscle sinews sticking out of the stubs of missing limbs. Wondering with each body who I was looking at. Harvest View only had one service, so every corpse was a friend. It hurt more when they recovered the bodies of children and babies. Imagining it could've been Vonnie." She pauses to swallow tears. "I wanted to protect her, but I didn't know how to protect myself. I called for Mom and Dad. They didn't know what to do, either. If anyone else stayed home that morning, they disappeared after the explosion. To this day, we haven't found anyone."

Kaitlyn fades farther into the distance. She's not here with me; she's reliving the horrific moment that changed her life.

"We were wearing the armor of God like any other day, but that morning a grenade went off under our feet. All of us changed. We stopped talking about God. We'd catch ourselves remembering someone from our church and cry.

"Mom was distraught for a long time. She struggled to hear God and wanted counseling, but announcing her faith to a stranger would've endangered us. She spent months locked alone in her room, talking with God and reading her Bible. Out of all of us, she came out of the tragedy closest to her old self.

"Dad was distant. He became different. More protective of us. Less trusting of others."

That explains why Stanley was startled when he saw me in uniform. He's shielding his daughters from a fear of the known, not a fear of the unknown. In today's world, reality can be more frightening than any nightmare.

"We never attended another church. We were afraid to die, and most churches weren't welcoming because they suspected newcomers might be terrorists."

Still gazing out the window, her expression softens. "And then there's Vonnie. She lives deep within herself. Been quiet since birth. I remember when Mom and Dad brought her home. I was excited to have a sister. I tried playing with her, but she'd pull away and whimper. She wasn't much fun until she was two, but she changed after the bombing." Kaitlyn shrugs. "She stopped eating for weeks, and hasn't eaten much since. I wondered that day, as our church smoldered on the news, how much she understood. She was little, but I suspect she comprehended more than we realized. She dug deeper inside her shell; it's where she feels safest. It might be the only place she feels safe.

"Then the Burning almost broke us. Dad went through the house and took away every sign we believed in God, except for our Bibles; he built a special hiding spot for those. I was mad." Her voice cracks with regret. "But not with him. I was angry with the Government for putting him in that position, to feel as if he had to choose between serving God and protecting us. I feared for him, thinking he was giving up his faith, and with it his eternity.

"As difficult as life was after the Burning, it was still simple to me: We continue obeying God. But Dad was so afraid of losing us he was paralyzed, yet willing to do anything. He's always taken his role as the family's guardian seriously, and he felt obligations and burdens I don't know.

"The first year after religion was outlawed was scary; I clung to God and His promises and I grew in faith, but I was constantly wondering if my parents and Vonnie would make it home at the end of the day. We didn't move like a lot of Believers; Dad said it would be too suspicious. If anyone from our past asked if we were still Christians, we could've been thrown in jail or worse. No one did. People must've believed that we gave up on God after our church was destroyed. It was difficult, but Dad might've saved our lives by not bringing us to another church."

Lashes locked with moisture, her eyes meet mine. She smiles faintly, as if it's obligatory. "Whatever happened, at least we lived. Thank God we were sick."

Thank You, Jesus, for saving her. I can't imagine having never experienced her.

I extend my open palm over the table and she takes it. My thick fingers wrap around her petite hand. "I'm glad you're here."

She rubs her tears, peering out the window again. I want to hold her. Seeing her hurt, my love for her becomes undeniable.

I give her a few moments to compose herself. It's all I can do. No one, nothing, can bring back the friends she lost that day.

Turning toward me, she wipes away the last of her tears. "I'm sorry. That was my first time telling my story."

"It's okay." I rub her hand. "I'm glad you got a chance."

Her grin catches me by surprise. "My dad thought you were a Christian. You made quite an impression on him. That isn't easy, considering your goal was to take me out."

Smiling with the compliment, I squeeze her fingers. "I live how God wants. He opens doors with the right people."

"Did you go to church?"

Steam warms my hand as my thumb traces the rim of my mug. "Yeah. A close-knit one, but I don't know them anymore. They probably feared for their lives and scattered to unfamiliar places. I reached out to a few the day after the Burning, but they avoided me. Maybe because I'm a cop. I considered using the System to find them, but I never did. I didn't want to invade their privacy, and it would've been heart-wrenching to see how many of them died."

I sigh, afraid to admit the whole truth.

"It's my fault I don't have contact with them. I made a mistake."

Kaitlyn's head leans to the side, her eyes narrowing without losing their brightness.

"Like most Believers, I knew in my heart that religion wouldn't be free much longer, but I stopped talking to my brothers ages ago. Between working complicated cases and during services, I told myself I was too busy for friends."

She raises her brows in acceptance while I think about how many hours I work every time a girl disappears. How many hours I spend every week analyzing what evidence I have. I didn't make time for my friends, and I paid a huge price. If God permits Kaitlyn and me to commit ourselves to each other, I have to make her a priority. I can't lose her the way I did my brothers in Christ.

"Because I distanced myself, anyone who survived doesn't trust me. I haven't talked with any of them since before the Burning."

"I'm sorry." Returning the favor, she pauses so I can recover from the sting of losing my friends.

"We didn't move, either, and no one mentioned our faith. I think everyone assumed my parents and I ditched God when the Burning happened because I'm a cop, and the Government must've gotten the impression that I'd forfeited my beliefs because it had been so long since I'd spoken with anyone in my church. That's what spared us from death." I bite my cheek as currents ripple through the black liquid in my mug. Whenever I remember the brothers I lost, the defeat still feels as heavy as the night faith burned. I don't know if any amount of time will heal it.

My eyes shift to Kaitlyn. Her compassion makes it easier to talk about the pain.

"Plus I believe God sheltered us. Christ warned us persecution would happen so our faith wouldn't be shaken. We don't stumble over what we see in front of us, and God is always guiding our paths."

Her fingers squeeze my hand as she gives me a sympathetic smile. A silent moment trickles by, and her grin never leaves me.

"You only mentioned your parents. Do you have any brothers or sisters?"

"No. I was a handful." I laugh and sip more coffee, placing the mug on the table.

She lightens with wonder. "What's the worst thing you did as a kid?"

"Jumped out of a tree and broke my ankle."

"You jumped out of a tree?" One hand rises in astonishment.

"I had a cape on."

Kaitlyn shakes her head with a giggle. "Not every hero flies."

"Yeah. I learned that." I chuckle with her. "What's the worst thing you did?"

Her eyes roll to the ceiling and stick there.

"Are you thinking this long because you're a saint or because you've done so many things you can't remember what's worse?"

"The latter."

"What am I getting into?" My laughter breaks her trance.

"I colored Vonnie."

"You colored your sister?"

"I had new markers. Mom told me not to color the house, so I scribbled on Vonnie. It tickled her, and I thought her giggles meant she liked it. I colored her more when I realized she was letting me play with her for the first time. She was blue, green, and purple for days." Cheek in hand, she laughs. I join her.

"Mom was mad until she read Vonnie's back."

"What did you write?"

"'Jesus loves me.' When she read it, she set Vonnie on the floor and scooped me up in a hug. She whispered, 'So do I.'"

"Talk about a get out of jail free card." My nervous energy comes out through my fingers, nudging my mug away as a new thought consumes me: *I can't lose this girl.*

"I have a lot of them." She giggles, her smile reaching her eyes as she slurps another sip. I've never had this great of a time with anyone, and the more I get to know her, the more beautiful she becomes.

"So what do your parents do?"

"Mom's a child development coordinator. It's a fancy title she gave herself because people turned their noses up when she said she was a stay-at-home mom. Occasionally she tries doing stuff from home. She's sold candles, cupcakes, headwear, handbags, makeup."

Her face slants to the left as her brows scrunch over her nose. "Don't you know what my dad does? He mentioned something about you two meeting through work."

"We did, but I don't know much other than he works at a security company."

"Dad's a Chief Executive Investigator for New American Securities. They monitor businesses' surveillance feeds around the clock for break-ins, thefts, robberies, fires, the works. He steps in for the big cases leading to felonies. He gathers details and hands them off to authorities. What was the case that brought you two together?"

"I can't say. It's an ongoing investigation." I edge it out with a smile, hoping I haven't offended her.

"Wow." Her eyes slide to the left and back to me. "Wasn't that years ago?"

"Four." I sip my coffee before changing topics. "Your father seems observant. Meticulous."

"Very!" She gleams, and I'm glad she's distracted from asking about the missing girls.

"There was this one case that had him fuddled for a couple days. He woke up one morning with a grand idea, ran through the house—didn't eat breakfast—and left for work. He came home with the biggest grin. I don't know details, but he had caught an employee doing something shady on camera but couldn't find the crime. He asked the business for permission to review their financial records since the date she was hired, and he caught a seven-figure embezzlement scheme and busted all of her partners."

"Was that in August of forty-five?"

"Yes . . ." Kaitlyn's face turns peculiar.

"That was him?"

Eleven million citizens, and Kaitlyn's father and I have shared *two* assignments?

"You worked the case?"

"I made the arrest. She was a crafty one . . ." I shake my head and slurp my coffee. "I read the file. Your father's work was remarkable. The detectives were impressed."

She pokes her cup with the tips of her fingers. "I'm glad you two have more to talk about."

"We have lots to talk about." I have so many questions about Kaitlyn: her childhood, her habits, her favorite things, her personality.

Her lips twist to the side, her brows furrowing as she leans over the table. "Why'd you stay a cop after the Burning? How do you balance it with your faith?"

"Carefully. God led me into public service, but it's tricky." I blow out a deep breath as my scariest moments come to mind. "Every day I find myself in situations where I have to ask God what I'm supposed to do. Most of the time, it's difficult to hear Him over everything that's happening and everyone talking to me. I've made bad calls. The world's too noisy, but I do my best to stay loyal to Him. It's a rare officer who can do this job and keep their faith in God, but I've known from a young age who I want to be. That makes choices easier. So far, I've never had to arrest a Believer. If the day comes, I trust God to provide a way out, or I'll die for Him.

"My biggest struggle is the Galleys. I fall asleep every night praying I can find a way to rescue Believers."

Her eyes flicker from my badge to my face. "Galleys?"

She's not on the inside yet. Everyone knows the Government kills Believers, but few outside of Security have heard of the institutions. The Government doesn't mention them, but word has been spreading.

"Where convicted Believers are executed."

Her countenance falls as reality sinks in.

"Why are you joining Security when you're a Christian?"

"Same reason. I'm following God." She takes a swig of caffeine.

"What will you be doing?"

"Counter-terrorism." She fades away, a slight smile pulling at the corner of her mouth. "God warned me about the Burning the night before it happened. He said the Government would consider Believers terrorists and their lives would be at stake. Then He asked me to work in counter-terrorism, but He promised to protect me from having to betray other people of faith."

A calm joy washes over her. "I'll always remember the peace He gave me: It was perfect, beyond comprehension. He said if I join Security, He'll work through me to save someone I love. I don't know who it will be, but I felt so alive, almost on fire, like I was meeting the purpose God called me to. I enrolled in college and I've been taking classes every semester, even through the summers. I'll scan surveillance, find terrorists, and organize leads and raids. That's why I want to shadow an officer. So I can understand how they work before sending them into danger. Maybe I can go with you tonight?" She jokes, beaming at my uniform.

I smirk, memorizing the sparkle of her sepia eyes as my fingers lock around hers. "Sounds like you're the boss."

Giggling, she stares at our entwined hands. Her skin is soft. Everything about her feels fragile. All I want to do is protect and care for her.

Her spoon falls from her other hand, clinking over the table before thudding against the floor. "Crap!"

My chest heaves with laughter, but I stay silent to avoid embarrassing her more.

God, I love her.

"I'm sorry. I'm clumsy when I'm nervous." She bends down to grab the spoon, her head smacking against the underside of the table as she rises. Rattles crash through the diner, the silverware and cups on the tabletop bouncing with the collision.

"Are you okay?" I hover out of my seat.

"Yeah. I'm fine." Rubbing the back of her head, she grins sheepishly as she straightens. "Where were we?"

She reaches for my hand, and I lay my palm in hers as I rest in the booth.

I smile at her and contain my laughter, though it carries through my voice. "So you're graceful when you're not nervous?"

"For the most part."

This girl has me hooked. Every part of her is perfect, even her clumsiness. I can't let her leave my life.

"Kaitlyn, I want to know you better. Can we make a commitment?"

She freezes. "Like what?"

I've turned down every woman, preserving myself with the knowledge that when I found the one, she would be obvious. I was right, and she's sitting in front of me. The joy God puts in my heart when I look at her tells me so.

"Will you be my girlfriend?"

Without hesitation, she squeezes my hand and beams.

"Yes!"

Chapter Sixteen

God has given me my mate, the man I'm marrying.

His name's Peter Tryndale. He's a police officer who came into my class yesterday. I loved him the first second I saw him. He is <u>gorgeous</u>! He locks his dirty-blond hair with a dash of gel, and he's almost six feet tall. I could drown in his coffee-colored eyes, splashed with golden streaks. His jaw is square; his cheeks were chiseled out of stone, but his tender smile softens his face. I tripped when I met him, and he caught me! His arms were thick and strong and made me feel safe. He didn't hesitate to call my dad; he was happy about it.

I spent the rest of my day thinking about him. I couldn't focus in class; I kept wondering what he was doing and if he was safe.

We had our first date today. He's so handsome all the women were staring. I am the luckiest girl in the world to be the one he's with. To be the one he smiles at and holds hands with.

He's a Christian, too. There's something about him. With him, I feel safer than I've ever felt before. A frenzy sweeps through me every time I see or think about him. When we touch, I'm whole. I didn't realize how much of me was missing until I found him. He's my strength.

He asked me to be his girlfriend. Guys never ask anymore. Men lack chivalry. Women have no modesty. Couples today have sex. Move in, move out. One-night stands. There's no commitment until they're married, but most marriages end in divorce because both people were in it for the wrong reasons.

But not Peter. He wants me to see only him, and he's promised he'll see only me. He won't kiss me until I'm ready, and he likes that I protect my honor. I told him I don't want to kiss anyone but my husband. His smile grew huge, almost humanly impossible. He doesn't expect me to give any part of myself to him. There is no gray area: we are reserving ourselves for each other. We're seeing where this leads, but I already know—because <u>this</u> is how a man treats a lady. Have I mentioned he's gorgeous?

On my thirteenth birthday, Mom gave me a present. I ripped off the giftwrapping, pulled the lid off the box, and gaped at the beauty of the cross necklace. Mom told me the moral she wanted me to remember every time I saw it: Keep my purity. Wait for the man God intends for me. She warned me that my teenage years would be tumultuous—full of boys, crushes, and strong desires—but God has one man in mind for me. It will be hard, but wait for him.

I'm glad I listened and didn't settle for anyone less than Peter. It was tempting: Every girl wants to feel cherished and special. It hurt watching girls accept attention from guys while rejecting it for myself so boys would leave me alone. But I've never wanted to live as other girls do—giving my heart and body to whomever will take it, desperate for love in return.

It's like giving yourself away and expecting something better, only to discover you lost yourself completely. You keep selling what little pieces you have left of your soul in hopes of finding the morsels that are lost. Your heart is all you have. Give away your heart, and you give away everything.

There was a time when I doubted I would find my mate or know when I met him; I questioned if I'd always be alone. Now I know it's true: You don't have to date losers to find the winner. Someday I'll have children to teach this lesson to, and I can tell them about my life. How I found Peter without dating anyone before him.

I'm in awe that a man like him exists, and I'm grateful to God for putting us together.

Thank You, Lord, for Peter. Please change me and help me be the best girlfriend I can be. To love and support him every day. Help me guard my heart from hurt and not give him too much too soon.

—Kaitlyn

Chapter Seventeen

Peter
Thursday, February 21, 2047
10:16 P.M.

"Ninjas."

"Pirates."

Kaitlyn sits beside me as I patrol the city and show her my job. It's been a slow night, a rarity allowing us plenty of time to learn about each other.

"Ninjas."

"What are you talking about? Everyone fears pirates!" Her energy level rises.

"And pirates fear ninjas. Ninjas win, hands down."

She crosses her arms and shakes her head, as if the gestures add any merit to her argument. "Says who?"

"Says the fact that one ninja could take out an entire ship of pirates without any of them realizing there was an intruder on board."

"Whatever. My pirates would feed your ninjas to the sharks."

"How?" I take my gaze off the road for a split second to scrutinize her. "Even if the ninjas were caught—and they wouldn't be real ninjas if they were—the ninjas would win."

Her lips pucker in a friendly snarl. "Pirates fight dirty and have guns."

"You must know some lucky pirates. It's hard to hit an invisible target."

"Maybe the pirates attack the ninjas and catch them off guard."

I glance at her with doubt. "Ninjas train and pirates are lazy. Plus ninjas have moves pirates would never see coming, even when they're smacked in the face."

Kaitlyn opens her mouth, but my dash's SimLink chimes before she says a word. The purple-bordered screen pops up as I answer the call.

"Tryndale," the officer asks, his baggy eyes revealing how tired he is. "Can you come get this guy?"

"Sure," I volunteer, the projection shutting off as I head to his location. I glimpse at Kaitlyn. "This is the illegal prostitution bust we heard on dispatch earlier."

Oblivious of what she'll soon see, her expression remains innocent. Law enforcement changes every agent. She will see darkness in the world, discover the existence of evils she could never comprehend, and it will change her. I like who she is now, but I'll enjoy her at every stage of her life, no matter how the job changes her.

"You should stay in the car."

Her head bobs as we drive in silence. Despite her presence, this night feels dark. Perhaps it's the call I'm responding to.

We arrive to a handful of police cars, their lights swirling in the blackness as they block the entrance of a run-down, abandoned building with boarded windows. A Security van is parked to the side, where officers are leading a line of women, wrists cuffed, into the back. The females, adorned in lingerie, are worn-out and sick-looking. Some of their outfits are torn, pieces of fishnet dangling from their arms, legs, and torsos. Their hair is frazzled, their skin worn, and their cheeks hollowed in from drug use. The older females are walking corpses, nearing death from addiction and disease. The younger ones possess traces of their former beauty, their sole proof that more innocent days existed, but—given a few more years, a few more men, a few more violations—they'll be as ill-looking as their seniors.

Lord, please help these women. Give them beautiful lives.

I've arrested prostitutes before; they're often more victims than criminals. Pimps train them never to snitch, making it difficult to arrest the real perpetrators: abusive boyfriends who brainwashed them, felons who coerced them with blackmail, traffickers who forced drugs into them.

But sometimes, like tonight, we arrest the pimp who didn't pay taxes, making the services illegal. The prostitutes are taken to jail also, but they come out with freedom.

"Oh, my gosh!" Kaitlyn gawks, palms pressed against the glass. "Will they get help?"

"Maybe." I exit my squad car and close the door. She'll want to talk about this later. Right now, I'm needed on scene.

The dungy aroma of mold assails me from a few feet outside the open entrance. Old, battered mattresses rest on the floor. Cockroaches scarper by. I need a shower just seeing this place. I hope I don't have to enter.

I slip on leather gloves as the officer who asked for help paces down the sidewalk, pushing the detainee toward me. Wearing a long brown coat and baggy pants, the criminal's brown eyes are clean; he's not addicted to the drugs he likely force-feeds the girls. Despite that his hands are cuffed behind his back, he smiles at me. One of his front teeth is gold. Some clichés never change.

"Here." The officer shoves him at me. "I booked the charges, but I gotta finish gathering evidence."

The felon and I journey to my car in silence, my hand fastened around his arm as I guide him to my trunk. "Do you have anything sharp on you? Any needles or weapons? Drugs?"

"Nah, Bro. I'm clean."

He wouldn't be the first criminal to lie. I instruct him to set his hands on the car and I pat his frame and under his coat. To my amazement, he's right.

Kaitlyn scans him over as I open the rear door. She cringes toward the front as he crawls into the backseat. A muted growl escapes his throat.

I know his game.

He makes his perch in the center, his eyes never leaving my girlfriend. I sit behind the wheel and let headquarters know that I'm en route with the suspect.

The ride isn't smooth. His face burns in the rearview mirror every time a street lamp passes over us, his eyes devouring Kaitlyn. I'm glad she doesn't see him.

As I suspected, he can't keep quiet.

"So," his eyes dart to me then back to Kaitlyn as he licks his sick grin. "You bangin' this chick?"

"Don't start." I stay neutral and give his reflection a firm glare.

"You score good meat."

Kaitlyn twists around, her fingers clutching the headrest as fury replaces her astonishment.

"Hey, Sweetie. You wanna feel a *real* man between your legs?" He kisses at her from his seat, laughing.

She snaps forward with crossed arms. I pull over, glad for his sake there's bullet resistant glass between them.

"Whatcha doin', Bro?" He inquires as we come to a stop on the side of the road. He appraises the darkness with paranoia, afraid of what I might do. Amusingly, he gawps at my girlfriend with desperation, as if the woman he insulted seconds ago will save him.

I flip on the dome light and light bar as I step out, leaning inside to peer at Kaitlyn. "You got this?"

Curled in her seat, she nods, the overhead light bouncing off her hair as she pouts through the window.

"Got what, Bro? Got what?"

I close my door and turn on my body camera as I open the back.

"C'mon. Get out." Maintaining my self-control is effortless because I'm not playing his game.

We're playing mine.

"Bro, what?" His jaw hangs in the car's interior glow.

"I'm not your bro. Get out."

He reluctantly scoots over the seat and stands out of the vehicle. "What're we doin'?"

"Walking." I nudge my head toward the bridge ahead. There's no sidewalk, cars race by at highway speed, and the blackness is only broken by a few street lamps and the flashing light bar.

He gapes with an open jaw. "Walking?"

I nod.

"Where?" His eyes bulge.

"Jail."

"In the Security Building?"

"Yep. Let's go." I tug on his arm. Gently, so he can move away.

He does.

"That's five miles!" He bends his knees and bounces in protest.

"More like eight."

He balks, and his mouth is so wide I'm waiting for the fake tooth to fall out.

"Can't handle eight miles?" I ask with mock compassion that sounds genuine.

He fervently shakes his head and wiggles his leg. "Nah, Man. My knee. Gives me problems."

"Hmm. Well, I have a dolly in the trunk. I can tie you to it, hook it to the back of my car, and tow you to jail."

He swings toward the tail end of the vehicle, his gaze returning with distress. "Why can't I ride in the backseat?"

I point through the window where Kaitlyn is sulking. "Because she's a lady, and you're not treating her with respect."

He tries speaking, but his first words are stuck together in a tongue-tie. "I can be respectful."

"Really?" Obvious doubt taints my voice.

His head bounces with urgency.

Anxiety dulling his awareness, I yank my flashlight out of my belt and blind him. "Why should I believe a tax-evading pimp?"

Wincing in the brightness, he breaks under my interrogation. "I know, Man. I know. I use women, and I don't pay my taxes."

He's convicted himself. He'll do time, and the streets will have one less pimp.

"But give me a chance. I can be respectful."

I push the light closer to his eyes. He bows to the side, but I keep him blinded and lean my face closer to his. Tobacco and alcohol reek off him. "Then when I allow you inside, you're giving her a sincere apology and not saying another word. If you look at her *once*, you're walking. Got it?"

His head bounces in earnest agreement.

I open the door and shut off the camera as he shuffles into his seat, sheepishly staring at his feet while muttering: "I'm sorry, Ma'am."

She ignores him, her arms crossed and back turned for the rest of the drive. Her glower reflects in the window when we stop in the dim parking garage. She steps out and stretches her legs as the felon exits the rear.

"I'll meet you in the lobby." I instruct her as I escort the criminal to the prison; he locks his vision far from her. I need a few minutes to check if any women have gone missing. Kaitlyn will be more comfortable in the vestibule than the garage.

The clerk is processing reports on the prisoner when we enter. An officer assigned to the jail frees me of him.

With a few minutes of freedom, I head upstairs to my office and close the door. I pull off my gloves and slip the SimLink out of my pocket to see if anyone new has been reported while Kaitlyn and I were on the town. Maybe a victim was assigned to another officer, though I doubt it. Searching through the System, no one else has disappeared.

Considering how many cops work my precinct, it's odd for the same officer to receive every call involving a serial criminal, and it's even odder that dispatch informs me about these women but doesn't tell me how it knows about them. The perp caught me searching for Ms. Black years ago and has assigned me to every victim since as part of his game.

When he strikes, I want to slide on the small things at work. Let people off the hook for lesser infractions so I have fewer reports to do, freeing my time to search for the monster and his victims. But that's a slippery slope, and I'd let bigger and bigger crimes go unpunished until

I'm not serving God anymore.

But despite the perp's power and wickedness, God is in control. He gave me the dream before the crimes started.

God, the perp's thorough and diligent, covering every track. Does he know I'm searching for him? If he studied me half as thoroughly as he does his victims, he's seen Kaitlyn. He's allowed me to search for him thus far, but loving her could change that. He could come after her to get to me. What do You want me to do? How do I protect her? Should I break up with her?

A blade slices through my heart.

She'll work Security anyway. If the perp is one of us, she'll be safer if I'm in her life. The closer I am to her, the better I can protect her.

Am I being selfish? We've been dating less than a month, but I'll be miserable without her, God. You put us together. I love her.

He gives me peace about staying with Kaitlyn, but I still have concerns.

I might be jeopardizing her. Losing my life to rescue the women is a sacrifice I have to risk, no one else. You called me to be the Exodus, not Kaitlyn. Please protect her, Jesus. Help me keep her safe, even when we're apart.

I leave my office and take the elevator to the lobby. As I come out, I see Kaitlyn munching on cookies with Zaranda, the third in command of Security. I'm not shocked to see her in the middle of the night, she works all hours, but I am surprised to see her with my girlfriend. And cookies? I've never seen Zaranda talk with anyone, let alone eat. She's standoffish and unsocial; I only know her name by virtue of her rank.

"Peter!" Zaranda exclaims, as if we've met. Kaitlyn must've told her my name.

"You two know each other?"

"We do now." She beams at me, covering her mouth as she chews. The overhead brightness shines in her fiery red curls as she turns to Kaitlyn. "Keep in touch."

"Mm-hmm," Kaitlyn hums, feasting on her cookie. She seems to be enjoying her dessert so much she barely remembers to smile at

Zaranda as she vanishes around a corner.

Squinting with furrowed brows, I tilt my head toward Kaitlyn, who's still enjoying her treat. "What happened?"

"I bought these in the snack machine and offered one to her when she walked by." She tosses the wrapper and licks crumbs off her fingers.

"Huh."

I lead her to the parking garage. She breaks the silence as the cruiser comes into sight.

"What did you do?"

"What?"

"That creep. Why'd he apologize?"

"Oh, that," I chuckle as I open her door. "I almost made him walk."

"All the way here?" Her hair falls against her collarbone as she stops short.

"Yes."

"Were you going to walk with him?"

"Yeah. I could've called another officer to transport him, but I had it handled." I motion for her to sit.

She watches me with confusion. "Why would you do that?"

"I won't allow anyone to disrespect you. I'd walk a hundred miles to protect your integrity."

The smile growing over her is a great reward, though I'll do anything, give anything, and be anything to protect her, even if I receive nothing in return. Knowing she's cared for is its own prize.

She wraps her fingers over mine on the car door, passion searing through her eyes. "Thank you." Squeezing my hand, she rises to her tiptoes and kisses me on the cheek. Her tender lips make me beam.

Her face comes into view, and she's as jubilant as I am.

"You never have to thank me. It's my job to protect you. My favorite one." I run my fingers through her hair, tucking her locks behind her ear. I kiss the top of her head and gesture toward her seat.

She makes herself comfortable, her hair shining in the hazy light. Her shirt flows over her lap, her jeans hugging her legs and her lips carrying the smile I gave her.

With a spirit more gorgeous than her body, my heart trusts in her. She works hard toward the goals God sets for her. She inspires and believes in me. She's faithful and kind, analytical and determined.

Thank You, Lord, for bringing Kaitlyn and me together.

Closing the door, I'm honored to be the man who's winning her heart.

Chapter Eighteen

Kaitlyn
Tuesday, March 12, 2047
1:49 P.M.

Two taps against my doorframe wake me up. I must be dreaming. When I open my eyes, a gorgeous police officer is standing at the entrance with a paper bag in his hand.

"No fair," I croak, my throat irritated from coughing spells. Vonnie's hack carries down the hall.

My boyfriend beams at me. "What's not fair?"

Sunglasses on top of his spiked champagne hair, brilliant white teeth contrasting against his sun-kissed skin, thick muscles rounding under his short sleeves. I can't believe I have to spell it out for him. "You're looking perfect in your uniform, and I'm gross and sick." I lift my head off the pillow, wondering if it's reckless to reveal my knotted hair.

"You look beautiful to me."

His smile tells me he means every word.

"Hungry?"

Nodding, I rise from bed. Peter's laughter fills the bedroom as I gain my balance.

"What's so funny?"

Still in the hallway—he's too gentlemanly to come into my bedroom—he stares at my clothes. "Your pajamas are pink."

"I know," I groan as my feet kick my slippers out from under the bed.

He laughs harder as my toes glide into the cotton. "Your slippers are pink, too? Do you have clothes in any other color?"

"I have green slippers," I say, almost defensively, as I saunter toward him. "But I don't want to puke on them."

His brows press together. "Have you been throwing up?"

"No, but I've had every other problem you can imagine. I wouldn't be surprised if I tossed my cookies."

"Well, if you do, I'll clean it up." He gathers my sweaty hair behind my ear. "Think you can keep down some soup?"

I nod, and he wraps his arm around me to guide me toward the stairs. Despite how ill I am, his hand doesn't leave my shoulder as we make our way to the dining room.

There's orange juice and a packet of paper waiting on the table as we take our seats. I sip the tangy fluid as he sets the bag on the table and unfolds it. He lifts out a plastic bowl and places it in front of me before popping off its lid and handing me a spoon and napkin.

Feeling more alive with broth warming my throat, I make conversation to hear his deep voice. "Are you off work?"

He smiles, head in hand. "Nah. It's my lunch break. I don't get these often."

"Where's your food?" I slurp another spoonful.

"I ate on the way." He gazes toward the violent coughs clunking down the bedroom hallway. When the hacking ends, his compassion returns to me.

"There's soup in the bag for your family. Their juice is in the fridge."

Forgetting to blink, I gape at him.

Yep. I'm marrying this guy.

"What?" He glances over his top, as if he's searching for a stain, and focuses on me with a half-cocked grin.

"You're amazing. That's all." I sip more broth, this time to calm my excitement instead of my cold. "Don't take this the wrong way, but you shouldn't be here. I'm getting everyone sick. It's only a matter of time until Dad comes down with it."

"It's worth the risk to take care of you. Besides, I need to give you this." He slides the packet toward me.

"What is it?" I ask, noticing how unnecessary the question was as I read the top line.

"A Bible study I did years ago when I was miserable with the stomach flu. Thought you might enjoy it."

"Thank you. I need something fun to do. I'm tired of feeling under the weather." My nasally voice exaggerates my whine.

Peter rises from his seat and kisses my head. "I love you."

I almost choke on my orange juice. "You do?"

He leans back in his chair, and his smile is so bright I hope I never forget it. "With all my heart."

It's good that I'm sick, because I'm so crazy for him that flu germs are the only reason I'm not jumping over this table and kissing him. Something I'd regret later, as we agreed to wait for the altar.

"I love you, too."

"I know." His mouth curves with laughter as daylight shines in his hair.

"Ego much?"

"Only with you." He kisses my cheek. "I have to get back to work, but we're celebrating when you feel better. Anything you want to do, I'll take you. My treat."

I'm awestruck that God made a man this perfect for me.

"Think about it while I'm away." He stands, smiling down on me.

Forgetting my soup and juice, my eyes can't leave him as I escort him to the door. "I'll be thinking about you more."

He pulls me against his chest, pressing his lips into my hair. "I love you."

The moment doesn't last long enough as he releases his grip and opens the door, winking at me before he departs.

The ill sensation returns as my euphoria fades in his absence; the giddiness feels odd in my sick body. I go back to the table and give in to another coughing fit that synchronizes harmoniously with my mom's and sister's. I pick up the packet and read Peter's notes and the fifteenth chapter of First Corinthians.

Chapter Nineteen

Peter
Wednesday, March 20, 2047
6:38 P.M.

Lord, I can't express how fascinated I am with Who You are. Kaitlyn is beautiful and kind. I love every part of her. Whenever I see her, hear her, or think about her, I'm overwhelmed with certainty that You made her—inside and out—for me. To fulfill me and give me joy. Thank You, Jesus, for giving me a companion who's not just a woman, but an experience. Somebody who makes my heart light on the heaviest of days.

My truck stills as I shut off the engine, parked in front of the Reeds' home. Light peeks through trees as the sun prepares to set. I admire God's beauty before grabbing the package and hopping out; the sound of my door closing behind me echoes over their large lawn.

Gift tucked under my arm, I climb the steps and ding the bell. Lorraine answers with a smile, her nose red and lips dry from the cold that she recovered from a few days ago. Their illnesses overlapped for half a week and all of them were too sick to leave home. Since their few extended relatives are on the West Coast, I did what I could to support them: Delivered tissues and food. Cooked a few pots of soup. It wasn't much, but it meant a lot to them.

"Oh, Peter! I'm glad to see you! We're not contagious anymore!"

Her arms fold around the bottom of my torso as I enter the foyer. She pulls away, gaping in horror. "Kaitlyn can't see that!"

Bewildered, I peer at the box I'm holding, decorated in blue and green paper with a white ribbon and green bow. "It's wrapped."

"You don't know Kaitlyn." She shakes her head, the tips of her short black hair stopping against her neck. Without taking her eyes off the gift, she grabs Stanley's leather coat off the wall hook and extends it toward me. "Cover it in this."

"What?"

"Kaitlyn guesses everything. Concealing it in this is your only hope at surprising her."

"Everything?"

"Ev-ree-thing." Lorraine's brows rise as she emphasizes each syllable.

I obey her while inwardly debating if it's possible for someone to guess with one-hundred percent accuracy.

A buzzer rings in the kitchen, its chime muted with distance. Lorraine leaves as I remove my shoes. The aroma of chocolate cake becomes noticeable as I step into the living room. Every time I've visited, she's been cooking. She loves serving food, and every dish has been mouthwatering.

"Hey, Peter." Stanley comes from out of nowhere; he must've been sitting in the corner next to the fireplace. He moves forward with his hand outstretched for a shake. "Thanks for helping out last week. That bug was wretched."

"No problem. I enjoyed it."

He draws me close for a quick pat on the back; he doesn't know how similar his embraces are to my dad's. There's comfort and strength in his presence.

We wander to the dining room; Lorraine's in the kitchen to the left, whipping frosting while the cake cools. The dimming sun glows through large windows fixed behind the dining table. The panes stand tall, sloping upward to the left, the angle paralleling the ceiling's slope.

"Under there." Stanley points to a white patio chair that doesn't complement their wooden dining set.

I place his jacket, with Kaitlyn's gift inside, beneath the seat.

Yvonne, prompted by the sounds and smell of dessert, comes toward us from the hallway passing the kitchen. I met Kaitlyn's little sister weeks ago, and she always wears her straight, black hair in a low ponytail, dresses in a white shirt with black pants, and walks with a timid posture. Excessively thin, her arms are crossed and her shoulders slouch forward, but she's not cold; it seems like an outward expression of the shell Kaitlyn said she lives in. She's protecting her heart.

She smiles her greeting; I've only heard her say a few sentences in the time I've known her.

"Peter!" A familiar voice shouts.

Turning left, I see Kaitlyn standing at the top of the staircase, beaming at me before barreling down the steps and into my arms. "I'm so glad you made it!"

I kiss the top of her head, growing to love the sensation of her tresses between my lips. "I wouldn't miss your birthday for all the world."

She hands me a packet of lined paper. "Thank you. I never thought about it that way, but you're right: Our bodies aren't meant to last. They're seeds that must die to bring forth the plants—our heavenly bodies. Death is germination. A rebirth."

I recognize my writing and remember the Bible study. "Keep it. You never know when you'll want to read it again."

Kaitlyn smiles her gratitude, and I rub her back as we approach the table. She puts down the packet and eases into the chair I pulled out for her. The chandelier bounces light around the room as its white crystals swirl in the breeze of the ceiling fan.

With everyone seated, Lorraine enters the dining room and focuses on Stanley. "Should we open gifts now?"

He searches over his family with his chin in his palm, the cuff of his blue satin shirt framing his wrist. "Who wants to go first?"

I find it odd nobody volunteers.

"Her grandma." Lorraine passes a small tree butted up against the breakfast bar in the back corner of the dining room. She grabs a slender present on the counter.

Kaitlyn accepts the gift, and she's not as excited as I expected. Her fingers are under the paper when her mother interrupts.

"Do you want to guess first?"

"Pink shirt." The response doesn't slow Kaitlyn down as she shreds off the paper and opens the lid. Her hand digs through baby pink tissue paper and emerges with a button-down blouse, a pink so light it's almost white. Everyone stifles their laughter.

"Her cousins buy her a lot of pink, too," Lorraine giggles. "One time they saw a picture of her in a green shirt and thought she needed more pink tops. They sent a pack of twenty."

My girlfriend analyzes her sister with a mixture of gratitude and confusion. "Why don't they buy you pink?"

Yvonne shrugs.

Kaitlyn holds the top with a smile, assessing its potential before folding it on the table. "I'm thankful they care about me. Pink's not bad, and the clothes remind me of family."

"Okay, Dear. This one's from your father and me." Lorraine grabs a large box—two feet by three feet by two feet—off the breakfast bar and hands it to Kaitlyn.

Package next to her ear, she shakes it with a grin. "A new journal?"

Her mother's head drops; Stanley's lips hug his tongue as he licks his front teeth in dismay. They hid a book in a box this size and she guessed it?

She rips off the paper and flips open the flaps, sending crumpled, colorful balls of tissue paper to the floor. With wide eyes, she draws out an elaborate notebook—a brown leather hardcover bordered with gold, the metal strips enlarged to triangles at the corners. Its pages are also rimmed with gold, and slipped between them is a mahogany-brown ribbon. She raises it to her nose, smelling the paper as she thumbs through blank pages.

"How?"

Stanley smirks. "Surprising her isn't easy."

Kaitlyn gives her parents a heartfelt thank-you as she rests the book on the table, ready for the next gift. Everyone studies me.

"I'm going last."

Lorraine stares at Yvonne. "You're next."

Kaitlyn's sister sticks out her hand; Lorraine gives her the last present remaining on the breakfast bar: about one foot long, half a foot wide, and a few inches thick. The package jingles as Yvonne passes it to Kaitlyn with a sinister smile. Their narrowed eyes fix on each other. Yvonne's brows rise and lower, daring Kaitlyn to test her. Kaitlyn presses her fingers over the giftwrap, squinting as she accepts the challenge.

"Pens. Colored."

Before I can think *pens don't jingle*, Yvonne's head falls back, eyes rolling with restrained emotion as Kaitlyn tears off the paper. Wedged between two wooden boards is a package of bright pens with bells taped on either side.

As Kaitlyn admires her ink, I gaze in shock at Lorraine, then Stanley, then Yvonne. Kaitlyn's oblivious to all three of them nodding.

My girlfriend isn't human.

Then again, she's never dealt with me. "Alright. My turn."

Kaitlyn sets down her pens, her golden tresses flowing over her shoulders. "New running shoes?"

My jaw drops.

Her expression doesn't change because she knows she's right.

"What kind?"

"Lime green, size eight, made by Rundico."

"How'd you know? How?" My voice cracks as my hands flip. I glare in shock at Lorraine and Stanley; they helped me pick out a pair Kaitlyn would love, vowing they wouldn't say a word to either of their daughters. "Who snitched?"

Kaitlyn's serious, focusing on me while her parents laugh.

Lorraine grabs her camera. "This is Kaitlyn. Maybe one day you'll pull a fast one. We haven't surprised her since she was nine."

"Nine?" My mouth makes the word but my voice doesn't come out. I shift my attention to Kaitlyn. "What color are the laces?"

"Blue."

I drop my face in my hands, muffling my words. "How. Do. You. Know? You don't even like blue!" My eyes narrow on her.

"Because your uniform is blue and you want me to remember you. That's why I like blue now." With a perky grin and anxious eyes glimmering in the crystal light, she stretches out empty hands.

I shake my head and lift my gift out from under my seat, letting the jacket fall to the floor. "Here. I guess wrapping paper isn't required with you."

Lorraine puckers her lips to the side, shaking her head in agreement as Kaitlyn yanks off the paper and digs through the box. She presses on the soles of her shoes, her bliss so strong it's tangible.

"Smile!" Her mother shouts with a broad grin of her own.

Kaitlyn clutches her shoes and beams at the camera until it flashes.

Yvonne tilts forward in her seat, reaching below the plank of wood she's sitting on. At the sound of tape unpeeling, everyone circles around as she separates a gift from the underside of her seat. With a ninja for a sister, I wonder why Kaitlyn has a fondness for pirates.

"Here." She hands Kaitlyn another present, this one small enough that I doubt it's concealed with anything other than paper.

Lorraine and Stanley are as perplexed as I am.

"Inserts!" Kaitlyn tears off the wrapping. I'm baffled to see her holding shoe inserts made for arch support while running.

I squint at Yvonne. "Did you—?"

"It was obvious." Her eyes widen with a roll, as if a child could've guessed my surprise.

Stanley is a man of silence; he wouldn't have talked about my gift. Naturally, I examine the one person who could've told Kaitlyn's sister what I bought.

Lorraine throws her hands in the air. "I said nothing!"

Scrutinizing Yvonne, I may have to accept forfeit from a teenager. "How'd you know?"

"You guys don't see how obvious it was?" She gapes from one person to the next, hoping someone understands her reasoning. "How do you think she knew?" She points at Kaitlyn, who isn't paying attention to anything but her sneakers and inserts.

"Her shoes are falling apart, but why would she buy a new pair when her birthday was around the corner? You guys told me you were buying her a journal, so that left Peter to buy the shoes. It's the one thing he sees she needs."

I'm a cop, and I've been made by a thirteen-year-old.

"Not everyone's as observant as you, Dear." Lorraine kisses Yvonne's head and leaves for the kitchen.

Both seeming content, Kaitlyn plays with her shoes while Yvonne, head resting on the chair, stares at the ceiling. They fist bump over the table without looking at each other.

"You'll have company." Stanley, sitting at the head of the table opposite from Kaitlyn, turns toward me. "One day Yvonne will have a boyfriend, and he'll have it as hard as you."

My nod's slight. "Hmm."

"They feed off each other."

I see what he means: Kaitlyn appears as delighted with her gifts as she is with having guessed them all, and Yvonne seems satisfied with her superior deduction skills.

Preemptive strikes will be key to surprising Kaitlyn. "What's her weakness?"

"Patience when she wants something."

She puts on her new shoes and jogs to and from the living room.

"They're perfect! Thank you!" She kisses me on the cheek, her hair swinging in front of my chest before she pulls away with a huge smile.

She charges to the kitchen. "I'm running tomorrow!"

"Indoor feet!" Lorraine yells, fumbling the cake pan as Kaitlyn collides into her with a hug.

"Thanks for the journal, Mom!" She kisses Lorraine on the cheek before scurrying to her seat and pumping her shoes. Lorraine follows and sets the frosted cake on the table.

Twenty candles burn on top.

Chapter Twenty

Peter
Sunday, April 7, 2047
4:37 P.M.

"So you're Kaitlyn?" My dad adores her with awe, understanding how important she is. His bright blond hair makes his loose, pale-yellow top appear washed out by comparison. He dressed up for the occasion: Repairing floors destroys his clothes, so he wears holey pants. But today he's in crisp, new jeans and an ironed shirt. "Peter's told me quite a bit about you, but he understated how pretty you are."

Adorned in a lime-green blouse and khaki capris, Kaitlyn ducks her head in modesty. "Thank you. It's wonderful to meet you, Mr. Tryndale." Resuming eye contact, she reaches for a handshake.

"Ah, call me James." Dad's grip tightens around her delicate fingers.

People hustle through Imperia's largest mall. Teenage girls pass, locked arm in arm, giggling and pointing at shop windows. Young men and women traipse around holding hands. Several men gawk at my girlfriend, some with an inappropriate hunger. Without Dad or Kaitlyn noticing, I glare at the few who seem threatening until their gazes retreat. Numerous ladies scowl at Kaitlyn with envy; little girls admire her like she's a princess. This is the reaction my girlfriend receives in public.

"Shall we? I'm treating." Dad hikes his thumb over his shoulder.

Kaitlyn looks to me for an answer.

"Sure."

She wraps her arm around mine as he leads us to the smoothie joint. I enjoy their open fountain, allowing patrons to create custom flavors. Because of this luxury, the line is usually long, and today's no exception. I'm glad we ate on our way. Kaitlyn, who eats as much as any man and stays petite by running miles a day, fixes her attention on the lit menus hanging overhead. Her hungry expression is identical to Dad's.

Mom comes out of the restroom hallway, eagerness in her step as she approaches. Her shoulder-length hair flows back with her speed, her purple blouse clinging to her front.

"Kaitlyn? Our son has told us a lot about you!"

Bewildered, my girlfriend spins around, her eyes widening as she realizes the stranger beaming at her is my mother. "Mrs. Tryndale!"

"Please. Dianne." Mom wraps her in a hug, both of them smiling. I memorize the sight of the two most important women in my life embracing for the first time.

The four of us fill our cups at the fountain and journey to the only clean table. Kaitlyn flashes an appreciative grin as she leans into the chair I pulled out. Dad draws out Mom's chair, and he winces as he sits beside her. He hides the pain for her sake—and because no man wants pity—but the decades he's spent handcrafting floors has taken a toll on his knees. I'm not sure how much of it is hereditary, but police work isn't much easier than kneeling on hardwood nine hours a day. Someday my knees will be screaming at me, too.

I bring the straw to my lips. Cold, refreshing cream washes down my throat as I wait for conversation.

Mom relaxes across from Kaitlyn, staring at her with admiration. "You must be special. You're the only girl Peter's dated."

Tucking her hair behind her ear, Kaitlyn's apprehension edges through her voice. "Thank you."

Jaw in palm, Mom's eyes dart back and forth between us. "How'd you two meet?"

"She fell." I lick pureed fruit off my straw.

Kaitlyn's cheeks puff out with a playful glare.

Mom gapes at me. "What?"

"I went to her class for an interview. She tripped as she walked up to me."

My girlfriend's betrayed expression is the cutest thing I've seen in months. She turns to Dad with hope when he speaks.

"Tell me you did the chivalrous thing and caught her."

"One-handed."

"Good for you, Son."

"Thanks."

We sip our smoothies as Kaitlyn switches her gaze between me and my dad, her admonishment settling on me with a shake of her head.

"Don't worry. It's better than how I met James. I fell and he *didn't* catch me. In a very crowded mall."

My girlfriend's shoulders bounce with laughter.

Dad scowls at Mom, his chin jutted. "How was I supposed to with all those shopping bags you were holding?"

"I'm sorry. I seem to remember you bragging about your days as a professional juggler." She eyes him with irritation.

"When I can see what I'm catching." Dad's face hangs in exasperation. "There wasn't a body visible behind those fifty jumbo tote bags. Watching you fall was like watching a can of silly string explode."

"At least the clothes broke my fall."

"Agreed!"

Returning to their beverages, they both raise their brows and shake their heads, neither agreeing on anything except for their gratitude that fabric softened her impact.

I'm glad I caught Kaitlyn, or I'd be hearing about how I let her fall for the rest of my life.

Mom grins at my girlfriend. "You two look happy together."

Dad gives me a sly wink and a nod. "It's a good thing you caught her." He swallows more of his smoothie, his head shaking again.

"Peter was excited when he told us about you, and he doesn't show his emotions often." Mom's fingertips and thumb brace her straw. "Meeting you, though, it's obvious why he couldn't contain his joy."

Kaitlyn sets her drink on the table. "Thank you."

"I knew letting him go wouldn't be easy, but I'm glad he's with you. I can tell you'll take great care of him."

Moved with great emotion, Kaitlyn's tone is firm, every word a promise. "I will do everything I can to keep him happy and safe."

Mom's face lightens, gratitude tugging at her lips.

Kaitlyn walks around the table and leans into Mom; their arms fold around each other. Mom smiles as she rocks my girlfriend side to side in a squeeze. Kaitlyn hugs Dad next, her yellow locks draping over his shoulder. He gives away his feelings as he closes his eyes with a grin.

No one can resist her love, kindness, and beauty.

She will be a remarkable bride. With God's blessing, I'll call her mine.

Chapter Twenty-One

"Do you like what I bought for you?" I point at the glass ordering screen extending out of the center of the table, lit with an image of an open-faced turkey sandwich with mashed potatoes and gravy. The first surprise I gave her was a sandwich with the one food I didn't know she hates: avocado.

Kaitlyn squints as she nears the table, returning from the ladies' room. A smile crosses her face. "Yes, I love it."

"I'm getting the impression you love all sandwiches, except for those with avocado." I lower the ordering screen into the table and close the lid.

She sits with a shrug, her movements graceful. She was right: She's agile when she's relaxed. I see the real side of her, full of flair, courage, and nobility.

"Pretty much."

"Pretty much?" I smirk. "Don't you live off PB&Js when your mom leaves town?"

One corner of her mouth twists slightly, her shoulders shifting in surrender. "They're quick."

It's difficult to focus when I'm with her. I cherish every second, but it's hard to see the present when I keep living in the future: I want to marry her. I want to spend the rest of my life with her.

I talk with God more than I talk with Kaitlyn on these dates. I ask Him to let me propose to her. I lie in bed at night and beg Him some more. Plead for patience to see me through until He says it's time.

Please, God, let me ask her to marry me. I want to wake next to her every morning, have children and grandchildren with her, grow old with her. I want to make her smile and laugh. I want to hold her when she's sick or hurt. I want to take care of her. I feel like my purpose as a man is fulfilled in her, that You made me to care for this beautiful daughter of Yours. Her heart is pure. Aside from You, no one has understood me so completely.

No matter how much the world hurts her, no one can hold her down. Even the assassin who bombed her church couldn't break her spirit because she's given You her soul. No one can steal her joy, her beauty, or her essence. Every time she smiles, I see how resilient she is; I understand her more than anyone because I know how much she's gone through, how much You've healed her to make her the person she is.

I want to do this in Your time, God. Every morning when I wake, it's her I want to see. I belong with her, Lord. She's my Eve.

"How are summer classes going?" I inquire as our food arrives.

The server places our dinners on the table and hurries for another guest.

She lays the napkin on her lap. "Good, but I'm a little disappointed. No gorgeous cops have stopped by and asked me out." She takes the fork out of her mouth and chews her first bite, the motion disrupting her smile.

I carve into my steak. "We'll have to remedy that."

Her grin reappears as she lifts her glass to her lips, sipping her water and setting it down with a thoughtful expression. "I was scared when we first met. You are the most attractive man I've seen, but I couldn't bring up *my faith*," she mouths the last words without saying them out loud in case anyone is listening.

"I was nervous, too. There was an intense desire in my heart to pursue you."

"What would you have done if I hadn't stayed after class?"

"I would've run in the hall and introduced myself. A weight fell on me the second I walked in the room, and it was you. I can't imagine life without you." A void of emptiness pulls on my heart at the thought of never knowing her. "I was watching you for a while before you noticed me."

Her fork clanks against her plate as she concentrates on me with a set jaw. "Are we competing? Because I stared at you the entire time you were speaking. You barely looked at me."

"I couldn't risk forty-plus students realizing I was crushing on you."

She swallows her bite, a smile of impending victory spreading over her face. "Yes, you could have."

My head tilts as I cock my brow.

"What? You're a cop. If any of them said anything, you could've arrested them for harassment." She reaches with her fork and stabs tomato and lettuce off my plate, shoving them in her mouth and simpering in triumph.

I shake my head in mock defeat.

She's the woman I need and want.

God, I love her.

Chapter Twenty-Two

Peter
Friday, July 12, 2047
5:06 P.M.

Really?

Wide awake, I shoot out of bed, tripping with my foot caught in a sheet. I hop my way to balance, charge through the doorway, run into my pants lying in the hall, and pull my shirt out of my jeans as I bolt through the door.

I scarper down the porch and into my truck. Fire it to life and leave the driveway. I press my foot on the accelerator and drive a few miles, not paying attention to the turns I take and the lights I stop at since I have travelled this route at least a dozen times to go window-shopping. But this time is different: God has given me permission.

I park in front of the brick building, dash out, and hustle through the glass doors. A chime alerts the owner to my presence. The older man, his citrus hair interrupted with patches of gray, peeks out to see me racing toward a long glass case. He relaxes when he recognizes me, his expression changing to happiness when he notices my exhilaration.

"Is today the day?" He moseys behind the counter, smiling at my nervous joy.

"That I buy."

Gold and silver and platinum jewelry shine in the overhead light. I glance at one diamond band after another.

Too small. Too thin. Too thick. Wrong cut.

There are over a hundred options; I have to ask Kaitlyn's Creator.

Which one, Lord?

He guides me to a set in the back left corner, and it's perfect for my bride.

"That one, please. Size four."

The owner chuckles as he pulls out my choice, placing the set on the counter for my inspection. I pull out a thin, gold band. The top half is wavy; a one-carat diamond rests on top, carried at the peak of a soft ripple. I twist it in my fingers as I search it for perfection. I do the same for the wedding band, also undulating to lock in unison with the engagement ring.

"Sold."

His grin reaches his eyes, buggy-looking through his thick glasses, as he finishes the transaction. "Congratulations. I'll miss seeing you every week."

"Thanks." I make a mental note to invite him to the wedding as I hurry out, ring box in hand, and restart the engine.

I call Stanley, but Lorraine's smile greets me. "Hi, Peter!"

"I have to visit right away."

Her face changes with worry. "Is everything okay?"

"Peachy. I need to talk with you and Stanley."

"Swing by. Dinner's almost ready."

I hang up and travel miles more, trying to concentrate on the road ahead as I drive out of habit again.

Paying attention to my surroundings is difficult while I'm driving, impossible when I'm idle.

I sprint up the porch steps and ring the bell.

Lorraine answers, squinting as she analyzes me. "Are you okay? Did you just get out of bed?"

"Yeah."

Stanley appears beside her, his face falling with concern.

She runs a hand over my cheek in a motherly gesture. "You look tired, Dear."

"I worked a fourteen-hour shift. Kaitlyn's at school, right?"

They nod as Lorraine's hand lowers.

I pull the ring box out of my pocket. Gravity grows stronger as Kaitlyn's parents realize what's inside before I open it.

Lifting the lid, I extend the set toward them. "May I ask Kaitlyn to marry me?"

Bouncing and screaming, Lorraine covers the smile flooding through her eyes, shining with tears. Her gaze darts between Stanley and the rings. Laughter breaks his calm exterior, his beam proving he is the donor of Kaitlyn's perfect teeth.

"I'm glad it's you!" His voice booms as he hugs me tight.

Yvonne, hands behind her back, comes from behind him as he steps aside. I bring the bands near to her; she admires them for a few seconds before shrugging. "Cool." The only change in her expression is the slight upward twist in her lips.

She's no threat to my secret.

My grin fades as I focus on Stanley. "Kaitlyn cannot know anything."

"Agreed."

We turn to Lorraine for compliance. Still jittery, she's our weak link. Stanley's face firms. "Lorraine?"

Yvonne, standing between her parents, stares at her mother.

He rests his palms on Lorraine's shoulders. "We can't surprise Kaitlyn if you're jumping."

She fights the excitement, but it quakes through her.

"Think about how much more rewarding it will be if we manage to surprise her." He holds her close, resting his chin on her head as she wipes at tears.

"I'll tell her I have another business idea." She pulls away and grabs the back of her neck, her countenance falling. "But I'll be lying."

"That girl leaves us no choice." Stanley's thumb rubs her shoulder. "And you've had a few dozen of those, so come up with one more and you won't be lying."

Yvonne laughs, recalling every flighty idea Lorraine's had. Undeterred by her mother's scowl, she hands me a comb.

I take it, baffled. "Why are you giving me this?"

"Mom said your hair was a mess. You'll want to look better if you're proposing."

Wedding rings in one hand, comb in the other, I gape at Yvonne. Lorraine and Stanley wear similar expressions.

"How'd you know?"

Emotions dulled, her shoulders rise a touch. "Lucky guess."

Ninja. I'm glad I've lived long enough to meet one.

Stanley gawks at the comb. "Is that mine?"

I hand it over, but he waves it away.

"Nah. Keep it."

"So it's a yes?"

All three of them beam, Lorraine bursting into tears.

"Welcome to the family, Son!" Stanley laughs and hugs me again.

Chapter Twenty-Three

Peter
Thursday, July 18, 2047
6:36 P.M.

Today I'm asking Kaitlyn to be my wife.

I've known since our first date she would be my bride, though I haven't told her yet. For five months, I've been living with an unquenchable thirst to spend my life with her. To marry her and have children with her. To be a husband, but to no one except Kaitlyn. I want to care for her and grow old with her.

My truck bounces over the Reeds' rocky driveway. Sun peeks through the canopy of tree branches hanging overhead, its rays shining on my blue hood. I bank left and the two-story home comes into view, light glimmering on its soft tan walls and brown roof and trimming. The place is inviting, despite how unornamented it is. They keep their lawn cut and free of weeds, but they aren't big with decorations.

I park in front of the door and travel to the entrance—tempering the exhilaration that threatens to spring through my steps—and ring the bell. No matter how many times I visit, I chat with Kaitlyn's family before leaving with her. A faint smell of smoke and meat is in the air; Stanley must be barbequing on the side porch.

The door flies open faster than usual, even for Kaitlyn—who's wearing an energetic grin. She's always elated about our dates, but tonight she's vivacious. Did Lorraine tell?

She hops out, her yellow tresses falling over the pink blouse she received on her birthday.

Aware of the strength of Kaitlyn's intuition, I have gone to great lengths to make the proposal a surprise. No matter how many years I spend with her, I'll never stop wooing her. There will be challenges, like finding new ways to catch her off guard as she learns my tricks.

I smile at Kaitlyn, beside me on the porch, watching me with glee. Lorraine's behind her, the corners of her mouth reaching her ears as she lifts two thumbs in the air, her chest lurching with silent laughter. Next to her is Stanley, who's observing me with reserved joy. Given their attempts to conceal their enthusiasm, I doubt they revealed my plan.

But Kaitlyn is overly excited. Did her sister tell? I dismiss that idea also: Yvonne takes pride in keeping secrets and likes me too much to risk hurting me.

Kaitlyn twists her arm around mine. "I have a present for you when we get back."

"Okay." I don't ask what the gift is for; if she knows tonight's agenda, starting that conversation could ruin my arrangements. The most I can do is act normal and wish for the best as I turn to her parents. "Mind if I steal your daughter for the evening?"

"No, of course not!" Lorraine almost shouts, nearly blowing my cover. Stanley cautions her with a nudge. My lips hold a tight line, scarcely faking a smile. My girlfriend can't see her parents, but she is so focused on me I have to feign normalcy or she'll suspect what I'm up to. As hard as it is to catch my girlfriend unaware, she wants a man who can and will surprise her, a mate who will sweep her off her feet.

Leading her down the porch, the warmth of her soft hand on my bare forearm makes me fantasize about walking down the aisle with her. Imagine how her lips will feel when I kiss her at the altar.

Her eyes are glued on me as I guide her to my truck. I'm tempted to ask why she's exuberant, but I bite my tongue.

"Are you having a good day?"

"Yes," I coo as I open her door. "Now that I'm with you, it's even better."

Kaitlyn freezes with a grin.

I motion inside the truck, breaking her trance and helping her in. I close her door, meander around the front, and enter on my side. The engine starts and I drive us to our date. A deep breath would soothe my nerves, but she'd notice. I have to relax without outward signals. I can take it easy in a couple of hours.

The sway of my truck eases my jitters and calms Kaitlyn. We enjoy the silence of each other's company on our way to the park, a common destination for us. I'm wearing normal date attire: a tan short-sleeve shirt and blue jeans. I have to make every detail as routine as possible or she'll guess.

Running through familiar motions, I park and help her out. Lead her to the path circling the water fountain.

She is beautiful, inside and out. I never tire of her sleek hair, the color of the sun. Her glowing skin and perfect teeth. Rosy lips radiating her soul's beauty every time she smiles. The way she writes every emotion on her face. Her heart is equally captivating with her kindness for others and her passion for life. She wants to make the world a better place. She does make it better, or at least my part of it. I can't imagine living without her. God is the source of my existence, and she is my reason for living. Now that I've been blessed to know her, I can't feel complete without her. I have to marry her. I hope she says yes.

In the beauty of orange evening sunlight and the relief of cooler air, I tuck Kaitlyn's svelte fingers between mine as we journey the paved path ringing the enormous, three-tier, concrete fountain.

My free hand traces the ring box in my pocket as I mentally rehearse the myriad of ways to arrange my words, but I can't think of a speech that tops the one I have memorized.

She notices my gaze and grins as I wrap my arms around her. "You're a miracle, and I'll never stop loving you." I kiss her head, silky strands of hair sticking to my lips. "Never forget that."

People pass by as we stand motionless in the center of the broad path. A few stare, starry-eyed with the admiration of young love.

Kaitlyn nuzzles in my arms, enjoying the warmth of my embrace before pulling away with a bright smile. "I'm the luckiest girl in the world to have you in my life. I love you." Grasping my hands, she rises to her tiptoes and presses her tender lips against my cheek.

She lowers to her heels and we resume our stroll with entwined fingers. She watches birds play in the trees as I appreciate her elegance, a gift from God I'm thankful to see every day.

I nudge her toward a wooden bench. "Let's sit down."

She takes her seat, the sun setting behind her.

I bend on one knee.

Her hands cover her mouth and nose, euphoria sparkling in her brown eyes. Her shock and delight make everything worthwhile: the waiting, the patience, the prayer. Her glee is more boisterous than it was when I asked her out five months ago. Seeing her this alive and knowing I'm doing what's right for her makes me proud to be a man. Every day I spend with her makes me more grateful to God for guiding my steps and helping me understand right and wrong as I walk through life.

Kaitlyn doesn't ask for much. Though she enjoys dressing nice, she would be just as ecstatic if I gave her a band with no stone at all. She loves me for who I am, not for what I give her. But she's my future wife, and I'm giving her the best. I have the funds, and I have the desire.

I pull out the box and open it; the rays bounce off the one-carat diamond.

Her right hand races to her chest; she gives me her left before I utter a word.

My broad smile stills my tension as I wrap my hand around hers.

"Kaitlyn Anna Reed, you are the only woman I need. You are beautiful inside and out. You make me laugh, and you give me purpose. I can't live without you. I'll be forever grateful if you'll do me the enormous honor of being my wife. Will you marry me?"

"Yes!"

Still on bended knee, I slide the gold ring on her finger. Lift the back of her hand to my lips. Nerves gone, my mouth relaxes into a grin of relieved ecstasy. "This ring wasn't beautiful until it was on you, Mrs. Tryndale."

She rushes into me, her small fingers tugging on the back of my shirt as she squeezes me in her tightest embrace. Her tears fall on my neck as I press into her soft hair. My smile brightens with the aroma of her perfume; every time I breathe it in, I'll remember this moment. The instant she changed my life forever by becoming my bride.

"Look!" I point at the corner of the park where my dad stands, holding a recorder. Kaitlyn rests her cheek against mine. We wave, laughing as we celebrate joining our lives together in God.

I love her with every part of my being.

She loves me just as much.

Kaitlyn kisses me on the cheek. Her smile grows on my face, and it's the biggest grin she's ever worn.

Chapter Twenty-Four

Peter
Thursday, July 18, 2047
9:39 P.M.

Kaitlyn's golden hair drapes around her face as she sits in my truck, admiring her diamond as I drive her home. Her family is waiting to celebrate with us; though I was nervous, they never doubted she'd say yes.

She turns to me with creased brows. "Did you time this?"

"Come again?"

"Today's your birthday."

Now her excitement makes sense.

"I forgot."

"You forgot your birthday?" Never one to miss an occasion for gifts, she can't envision forgetting a birthday, especially her own.

"I'm more excited about marrying you, Mrs. Tryndale."

The corners of her beautiful chocolate eyes wrinkle with delight. It's hard to break away from her, but I fix my gaze on the Reeds' driveway. "The best gift I could get was for you to say yes. Nothing else matters."

She rustles in my peripheral and the warmth of her supple lips presses against my cheek.

"I love you."

"I love you, too." My face aches from wearing the largest grin of my life, but it's the best pain I've ever felt. I put the truck in park and walk to her side.

She slides down the tan upholstered seat, moonlight glowing around her as frogs and crickets sing in the background. Her arm winds around mine, her hand gliding along my forearm, over my wrist, and into my palm before she leads me up the porch.

Kaitlyn's grip is fierce as she drags me through her home like a six-year-old with a ragdoll.

"Mom! Dad! Vonnie! Quick!" Her voice rings through the living room, bouncing off the vaulted ceiling and echoing through the halls and upstairs chambers.

We scarper through the living room and find her parents beside the kitchen.

Kaitlyn flashes her jewel. "I'm engaged!"

Lorraine grabs a professional camera sitting on the breakfast bar. Kaitlyn beams at her father, who is glimmering with a quiet but powerful joy.

"That's wonderful, Dear." Lorraine wraps her daughter in a hug, running her free hand through Kaitlyn's hair. "Let's get a picture of you two."

Kaitlyn's expression changes from ecstasy to puzzlement as she pulls away from her mother's embrace, her voice falling. "You guys knew?"

Their reserved excitement has given us away.

Tears pool in Lorraine's eyes as she rubs Kaitlyn's shoulder. "Peter's a wonderful man. He asked for our permission to take your hand in marriage. You should be proud of him. Men don't do that anymore."

Kaitlyn cocks her hip in her hand. "But your muffin delivery business!"

"Oh, Dear. I learned my lesson with the cupcakes. Do you think your mother would make the same mistake twice?" She pats Kaitlyn's arm with a chuckle and leaves.

Stanley, hands in pockets, lingers on the other side of his daughter. Overhead light reflects off his golden hair as he observes Kaitlyn and me with a perceptive smile, pleased the muffin business threw Kaitlyn off my trail.

Too many emotions are spilling over Kaitlyn's face to read her, but confusion dominates.

"You asked them?"

"Okay, you two! Picture!" Lorraine dances beside the couch for our attention.

Feet shoulder-width apart and arms crossed, I keep my sight on my new fiancée. "Yep."

"When?" Her palms flip in heated surprise.

Her mother shouts again. "Picture!"

"While you were in class last week."

"You sneak!" She winks at me with tousled hair. Her grin has changed; it's brighter, as if a piece of her heart was dormant until tonight.

Wanting to feel her soft lips against mine, I lose my breath. I want to run my fingers through her hair and smooth down her satin tresses.

Following her to the couch, I can't believe I'm marrying this woman. I can't take my eyes off her shimmering yellow hair and her slender frame. Her smile is so brilliant I'll never forget its radiance. I could see an angel and find their beauty dims in comparison. She is wonderful and beautiful and loving and glorious and God made her for me.

"Sit down! Right there!" Lorraine points to a specific spot on the couch. If she's this demanding over an informal engagement photo, what will she be like as the wedding planner? I'm certain Kaitlyn will put her in charge. Thankfully, I'm not the bride.

I relax in my seat, grateful I'm past the anxiety of proposing and Kaitlyn is rejoicing over my promise to her, my vow that I will spend the rest of my life loving her and only her.

My arm lying on the back of the couch behind my bride, she tilts forward and flaunts her diamond near her mother's camera. Her euphoria is electric; if she's this exhilarated over our engagement, how magnificent will she be on the day we marry? On our honeymoon?

"Say 'Wedding!'" Lorraine smiles behind the lens.

Kaitlyn screams the word, her teeth showing through her beam.

I memorize my fiancée in silence, grateful to God for creating a woman perfect for me.

Lorraine sets the camera on the coffee table. "Let's look at that ring closer."

My fiancée lengthens her arm, flipping her wrist down like a princess. Her mother takes her hand and inspects the stone in detail.

"It is gorgeous. Looks nicer on you than I imagined. He has excellent taste."

"You saw my ring first, too?" Kaitlyn's tone drops, her mouth hanging open.

Armed with sugar, Lorraine smooths Kaitlyn's hair at the temple. "Do you want pie, Dear? We have celebrating to do."

My distracted fiancée bolts to her feet; I follow her.

"Yvonne! Come down for dessert! Peter popped the question!" Lorraine hollers, peeking upstairs but not moving toward it.

"She knew, too?"

Her mother nods, prideful we finally surprised her.

"How did all of you keep this from me?" Kaitlyn's hands shoot in the air; she can't believe she missed the hints written on four people, but she shouldn't be shocked that her sister kept my secret: Yvonne's quiet enough to earn national security clearance. I wonder how many secrets that thirteen-year-old has.

"It wasn't easy," Stanley booms from the dining room. "But Peter's good at what he does."

Kaitlyn turns to him. Staring at the back of her head, I imagine she's pouting. Her mother strokes her hair, disrupting her focus. When their gazes connect, Lorraine rises to her tiptoes and kisses her on the forehead.

"We love you." She leaves the living room before Kaitlyn can object, passing the kitchen as she disappears in the hall.

No longer insulted, my bride curls her hands around my biceps. "I'll be right back."

Before I can speak, she's racing up the stairs, her brilliant hair dancing behind her.

Stanley's sitting at the dining table when a crash sounds down the hall. He stands, but a muffled *"I got it!"* echoes toward us before he takes a step. Back in his seat, he sighs as he rests his cheek in his palm. I wonder if he's groaning because he wants to help Lorraine more often and she's too sovereign to allow it; I have that issue with Kaitlyn at times. Reed women are independent, though that trait is a big reason why I'm drawn to my bride.

I couldn't have wished for a better family to marry into. Though I've been in their lives for less than half a year, they've welcomed me as one of their own. In many ways, they've been the answer to my prayers. Stanley, Lorraine, and Yvonne are a great foundation of extended family for our future children. I didn't realize how much I yearned for more family until I found them. They value me. They trust me with Kaitlyn, and she believes in me to protect her, cherish her, and provide for her.

Yvonne arrives out of thin air, her stunning hazel eyes piercing mine. She shrugs at me with a small smile on her way to the table. Her thin hair, black like her mother's, is tied in another low ponytail. I can't get over how different Kaitlyn and Yvonne are, despite being sisters.

Kaitlyn appears behind her, running to me with a package. "Happy birthday!"

Analyzing her with a controlled grin, I accept the present and slip off the teal ribbon and blue wrapping paper, dropping them to the floor. A white, paperboard box rests in my hands; whatever's inside must be wonderful because Kaitlyn's giddiness is growing. No one is in the living room with us; maybe her parents and sister know it's private.

I pry off the lid to reveal . . . *The Everyday Teen Girl's Bible.*

My jaw hangs halfway open. I glance from the Bible to her and back in confusion. "Umm?"

"Open it!" She clasps her hands as her weight bounces side to side, her tempo increasing with excitement.

Pages are tattered and beat around the edges from obsessive use and spotted yellow and brown from spills. Crumpled note tabs and bookmarks stick out the top. My index finger runs along the front, pulling back the hardcover.

This Bible Belongs To: Kaitlyn Reed   The handwriting doesn't match the beautiful penmanship she possesses now.

"My parents got it from someone they trusted after our church—" She shies away to a distant point on the floor as she cradles herself, her voice cracking before she finds the strength to bring her eyes back to mine. "You know. They suspected churches wouldn't be around much longer, but they wanted to help me through my teen years.

"I want you to read the notes and prayers I wrote in it growing up. I want you to know how hard I worked to stay pure for you. Every guy I turned down, every date I rejected . . . it's you I've been waiting for. I love you."

"Thank you." The words come out in a hushed awe. Saving herself is the greatest gift she could give me, outward proof of her inward commitment to honor her God and the husband He created for her. But, as for tangible objects, this is the best present. I can watch her journey unfold as she matured, see how her choices molded her into the woman she is today. Different from her peers. Unique from other women.

Still in amazement over what a breathtaking bride she is, I wonder what I've done to deserve her. Then I remember the best relationships are based on love that's freely given, not earned.

Her arms twist around my torso, and strands of hair catch between my lips as I kiss her head. "This is the best present I've ever received."

"You're welcome. I love you, Peter."

I love her more than ever. I shut my eyes and clutch my bride against my chest, savoring her scent. We lose track of time until our arms fall.

Lorraine returns with a fifth seat for the table, the white patio chair stashed in storage because it doesn't match the cast iron arrangement on the side deck.

I place my gift on the coffee table and lock hands with Kaitlyn, whispering three words I've spoken to no other woman: "I love you."

She remains quiet as we head to the dining table, her luminous joy assuring me of all I need to know: She loves me more than I can imagine.

We take our seats with Yvonne and Stanley. Our reflections glow in the dark windows as we celebrate. A miraculous day is ending, but many miracles wait ahead.

Kaitlyn sits to my left, our hands entwined over the corner of the table. She examines the ring on her finger, admiring its sparkle. She peeks in my direction and catches me studying her. I don't dim my delight: I enjoy watching her radiate ecstasy as much as she appreciates the glint of her gem. She is my treasure.

Blushing and biting her lip, her eyes dart away as she hides her left hand under the table. I lift her other hand to my lips and kiss her soft skin without breaking my smile. Her grin reaches both ears. She's all I can see. Even with her family surrounding us, it feels like we are the only people in the room.

Her mocha eyes gleam with flecks of gold. "How'd you know my ring size?"

"You forgot a ring in the bathroom. I traced the inside of it."

Her white teeth shine in the chandelier's light, her jaw dropping with laughter. "You cheated!"

Lorraine, standing on the other side of the table, freezes with the chocolate cream pie. "You fooled her twice?"

I wink at her, one corner of my mouth curved.

Astonished, she sets the dessert on the table and makes a separate trip for plates and forks. She serves everyone a slice, helping herself last. My mouth waters at the sweet scent of cocoa and whipped cream.

This pie tastes richer than the store-bought variety, and its texture is creamier. "Did you make this from scratch?"

"Even the whipped cream." She sits in the chair across from me, pride holding her shoulders higher. "It's a special occasion."

Lorraine doesn't need one; she loves cooking. Amazingly, given her love of food, Kaitlyn didn't inherit her mother's culinary expertise. I've only witnessed her cook the most basic of dinners, like chicken and rice. Even then, the rice on the bottom was burned.

We savor our dessert in quiet, forks clanking against ceramic plates. Sweet, fluffy pie collapses in my mouth.

Stanley breaks the silence. "When are you two getting married?"

Kaitlyn and I answer at the same time:

"Next month!"

"After she graduates."

We scrutinize each other with mutual defiance. Only one of us will have our way.

Her father snickers. "Welcome to marriage." Another bite of pie smacks in his mouth.

My eyes are locked on Kaitlyn's as Stanley chuckles; I wonder if he knew this would happen and he asked because he wanted the entertainment. Yvonne–sitting on the other side of her sister, a forkful of pie suspended halfway between her plate and mouth–gawks at us with disgusted curiosity.

After we've finished our servings, Stanley helps Lorraine clear the table. Kaitlyn and I stay seated, hands clasped over the corner of the tabletop. We beam at each other, though Kaitlyn periodically breaks her gaze away to the rock on her finger. I love putting joy in her heart. I love adding purpose to her life, and I cherish the definition she brings to mine.

She leans in close. "Why not next month?"

"Because I love you; I don't want to be a distraction." I kiss her forehead before resting the top of my head on hers. The smell of flowers makes her feel all the more precious and fragile.

"You distract me more this way." Her whisper rings in my ears.

"We'll be leaving you two alone."

Lorraine, smiling with tears, pats Yvonne's shoulder.

"We couldn't have hoped for a better man for Kaitlyn. She'll forever be our baby, but we know she's safe in your hands. Thank you for taking care of her. It's your birthday, but we received the greater gift–you for a son. Happy birthday, Peter."

"Thank you." I notice Stanley's gone; he rarely stays longer than his presence is required. He trusts me with his daughter and knows we want privacy to discuss wedding plans.

Lorraine and Yvonne walk upstairs, leaving us alone. I lay my forehead on my bride's, my fingers tracing her supple hands. "Kaitlyn, I'll distract you more after marriage. Trust me."

"I do trust you, but do you realize how long we have till I graduate?"

I kiss her head, wrapping her in an embrace as I stroke her back. "Two years."

"Do you know how long that will take?"

"About seven hundred days."

She cocks her head. "Way to make it sound longer."

"I can support you just as much while being your fiancé. You'll need your space to focus on school, and marriage will distract you more than engagement. You're twenty, Kaitlyn. We're young. We have all the time in the world."

"What if we don't?"

I grab her shoulders. "Why do you say that?"

"You know about my church. People die every day in accidents and violence, and our faith makes us targets. Especially you—you're a cop. What if we never live our dream?" Her voice cracks as she wipes away tears, trying not to smudge her mascara.

She doesn't know how right she is, that there is a serial criminal hunting Christians. But I don't want her to worry about me when we're apart; I don't want her to fear with every shift that I may encounter the killer and lose.

"I can't promise we won't . . . die." I choke on the word. "But I can protect us better *because* I'm a cop. God is watching out for both of us, and I love you more than life. I will die before I allow anyone to hurt you."

Tears paralyze her against my chest. I hold her, her arched back heaving with grief beneath my hands. Her jaw on my shoulder, she whispers: "Tomorrow isn't promised to anyone, Peter."

I squeeze her tighter; I don't want to think about losing her. She's my Eve, my bride, my better half. I can't imagine living without her.

"That's true, but we still need to plan for it. If we marry now, you might not finish school. You might get pregnant. You might find more interest in our family—"

"What's wrong with that?"

"Nothing, Kaitlyn."

She tugs away, but I keep her close and kiss her behind her ear.

"But didn't you say God called you to Security? To save someone special?"

"I'm not giving up my calling." She draws back, her hands lifting a few inches off her lap. Her face is torn, as if she'll have regrets about waiting. "Yeah, I might enjoy you and our children more, but I can work and have a family. Maybe God will use you to help me in counter-terrorism, or maybe leading me to you is part of why He asked me to enlist in Security."

She might be right; what if God will use our relationship to create the Exodus He told me about? But I won't disobey the Lord or take a chance that she'll forget her calling because of me. She has to train for her mission as I did for mine.

"I've been praying about you since the first second I saw you, and I want to live God's way. He gave me permission to propose to you, but He cautioned me to wait until you graduate before we go any further. Talk to God about this, Kaitlyn. We can't rush Him."

"I know." She wipes away more tears, still trying to avoid mascara, but it's useless. I rub away brown streaks running down her face. She presses my hand against her cheek, cool and damp with moisture.

"I don't know why God wants us to wait, but it's my duty as a man to help you and not hinder you," I whisper. "Married life will be different; something might happen, like having a baby, that will distract you from finishing school."

Or the reason I most suspect: If I marry her, if I make the declaration that this is the woman I can't live without, the perp will take her. Maybe God wants me to stop him before tying the knot.

"Please respect my decision. I love you, and I want to see you go hard for God. He wants to do great things in you, Kaitlyn. Focus on your studies and prepare yourself to protect others. To save that person you love."

She sighs as she relinquishes control. Her whisper, thick with emotion, tickles my wrist. "I do respect you. I'll wait, but it won't be easy."

I bring her into my arms. "It'll be hard for both of us, but it's best we do this God's way. You're my Eve. I love you." I kiss the top of her cheek, her heavy breath falling against my chest.

She clutches my shirt with both hands. "I love you, too."

Chapter Twenty-Five

I long for my husband, Lord, but I trust You more than I miss him. There's glory in this somewhere, though I may not see it until after death. I do wonder, though, why You allowed him to die. How will I teach our son to be a good man when I am a woman? What will I do for a living? My husband was my provider. Where will I work, and who will care for our child while I'm there?

Maybe Mom is right: I need to move back in with her and Dad. Let them help me. But they're a thousand miles away. Then again, there's nothing left for me in Imperia. We moved here a couple of months ago for his work, but that doesn't matter anymore, does it?

Peering at the piece of him growing in my womb, I pray daily for our son's health. I beg God that his birth will give me a reason to live again. I hope my boy takes after my husband and I can watch him grow into his father.

I don't care that we lost our home when he died. I don't miss it. I miss him. He was my best friend.

Our baby, sensing my heartache, darts in my womb. I rub over him, trying to soothe his anxiety. Intangible, invisible, but stronger than any umbilical cord, a wire connects our souls.

It will take all my strength to rise from the bench in the

supermarket's foyer and journey back to the shelter, where I'm living until I find a permanent place. I left for the store feeling like I had enough energy to buy kiwis. I guess I did, since I have the fruit, but I wonder if I have the stamina to return.

"Ready?" I stare at my belly, waiting for a response. One shopper smiles; another sneers like I need a paddy wagon.

I stand, the effort making my body groan loudly enough I'm certain others hear it. One glance around my surroundings tells me the screams were a hallucination. Pregnancy is making me crazy.

Kiwis in hand, I totter out of the supermarket and waddle half a block down the sidewalk when my legs grow dull and achy, unable to carry my weight another step. Somehow I keep walking, but each time one foot inches forward, I half-expect the ankle above it to snap.

I stop for a break, holding my stomach as it tugs my shoulders forward. Faint and short of breath, I stretch my gasps into full inhalations, expanding my lungs against the pressure of my womb. Darkness gives me anxiety, increasing my difficulty. Streetlights, traffic signals, business signs, and vehicles are my only sources of illumination. Maybe it's because I'm missing my husband more than ever, but this night feels evil.

Lord, I can't keep going.

Tears fall. Every part of me is shattered: My heart yearns for my husband. He won't hear our child's first cry. He won't hold our son. My soul thirsts for God. Scripture says He is near to the broken-hearted, yet I haven't felt His presence in ages. I'm homeless. My body is ripping, stretching, and contorting in impossible ways under the stress of a nearly full-term baby. My mind is a pretzel, having tried to think of solutions to my problems from so many different angles—while also thinking about my child—that it's tangled its own wires.

No one can see me crying. No one can help. It's just me and my son. He wants us to rest, but the sidewalk is too hard to lie on and I can't make it to the shelter. The kiwis I had to have an hour ago are now a burden.

A truck pulls to the curb. The window lowers, and a man with blue eyes smiles at me, his white teeth reflecting the overhead light.

"Would you like a ride?"

I never accept rides from strangers, especially men, but I don't know what I'll do without help. "Are you heading toward Monroe?"

"Driving right by it."

He's so handsome he's angelic, but I miss my husband too much to feel attraction toward another, even him.

Twisting the grocery sack left, right, left, I bite my lip and consider which choice is wiser: Walking and risking collapse? Or taking a ride with this harmless-looking stranger?

"Hop in."

Too tired to debate any longer, I traipse around the front of his truck. He leans over and opens his passenger door. I set the kiwis in his truck, and he moves them to the backseat. Unable to lift myself, I wrap my arms over his seat and pant.

"Do you need help?"

Embarrassed, I smother my face in the cushion. "Mm-hmm."

He steps out, races to my side, and helps me enter.

As soon as I'm comfortable, danger asphyxiates me. The door bangs shut, and panic pounds my heart. I reach for the handle, but something takes away my vision and traps me against the seat.

My chest too tight to breathe, I struggle to think through what's happening: The man was outside when the iron vise gripped me. Someone else is in this vehicle, and they threw a hood over my head.

Unable to shield my son from my fright, he pokes and kicks the walls of my womb with frantic terror. Knowing I can't protect him exaggerates my fear.

I wiggle for freedom. The pressure leaves my chest as big hands squeeze my throat. Without air, my only choice is to be still; movement uses oxygen my son desperately needs.

"Think about your baby." The driver posed as an angel of light, and— even with the cloak of deception removed—his voice carries the same smooth polish. "If you fight, we cut off your air. No oxygen for mom, no oxygen for baby. If you want your son to have a chance, you're doing what I say. Got it?"

Does he know me? How does he know I'm having a boy? Did he guess?

I hope we can stay alive long enough for the police to save us. Surveillance is everywhere; Security has to be on the way.

The truck bounces along for what feels like an eternity before coming to a halt. The hands stray from my neck as the fabric moves off my face; the man's eyes are locked on mine. They're still a startling shade of blue—but darker, burning so hot I can almost see flames. I keep my vision from the person behind me. Blackness makes it impossible to see what's outside, but the amount of time he drove and the absence of noise and light make me think we're secluded.

"Do you believe in Jesus?" A blade clicks out of his palm.

I fight shallow, forceful gasps of air. "Yes."

He runs the blade over my rounded middle, its tip lifting my shirt as he lowers the band of my pants with his free hand. My belly bared, his razor's edge follows the zigzag of a stretch mark. He gawks at my abdomen with perverted admiration, as if he can see my son through my paper-thin skin. "What if I told you that I'm making you choose between your God and your baby?"

Abraham loved You more than he loved Isaac. Am I strong enough to give up my child's life for You? I love You; I don't want to reject You. I'm tempted to do whatever it takes to give my child breath, but no one has life without You. I need Your strength, Lord.

Gulping for air, I pray the strongest Word in the universe, the Word that created the world: *Jesus.*

Hold truth to the lie. Shine light on the darkness.

"You don't have that power."

He presses the blade in, breaking my belly's skin just enough to draw blood. My child squirms with my fear. Eyes clenched and tears flooding down, I scream with the horror of our impending deaths. I clutch my son with open palms, wishing I could comfort him.

"You think I don't?"

"No." God's been quiet for a long time, but His voice is running through the emotional connection I share with my son as He soothes us both. He is with us always. The Lord's Spirit isn't the thundering crash I'm accustomed to; it's a gentle acceptance: My son and I will die. In a few minutes, we will wake in front of Jesus, reunited with my husband forever.

The knife runs up my naked belly, blood beading along the trail. The blade rubs against my top as it ascends my chest, grooving along my neck and under my jaw until the tip reaches my cheek. It pierces through my skin, stabbing into my gums and sliding between two teeth. Nausea railroads me; I'm not sure if it's from terror or the sickening taste of my blood.

"Do you want to hold your child?"

"Of course." I swallow my blood as my baby kicks with fear.

"Deny God, and I'll let you."

The murderer isn't at war with me. He's at war with Christ.

A tidal wave of God's courage consumes me. "Liar."

"What makes you think I'm lying?"

"Because I know who pulls your strings."

He blisters with rage.

"You want me to deny God so you can kill me with a one-way ticket for hell. Then my son will lose me forever. But you can't destroy my soul, and you can't touch my child's. God alone has that power, so why should I fear you?"

He stabs my forehead.

Chapter Twenty-Six

Peter
Wednesday, January 8, 2048
5:58 A.M.

I'm growing attached. It's hard not to feel as if I know these women, because in a way I do: I saw their fates before their nightmares began. I felt a connection with them in my dream, and every time one vanishes I have another sister in Christ to search for.

The tenth victim has disappeared: Holly White. Like her predecessors, she was mysteriously assigned to me through the System.

As usual, I conducted my investigation with a sense of caution, knowing that each step may lead me into an ambush. My quest for Mrs. White was fast, since her profile gave me system error messages for today and yesterday. She's in the System until Monday, though, and that's how I know she's homeless, pregnant, and soon to be a single mother, since her husband died two weeks ago surfing the Atlantic Coast. Would the perp stoop low enough to target a widowed, destitute woman and the life growing inside of her?

Error messages guarantee he has. Mrs. White will never hold her child unless I rescue them. I have to remain optimistic that she's alive, that I'll discover a sign that will lead me to her so I can bring her and her baby to safety. The perp hasn't won until I allow him to kill my faith.

I want to find this man and hurt him.

God, please give me Your strength and wisdom. Help me remember that vengeance is Yours, not mine.

The silent prayer renews my calm.

Mrs. White is five-foot-six. Pale blond, almost white, hair. Petite, with a big belly all out in front. A woman eight months pregnant stands out in public.

She had few people in her life: a couple of friends, two cousins, her parents, and a brother—all of them live over a thousand miles away. I scanned through their correspondences and finances. They seemed to care for her; no one wanted to harm her or her child. I called her parents, but they had no information. Now they're worried, and sleep won't come easily to them for weeks to come.

Her husband has one living relative, his mother, but she's senile and in a nursing home. His buddies are clean and also a thousand miles away. Mrs. White and her husband moved to Imperia recently and hadn't resided here long enough to make new friends. She hasn't gone to school or worked in years. Though she went to church in her hometown until the Burning happened, she parted ways with the Believers she knew, a frequent story for Christians. In a last-ditch effort, I checked every employee at the medical clinic where she receives her care. There, too, everyone had alibis and no one appeared to have motive for harming Mrs. White or her baby.

I have two hints so far. First, her husband's savings was used at a supermarket on Tuesday, the day she disappeared. He didn't have much left, but somebody used the funds to buy kiwis. The shop's surveillance system was black, so Mrs. White must've been there. Second, she stayed overnights at a shelter near the store; the lady who runs it remembered seeing her every night, but she claims Mrs. White left around ten-thirty last night and never returned. She stated Mrs. White was considering moving back with her parents, but she was hesitating because she and her mother share a hard past.

I hunted for clues in the surveillance from cameras neighboring the shop and shelter, looking for a familiar face, a suspicious vehicle, or a common denominator from the footage of previous abduction sites.

Like every other time, I struck out.

Driving through the darkness to the supermarket, I'm desperate to uncover the evidence I need to stop the perp for good. Holly White is Victim Ten; there are two more if I don't stop him.

Hurrying out of my patrol car, I hope I can save the girl this time. I rush into the store, rejecting the sharp scent of fermented beef sticks that have sat in the impulse aisles long enough to stain the air. Pulling up an image of Mrs. White on my SimLink, I show employees and customers her picture and ask if they've seen her. Most don't remember her, but one confirms she came in late last night and bought fruit. I interview more people, but nobody has more to add.

I locate the store manager, a peaceful old man with a broad smile. He leads me into his office. I point to Mrs. White's image. Inform him she's missing and was seen in his shop last night. Moving slow with age, his nod takes almost half a minute as he sits motionless behind his desk.

"What happened with your surveillance footage? It's not visible through our system."

His trunk pivots toward his computer. Then his arm . . . then his finger straightens . . . then its tip touches the screen. Then he can't remember his password.

"Hmm. Two-four-three-eight?" *Tap. Tap. Tap.* Reaching . . . Reaching . . . *Tap.*

Beep-Blurp.

"Hmm. Zero-four-one-two?" *Tap.* He tilts forward, his forefinger pushing his glasses up the bridge of his nose as he squints at the numbers.

Tap . . .

Tap . . .

Tap . . .

He leans closer to the screen and presses another button.

Beep-Blurp.

He gapes at the screen. "Hmm. I could've sworn it was my grandkid's birthday."

Head hanging with irritation, I catch myself rubbing the wrinkles in my forehead. My palm drags against my face as my gaze returns.

"Oh! That's right. I changed it yesterday." He gives me a goofy grin, as if he doesn't understand a missing pregnant woman is at stake. "Getting senile in my old age."

He pats the numbers on his screen—each stroke taking eons—before logging in. He pulls up his camera footage. "Hmm. I've never seen this before. It must be a glitch."

This is getting old, fast.

"Thank you for your time." I leave his office and bolt to my squad car, slamming the door and punching the steering wheel. Another woman has fallen dead—and a baby with her—and the trail is as cold as ever.

The perp is powerful. If any distant family or friends have tried to build awareness about the missing ladies, he has kept the media and online communities silent. He's kept the truth hidden with the girls, wherever they are. The nation is blind to his acts. He's stolen ten women; two more are destined if I don't stop him.

God, please. I'm begging You. Many Israelites died under Pharaoh's tyranny before You prepared Moses, but I'll go nuts if I have to wait much longer. Too many ladies have died, Father. Now a baby, too. I hate him, Lord. I want to break every bone in his body for what he's done. Please take my wrath. Help me forgive, at least enough to calm down and think objectively. Help me find him so I can end this and save the women who are still alive. Part the waters, Jesus.

Chapter Twenty-Seven

Peter
Wednesday, January 8, 2048
10:59 P.M.

Brisk air cools my face as I stand outside Kaitlyn's door, exhausted from searching for Mrs. White and her baby while juggling hectic calls along the way.

She answers with a smile, wearing faded green pajamas and furry slippers. Her shiny, yellow tresses are tied in a bun. Even in nightwear and no makeup, she is the most beautiful woman I've seen.

"Hi," she whispers, opening the door wider.

I enter her home; its tranquility grows more inviting in the silence of night. Her parents and sister are asleep, so I stay quiet. I want to feel guilty that Kaitlyn's staying up late for me, but I feel joy. I called to hear her voice before bed, and she insisted I visit. I can never pass an opportunity to experience her presence, to adore her gorgeous smile, to enjoy her tender caress.

Leaving my jacket on, I slide off my boots in the foyer and follow my bride. We pass the fireplace and she sits on the couch, leaning against the armrest and pulling her legs under her hip. She props her arm on the back of the couch and smiles at me. Light bounces off the stone on her hand as her fingers tease her hair. I'm glad I gave her the ring that I did: Impossible to miss, everyone knows she's taken.

She pats the cushion next to her, but I sit on the floor and incline against the couch instead; I'll lose consciousness if I get too comfortable. My eyes are sandpaper. The hunt has left me so fatigued I won't move for hours once I crash. Stanley won't be happy if he finds me sleeping in his living room.

Kaitlyn's watching me. "What's wrong?"

Staring in the distance, I accept the time has come to tell her. After five years, I can no longer bear this load alone.

I study her as I stuff my hands in my pockets, edgy with the idea of releasing my emotions; they'll fester as I recite the facts, but she is the one person who sees every side of me. She will understand my frustration.

"Can we go outside?"

She agrees, squinting with worry before leading me to the side patio. The chill of the deck creeps through my socks as I pull the metal chairs away from the table. After Kaitlyn is seated, I rest in my chair and support myself on the cast iron table. The crisp bite in the air is soothing to me, but she's not wearing a coat and is fighting shivers.

I slip off my jacket with a smile. "Get up."

She rises, her muscles tense with cold. I hold my jacket behind her and ease the sleeves over her arms. My coat reaches her knees, the sleeves curling over her hands. She folds the sides tight around her torso. The porch light shines on the reflective POLICE lettering on her back. She beams at me, her neck covered in the raised collar. Her petite body buried in my jacket and her innocent expression glowing in the night draw me deeper in love with her. All I can do is smile.

I kiss her cheek and wrap my arms around her. "I love you."

"I . . . love . . . you . . . too." Her words come out in pieces as chills lock her jaw.

My grin grows as I help her back in her seat. "You would not survive in a northern climate."

She shakes her head in agreement as she relaxes in my coat.

Rubbing my forearm to ease the trace of a chill seeping through my sleeve, I wonder how I'll tell her. Kaitlyn notices my anxiety, her focus on me forceful enough she seems to have forgotten she's cold.

"I wish I could tell you this inside where it's warm, but I can't risk anybody else knowing."

Please give me the words, Lord. I've never said them out loud.

"I didn't want to tell you about this until it was over because I don't want you to worry, but I'm at my breaking point. You're the only person I trust." I press on calluses under my knuckles, focusing on my skin to detach myself from the words. "I've been chasing a serial kidnapper for five years, and the women he abducts are never found."

Hunched over the table, the jacket hiding her frame, her curious peer changes to concern. "Surveillance doesn't help?"

"He's hidden from the System, and the girls are removed from the System on the days of their disappearances and never come back online."

Her jaw drops as she grasps the magnitude of my predicament. "Serious?"

I rub the fatigue from my eyes. "All I see when I search for victims is a message reading 'System Error.' Cameras that victims were recorded on are black all day for the days they were captured. Then, magically, they're working again at midnight.

"I've followed street cameras, hoping for a trail of blackness, but there was never one to follow. Maybe the victims enter a vehicle and leave sight of the cameras? And I can't find their cars. They're not at their homes or places of employment, and the System doesn't see them."

"This sounds like an inside job."

"Because it is." The table cools my hands as my vision fades into the darkness. "The perp is either a high-level Government Official or has connections to one. My guess is the former.

"On one occasion, I watched him steal a girl. His car was crazy fast, faster than my cruiser, but I saw his taillights. I couldn't recognize the make and model. It had to be custom. I spent days scouring surveillance feeds of Security's parking garage, waiting to see those brake lights again, but I never did.

"Right before he took her, somebody hacked my SimLink and

displayed his location; that's how I found him. I wondered if somebody else was trying to help me stop him, but I think it was him. He was playing with me."

Kaitlyn grabs my hand. "Did another woman disappear?"

"Last night. Dispatch assigned her to me. That's the other reason why I think the kidnapper works inside Security: Dispatch assigns the missing women to *only* me, and it won't—or can't—show who reported them."

Her head moves slowly as she processes the information.

"Kaitlyn—"

Her gaze drifts toward mine, filled with distress.

"The woman was homeless and eight months pregnant. When I failed, a baby died with her."

Disgust twists her top lip. "Are you sure they're . . .?"

"I'm certain. If I can find this guy, I'll prove it." I restrain the urge to pound the table so I don't scare my bride. "If I had found him by now, she and her baby would be alive. I want to tear him apart."

My stare is locked on the wooded area in front of me, barely visible in the night. Filled with dread, moonlight reflects in Kaitlyn's tears as she squeezes my hand.

"What do we do?"

"What can we?" My eyes gravitate toward hers as desperation sweeps through me. "The closest I've come to catching him was when he told me where he was; that's the only way I know he's a he. I have to catch him in the act, but I don't know how. I can't find a pattern."

I slump back in defeat and watch the stars. "When God revealed that I'd be a cop, I wondered why He wanted me to do this job when the Government stands against Him. My father mentioned Biblical examples of times God placed His children with His enemies and how their obedience led to the deliverance of His people. After I'd been on the force for a few months, God informed me I'd be an Exodus. Seconds later, a call came in about a missing woman. I found a trail of them, and they're all Christians. It's been five years; I'm not making a good Exodus." I rub my eyes to hide tears.

Her head hangs heavy. "Give it time."

"Kaitlyn, it was your dad who called."

Her eyes narrow.

"The perp chooses women with no local family or friends to report them missing, but the fourth victim worked at a facility that employed your father's company. He notified me of the surveillance glitch and asked if I could find her."

Kaitlyn scans the tabletop.

"Don't tell him. The Lord warned me to protect him; I don't want him snooping."

"Do you think he'll die?" Her face falls.

"If he digs, yeah. He might."

"Thank you. For keeping him safe." She rests her tiny fingers in my palm with a bleak smile, her tension easing as she rises.

I follow her to the porch swing resting in front of a tall window. I sit beside her and press her against my chest, folds of my jacket caught between her frame and my arm. Her head lies on my badge as my heel rocks us back and forth.

"I can't wait to graduate." She lifts her gaze to mine. "Once I'm working in Security, I can help."

Sighing with relief, I rest my head back. "I'm looking forward to that. I trust no one else. The perp might be any of the men I work with, and anyone could be his accomplice."

She relaxes her head on my shoulder and drapes an arm around my chest. No matter how difficult my days are, she can melt the stress away with a tender touch, a gentle word, or a fragrant kiss.

My lips descend to her hair. She flashes me a bright smile and curls her legs over my lap. She is all the beauty I need in life. My fingers stroke the nape of her neck to the knot of tresses on top of her head; her lids close as she focuses on my affection.

Though I try my hardest, it's impossible to express how thankful I am for Kaitlyn. She's my light and hope. Her hair smooth against my cheek, I notice she's wearing my favorite perfume, the intoxicating aroma I breathed in when she said yes.

God, I love her.

We sway in the cool night air; I keep her snug in my embrace, our hands clasped over her lap as she drifts off in my arms.

"Kaitlyn?"

Her head bobs. "Mmm?"

"I've known since our first date you're my bride." I kiss the soft skin where her hair and forehead meet.

"Me, too. My heart was racing in that classroom. And at coffee. And after you made the criminal say he was sorry." Her fingers rub mine, laughter waking her up. "I heard God say yes to you, and I knew you had to be the one He made for me, especially when you didn't mind calling my dad. I've never felt safer than when I'm with you." Her head cocking to the side, a wily smirk crosses her face. "But for the record, a ship full of pirates would totally take out your ninjas."

"Oh, whatever!" I reach under the jacket and tickle her shoulders. She curls with a squeal, but our laughter gives way to passion. I cradle her cheek, pressing my forehead against hers. She rests her hands on my chest as the air grows warmer between us.

"I miss you every morning when I wake up. I wish you were in my bed."

Her eyes widen, all traces of drowsiness replaced with anticipation. "Have you changed your mind? Do you think we can get married now?"

"No." I kiss her cheek. "I'm marrying you in God's time. I'm just telling you how I feel."

Her arms cross in a pout. "Tease."

I wrap my arm around her and squeeze as my lips fall to their favorite place in her hair. My mouth lingers a couple of inches over her golden locks as I whisper: "But that's how I feel about you. I can never live without you. You're the only woman in the world I see. That will never change." I kiss the tip of her nose. "I love you forever."

She lies on my chest, her fingers poking out of my coat sleeves and clutching my shirt. In this moment, with my Eve in my arms, I am whole and my world is perfect.

Chapter Twenty-Eight

Peter
Thursday, January 9, 2048
8:11 P.M.

Metal cools my fingers as I turn the key and twist the knob. "Here's what I'm dealing with."

Stuffy air, pungent with the smells of dust and old paper, smothers my skin as the door floats open. I converted a spare bedroom into an office where I study the missing women, and the door and window remain locked to protect my investigation. With no ventilation, the space has a perpetual sense of mugginess.

I flip on the light, muted by the drab environment. Kaitlyn's gaze darts around the room barely long enough to notice the stacks of papers, folders, and notebooks cluttering the floor, thin trails of exposed carpet the only safe paths to travel. Her focus narrows on the opposing wall where a giant map of Imperia hangs over the window, littered with tacks representing the last known locations of the victims. The pins are connected with strings to the peripheral of information haloing the map and flooding over the cardboard covering the glass: Victim photos. Notecards with the dates they disappeared. Dates of birth. ID numbers. Ages at abduction. Addresses. Hobbies. Education. Contacts. Sources of income. Places they were expected on the days they were kidnapped. In the upper right-hand corner of each card is a number counting the sequential order of the victims.

With an outstretched hand, Kaitlyn makes her way to the map, the physical representation of my conundrum. Her fingers trace the thread belonging to the first abductee. While the other strings are white, I made hers red.

"Are these . . .?"

"The girls who've been taken. That's Amy Pikes, Victim One."

Her hair trails over her shoulder as she glances at me, half worried and half repulsed, before reaching for another cord and viewing the photo attached to it.

"Veronica Steyer, Victim Nine." I can't read the number from the doorway, but I recognize her picture and know her data. I have every woman, every failure, memorized.

The paralysis of fear removes all expression as she turns to me. "There are so many."

"Ten, to be exact. There will be more if I don't find him . . . them. What if it's a team?"

Her nose crinkles in disgust. "That's a sick thought."

"But it might be. That time I suspect he baited me? I watched the victim fight him all the way to his car, even as he forced her in the backseat. But the door never reopened, even as he ran to the driver's side. Was a second kidnapper holding her down?" I moan, recalling the moment the pieces came together and slipped like sand between my fingers. "I had a recording of the whole event, evidence to analyze, a trail to follow. And the footage vanished a minute later when he deleted her."

Her hand rises to her falling face, grasping loose hair in desperation I'm all too familiar with.

"This is what I've been up against for five years. Sometimes he waits months, sometimes he waits longer. The first two victims were two years apart. Every time I think he's finished—dead, moved, got bored and quit—he strikes again."

She rubs her forehead. "I wish we could trust Zaranda. She's high up and could put an end to this."

"Yeah, but it's a risky play."

"Agreed. I don't know what to make of her. She hates Christians and knows we follow Jesus, but hasn't reported us. Is she waiting for the right time to betray us? Maybe she wants to find more Believers through us?" She cradles her jaw and re-centers our attention. "What else do you know for sure?"

Walking the narrow path to my closet, the carpet coarse against my bare feet, I slide the door open to reveal my board and point to the bulleted facts as I recount them. "The victims are female, between nineteen and thirty-nine, and they share three common denominators: First, they're stunning, though they may be any race or build. Second, they were dedicated Christians before the Burning. But after the ban on religion, it's hard to know if they still were. Third, they have no close contacts nearby who will look for them or report them missing.

"They vanish from the System the day they're nabbed. Searching for them after that gives me an error message. They're taken from Imperia, but anywhere within the city. The perp seems to strike at any time, and he's careful never to choose two victims with potential ties."

"What?"

"He must research them." I lean against the closet frame, crossing my arms and placing one ankle in front of the other. "If somebody told a friend that their co-worker was taken and the police can't find her, and their friend's accountant also vanished, people would talk and might blow his cover. Victims are always several degrees removed from one another, and their families and friends live hundreds—sometimes thousands—of miles apart."

Kaitlyn's mind drifts, her eyes glassing over. "This person is powerful."

"Very. Victims' residences hold no clues and sit empty until the owners or mortgage companies re-rent or repossess them. If landlords or investment companies have called to report a disappearance, there's no record of it in the System. Even victims' cars disappear without a trace.

"I assume people have approached the media or tried bringing awareness online, but the public still doesn't realize there's a serial kidnapper at large. He must be a high-ranking official, or have one in his pocket, to keep the news quiet and delete or disable online mentions of his victims."

"But wouldn't interfering with online communications tip people off?"

"Nope. They probably believe what businesses do when the perp deletes their camera footage: It's a glitch."

She shakes her head, the ends of her hair catching on her jungle green top. "Has anyone tried posting missing person fliers?"

"Not that I've noticed. Like I said, these girls don't have nearby friends or family, and no one's travelled here to search around. Most of them didn't have the funds to come here or hire an investigator. Another detail the assailant likely exploited."

I bend down, grabbing a folder next to my foot and handing it to her. The victims' most recent pictures spill out as she pinches it. Her jaw falls as images scatter the ground, her sickened visage fixing on the two photos in her hand before shifting to me.

Swallowing the lump in my throat, I lose my gaze on a victim's smile before staring at Kaitlyn. "These girls had decades ahead of them. I want to find them. I want to find the monster who's taking them. Show him how weak he is when he goes against a man instead of a defenseless woman. But I don't know what to do, and I've long suspected that asking the wrong person for help might get someone killed."

Kaitlyn scans the photos and piles on the floor as if they contain venomous snakes, capable of killing us within seconds. "Peter, if what you said is true . . . If women are disappearing, and this person has a vendetta against Christians, and you're seeking them . . ." Her tear-filled eyes meet mine. "Will you be okay?"

I crane my face toward hers, leveling our gazes. "He knows about me, Kaitlyn; I guarantee it. He's been at this for over seven years and has never chosen a girl anybody would find, never chosen two victims who are the least bit connected. Never permitted the media to disclose his activities. Never allowed online discussions. He's able to hide people from the System and order dispatch to assign victims to *only* me. He hacked my SimLink with his location so I'd watch him take a girl. I have a hard time believing he has that much power and doesn't see me poking around. He has to know I'm a Christian. He's toying with me."

"Why would he let you threaten him?"

"It's part of his game: The cop who can't bust him."

A tear splatters on a photo clutched in her hand. "I can't lose you, Peter."

"Kaitlyn, no matter how powerful this guy is, God is in control. Nothing will happen to me until it's my time, ordained by Him."

Droplets flow down her cheeks.

My voice softens, and I give her the expression I always do when she needs soothing. "This is my calling, remember? He's in control with this, even though I don't hear Him when I pray about these girls." My focus veers to the map plagued with pins. "He told me I'd be an Exodus seconds before your dad called and led me on their trail. This is what He wants from me. He has a plan in this."

Her face wrinkles in confusion.

"You've read Exodus, right?" I redirect conversation, hoping to distract her from painful thoughts.

"Of course." She glances at a picture in her hand.

"I studied it after my calling. When Pharaoh released the Hebrews, the shortest route to their new home would've been through the land of the Philistines. But God opted against it because those people were at war; He knew if His children saw battle they would return to their bondage in Egypt. That's why He led them the long way and through the Red Sea. It taught me that people, even God's children, are so fearful of the cost of liberation they would rather be slaves than fight.

"It's as applicable today as it was then: Terror attacks left Americans so frightened of the cost that comes with fighting for freedom they gave up their rights. We live in bondage of fear, not resisting the Government as they continue taking away our liberties. What has that forfeiture cost us? We've so willingly allowed the Government to spy on us that this monster has all the tools he needs to kidnap, kill, and stay untouchable."

I'm surprised when Kaitlyn smiles faintly. "But remember when the Israelites were terrified that Pharaoh would recapture them, his six hundred chariots overwhelming compared to their makeshift army? God parted the sea and rescued them. He proved to them, and is teaching us, that our darkest moments are when we see the greatest displays of His power." She picks up the remaining pictures and analyzes them one at a time, no longer afraid. That's Kaitlyn: Scared for sixty seconds, then ready for battle.

"So where do we start?"

I cross my arms and prepare myself for the inevitable conflict. "That's the thing, Kaitlyn. The more I talk about this with you, the more I think it should be me handling this, not we."

"What do you mean?" Her eyes sear into mine as her hand tilts at the wrist, a photo rustling between her fingers.

"The more you know, the more danger you're in. I'm willing to die for this if needed, but I'm not sacrificing you. You fit most of his profile. You're the right age. A Christian. Mind-blowingly beautiful." It's the first time I've said those words and didn't feel I was paying her a compliment. "The only way you're different from previous victims is that you have family in Imperia, but that doesn't mean you're safe. Later, when you work for Security, if you use your login to search for him, and he spots you . . ."

The stuffy air makes it harder to breathe as I imagine somebody hurting my bride. "You can't do that. You can't use your resources to help me after you're hired. This man is a sadist, Kaitlyn. I can't let him get his hands on you."

"I'm strong." Her attention shifts to the photographs, as if the matter is settled, but my hesitation throws a weight over the room. She focuses on me and, seeing my angst, sets down the pictures.

She's too weak to withstand this beast's wrath, but I don't want to tell her. "Kaitlyn, this monster is sicker than you realize. I'll do anything to keep you safe. I almost broke up with you the night of your ride-along because I feared he would come after you to get to me."

Her heart shatters, as if she's torn between a yearning to cry and the stronger desire to appear fearless. "You almost broke up with me?"

"Only to protect you. I prayed about it. The idea of not having you in my life hurt deeper than words can express. What grieved me more, though, was knowing how much pain it would cause you. But I've suspected since the beginning the perp is watching me. If he keeps track of me the way he does his victims, he's seen you, and you're his type. I asked God if I should let you go to keep you safe, if I should stay single until I bring the guy down. I would pay that price for Him. Yet, as much as I can't live without you, I didn't stay with you out of selfishness."

"Why'd you stay with me?" Her voice breaks, her tone beseeching. Neither of us can live without the other.

"Because God wants us together, and it was safest for you to keep me around; I can protect you better if I'm close."

She's powerless to fight the tears streaming down. I take a few steps toward her, rubbing my hand along her cheek and wiping away droplets with my thumb. I lean my forehead on hers.

"Since the moment you became my girlfriend, I've known I can never stop loving you. If I pushed you away, and later discovered you'd been hurt, whether by the perp or someone else . . ." The warmth of our breath lingers between our faces. "That crushed me more, because I could've protected you if you were in my life. Near or far, as long as you're alive I can live, too. But the second you die, I will lose the desire to breathe. I can't fail you. I can't let you die. That's why you can't help me: It would tick him off if a Christian woman looked for him. He might already know about you, but we can't fuel the fire."

She strokes my set jaw, but I keep my eyes away from her. I won't let her jeopardize her safety.

"I understand you want to protect me, Peter, but you know I'm strong. I can handle this. You've been working alone for five years, and this—" she pulls away as her arms wave around my office. "—is all you've gotten. You said he'll take more women if he isn't stopped. Work with me. Besides, he'll have a hard time covering his trail if he takes me when I'm a Government Official."

"No, he won't." My forceful words stun her. "He can kill you here in Imperia and say you were relocated to the other end of the nation and murdered there. He could place your corpse in a building he knows will blow up—"

"That's going pretty far." Her hand rests on a tilted hip.

"He goes to the ends of the earth, Kaitlyn. This man is greedy, destroying countless lives and robbing all these women of the decades they had left. This is a sick game to him. Who abducts a pregnant widow?"

Tears pouring down both cheeks, Kaitlyn examines the map, the strings and tacks, the notes pinned to the wall, and the pictures spread on the floor.

"Before I knew I'd become a cop—hours before your church was attacked—God gave me a dream, a prophecy. I saw a dozen women with their faces cut off. They were black and white, void of any detail. Except for one girl who was wearing a red coat. They dropped to the ground dead. The red coat turned to blood.

"There was a heavy rainfall." I squint recalling the imagery. "A dark ocean gripped me with sorrow. A coffin was floating on it, the waves of a violent storm thrashing around it as it sank to the bottom. Jesus calmed the waters and parted the sea. I pointed to freedom and thousands of people ran between the walls of water. They were escaping the government that was chasing them."

"Okaaay . . ." Kaitlyn's eyes dart back and forth, her shoulders rising and falling.

"What if you're the woman in the red coat?"

"What if I'm not? Or, if I am, do you know what I symbolize?" She points at the map. "Why is the first victim's string red?"

Observing Ms. Pikes' thread with regret, I imagine what her final moments must've felt like. "Because criminals usually make mistakes the first time they strike and leave behind evidence."

"So maybe the red coat means there will be a case that gives you the clue you need. Or that a woman will stand apart who helps you."

My lids close, my gaze drifting toward hers before reopening. "The coat turning to blood?"

"If I'm the woman in the red coat, maybe I'll get a paper cut sifting through evidence."

Impatience poisons my sigh. "And the storm?"

"Maybe my coat's a parka." She winks at me, a stray tear trickling down.

I glare at her morbid attempt at humor. "Kaitlyn—"

"Listen, I have the feeling one of us might die. But what's the alternative? Run from our callings? Disobey God? Let a hundred girls perish because we're too scared and selfish to sacrifice ourselves when we know God is always with us?"

I see the coffin floating on the water again, and the sea's growing darker as I barrel closer to my fate, taking my bride with me. I swallow hard, my throat almost too stiff to push out the words. "Do you think that coffin belongs to one of us?"

Kaitlyn's expression is solemn. "I don't know, but God does. He'll see us through this. Maybe we'll both come out okay. Maybe you are the person God meant for me to save. Stay strong, Peter. Don't let your emotions lead you. We're saved by grace through faith, not feelings."

This is the first time I've been told I'm relying too heavily on emotion. While they aren't the words I want to hear, they are what I need to hear. I'm not prone to strong reactions, but the idea of losing my bride threatens my ability to exist. My own death scares me just as much: If I'm not here, who will protect her? What assurance do I have the killer won't come after her once I'm eliminated?

A tinge of pain strikes my heart as I wonder if the real storm, the one prophesied in my dream, is yet to come. If the sea of sorrow represents trauma I've yet to suffer. If the coffin didn't symbolize the deaths of the victims, but signifies one of ours.

Staring at the wall, I recommit every victim's image to memory. "What do you do when God's silent?"

"Wait." She gives a coy smile. "Many great things are born in silence, like the sprouting of a seed."

She's right. I push out my fear. If I lose control of myself, I've lost all the control I have.

"We'll be okay, Peter. Sometimes God's quiet during the hard times so we learn to praise Him through every circumstance. God knows what's going to happen. He's planned for it, so we don't have to worry."

God has already prepared for what Peter's future holds. Dad's words to Mom when she doubted my calling.

"God made me a problem solver. Dad's taken me to work and taught me tricks. You've trained me a lot, too, and you'll continue teaching me." She smooths her hands over my tense biceps, her nails running down my arms and easing the stress building inside of me.

"Peter, I'm in this. Please, let me help you. I'm following God into this work, and if you're making us wait to marry so I can accomplish my calling, then you better let me do it. You brave danger every shift, and all I can do is trust God. But I can help you with this. He'll never run out of victims. I'm a Christian signing up for Security; my life's already in danger."

My frustration sighs out as I admit she's right: I have to let her help because sooner or later he'll take another woman or come after one of us.

"Genesis says woman is man's helper. God made Eve for Adam, and He had you in mind when He made me. Helping you is part of why He placed me here. No matter what happens, I'm not afraid. Do you know why?"

"Because God's with you?"

"It's deeper than that. Terrorism took my childhood. That bomb was meant for me as much as those it killed, and I was furious—*at Jesus*. My parents raised me to love Him, but I grew up thinking He was a pacifist, and the explosion cemented the idea in my mind.

"It rattled my faith, how weak He seemed. I wasn't sure I could serve a God Who expected me to love someone I hated while He appeared to do nothing. But He changed me."

"How?"

"I was reading the names of Christ, and one stuck out: Lion of Judah. I begged Jesus to show me the lion in Him, and He did. I discovered His restraint is temporary, and His might is powerful. I trembled in awe because no one can fathom His strength, and no one can withstand His judgment. Whatever comes to pass He has allowed. Terrible things will happen to us, but they will work for our greater good, even if we can't understand.

"That's why when something horrible happens, I seek Christ. He reveals mysteries and wonderful things, how He brings good from evil. That's what we should do here. Pray, and remember how big God is."

It occurs to me that she explained how her parents and sister coped with losing their church, but she never described how she handled it. That was how: Her faith reached its limit, she sought God, and she grew stronger with Him as a result. Kaitlyn lives how I imagine God must want all of His children to: Every hardship, every struggle, every explosion on the battlefield of life draws her closer to Him, renders her anxious for a deeper understanding of Who He is.

God is bigger than any problem I'll endure, and I trust Him with every heartbeat. Kaitlyn is my helper. I wrap her in my arms and kiss the top of her head, breathing in her floral aroma.

"I need your help, Kaitlyn. I'll share everything I have. Tell me what you see."

Her cheek presses against my chest in a smile.

Chapter Twenty-Nine

Kaitlyn
Sunday, July 11, 2049
2:12 P.M.

"Oh, a cop!" The plump brunette calls out as she shuffles down the driveway.

When Peter promised to inspect places with me, I pleaded for him to wear his uniform, assuming it would deter unscrupulous landlords. It's one of the smarter choices I've recently made. The first three property owners shied away at the first sight of him.

This landlady's obvious nervousness makes me question if she, too, is up to something unethical. As I study her frazzled hair, excessive makeup, the way she pats her pockets to remember where she put her belongings, and her unreasonably high heels—despite knowing she'd be treading a gravel driveway—it becomes obvious she's the scattered type.

Peter's face firms with her approach. I wonder if he's coming to the same conclusion I am, but he's hard to read when he's focused.

Meeting us at the end of the driveway, and nearly falling when her heel catches in a pothole, she reaches for a handshake. "You must be Kaitlyn, the one interested in renting this home?"

"Yes." I smile while wondering what she might be hiding from the cop at my side. I've been in Security for a few weeks, and already I've seen enough to suspect everyone.

She leads us toward the home without giving Peter another glance.

We step in after her. The kitchen is the first room we enter, and with no dining room, I imagine I'll have to set my table in front of the door, which will make the entrance clumsy.

My first instinct is to run. I want to blame it on the eccentric landlord and awkward entry, but my uneasiness stems from living alone. I've never been without my parents, and I haven't been without Vonnie since she was born. I'll sleep in an empty house. No one will be home when I'm off work. I'll have no one to talk to or play games with except when Peter or my family visits. There will be silence unless I make noise. There won't be food unless I buy and prepare it, and cooking isn't my forte. I'll be lonely. And I don't want to think about the bills I'll inherit.

I keep telling myself that it will be a good experience. I'll figure out how to cook and manage a budget. I'll have time to concentrate on God. Peter and Dad are right: Living by myself will be maturing, and I won't have another chance after I'm married. At first I told Peter I felt safer staying at home since there's a serial killer running around Imperia, but he reminded me that God is in control. We can't allow a criminal to determine our lives. He promised I'll be safe either way because he's protecting me.

I know he is.

He treads farther into the home. Maybe he wants to give the place the benefit of the doubt, or perhaps the cop in him is curious if he can find traces of previous crimes. He loves challenges.

I follow Peter past the landlady, studying him more than the home. I always feel safe in his presence, but nothing parallels the security he provides in uniform. The attire, badge, cuffs, spray, pistol, stun gun. I love being with him in public. He gave me a hard time when I nagged him to accompany me armed and in uniform, until he found out men have followed me to my car. Ever since, I have usually saved my errands for when he can join me. He doesn't know how many times I've caught a creepy guy coming at me, only to bolt once Peter appears. He is the best protector I've ever had.

"It's a simple tour," the owner states. "Kitchen and front closet. Living room with an exit to the back patio. Bedroom and bathroom with laundry machines tucked in between."

My fiancé investigates every nook and cranny, opens every door, and digs between carpet and baseboards.

The lady stares at him crouched in the vacant bedroom, the handcuffs on his belt shimmering in the light as his back straightens. He rubs something between his fingers, probably dust.

I saunter to his side. Not knowing what to do, I contemplate the boring white walls.

Peter stands and turns toward her. "Can you give us a minute?"

"Sure." She grins before leaving.

The front door shuts behind her and he beams at me. "What do you think?"

My knees weaken with the boom of his voice. Arms crossed, his biceps bulge under the short sleeves of his uniform. The navy blue fabric contrasts with his white skin, his tender smile softens his strong face, and his dark blond hair shines in the sunlight filtering through the window. Moments like this I don't know how I'll wait until my birthday. The closer our wedding day gets, the stronger my desires grow.

"When are we getting married?"

His laughter bounces through the empty bedroom. He wraps his arm around me and guides me to the open window. Relaxing in his embrace, I breathe in fresh air and his crisp cologne.

"Look around. The nearest neighbor is a half-mile away. The rent is cheap. This place is a blessing."

Peter's way of saying he thinks it's from God while staying vague in case someone's listening.

Though the privacy of trees and no neighbors invigorates me, I remain skeptical, a trait my father taught me well. "What if it's cheap because it's a dump and we don't know it yet?"

"You're moving into my place after we marry in March. You'll survive."

He brings me closer for a kiss; I melt every time his lips press into my hair.

"Do we have to wait until my birthday?"

He stifles a chuckle, squinting at me with curiosity. "Did we agree on the date? I didn't pressure you, did I?"

Shaking my head, I remember the moment we came out of prayer and decided on my birthday.

"I recall you wanting to marry on your birthday since I proposed to you on mine."

"I know, but–"

His fingertips, soft in his strong hand, trace my cheek, his caress weakening my will. I close my eyes and savor his touch, my heart pounding with passion. These moments never happen enough. My yearning for him grows unbearable, but so does my longing to follow him.

"We sent out the invites. It would be rude to ask our guests to reschedule their arrangements."

"I want to kiss you, though!" My foot rises for a stomp, but I catch myself in time to lessen the impact before I look like a three-year-old throwing a tantrum.

His fingers run through my hair, the faintest trace of laughter tainting his words. "But we agreed waiting for the altar was the best way to avoid temptation. You said you don't want to kiss anyone but your husband."

"That was before I knew our engagement was going to last two years," I whimper. "And I know you're my husband."

His thick arms pull me close. "Love is patient." His breath ripples through my hair, his strong jaw resting on my head.

I step back so he has a fuller view of my begging. "We never prayed about eloping. What if we married in secret and again on our wedding day? It would be so . . . clandestine." My hands clasp with excitement.

"And deceitful. We'd be living a lie."

My forehead slumps against his chest as I frown. He's always right, or at least it seems that way. His hard arms grip me tighter, making me weak with desire and strengthening my urge to marry him.

He kisses my hair again, his fingers stroking the nape of my neck. "I love you. I want you to be my wife right now, but love is patient." He scoops me in a side hug, gazing into the kitchen. His eyes sparkle with enthusiasm. "Live here on your own. You'll have nine months of privacy. Nine months to plan our wedding without distractions. Nine months to solidify your relationships–" he squeezes me with the word, his subtle way of indicating that he's speaking more about my connection with Christ than with anyone else, "–before you're focused on me as your husband."

I sigh in surrender. The wait will be long.

Hearing my sadness, he holds me against his chest in a firm embrace. I hear his grin. "I'll visit you a lot."

"How often?" My words are muffled against his solid build. I peer up at him and he kisses my forehead with a bright smile. I want to see his happiness every day.

"As often as I can."

"Then I'll take it."

I cling to him tighter, almost wishing I talked him into marrying sooner, but my birthday is the right date: It's meaningful, and it allows me time to adjust to a high-stress job, experience life on my own, and plan our wedding. I want everyone to see how much Peter and I love each other; I want food and games and music and dancing; I want to celebrate the love God gave us. It will take Mom, Vonnie, and I time to coordinate our ideas, time I didn't have when I was occupied with school.

Life will be perfect when I can wake in Peter's arms and kiss his smooth lips every day. Watch him bloom into a greater man each passing year. I'm ready for our future and our holy union, when we become one flesh. I'm eager to meet our children and raise them to love the Lord. I'm excited to walk hand in hand with Jesus and Peter as we bring up our family to love and serve God.

"I wrote my vows."

My face rubs against his chest as I peek at him. "You have?"

"Mm-Hmm." He caresses my back, leaning his cheek on my head.

"And I'm already fulfilling them."

Safe in his big arms, adrenaline courses through me, my heart racing with the resonance of his deep voice. I hug him tighter as he kisses me again.

"My favorite one is to protect you at any cost for the rest of our lives."

Chapter Thirty

Peter
Thursday, November 25, 2049
1:09 P.M.

"Can you believe we only have four more months?" Kaitlyn beams from the passenger's side of my truck. The midday sun shines in her golden hair, but the rays hold nothing against her splendor.

Smiling, I don't have a chance to speak before she continues.

"Where are you taking us for our honeymoon?"

My mouth straightens into a line, one corner curved. "Wouldn't you like to know?"

"Peter! I need to know!"

"No. You don't."

"Yes, I do." Her face tightens, her determination coming out in full strength. "I want to do a themed wedding. It should match with where we're going."

A restrained grin tugs at my lips, my chest giving way with laughter. "Nice try."

She snaps in a pout.

Knowing her emotional display is connected to more than just my refusal to spoil her surprise, I ask the obvious to further her unrest. "How far did you get with your mom and sister?"

A sharp exhalation shoots out her nose, her sulk deepening as she glares out her window. "They wouldn't spill."

I laugh harder than I have in years. "Because they don't know."

She jolts toward me, her chin hanging. "They don't?"

The truck cruises along as I shake my head, still laughing.

"Who does?"

"Me."

"And?"

"That's it. There's no one for you to crack."

Pleading, the center of her lips presses up and out as her voice breaks. "But the theme!"

Glancing at her again—learning by heart the way her sleek tresses fall around her face and how her eyes tremble when she's eager—I decide to compromise.

"Alright."

She claps, her smile glistening with brightness. "Yay!"

"Pick a theme you love."

Kaitlyn hovers in my peripheral, her brow furrowed. "What?"

I chuckle, raising one hand off the wheel as I explain. "You, your mom, and Yvonne will make sure you have a ceremony and reception you'll love. I'm taking you somewhere you'll love. We love each other, so love should be the theme."

She coils in her seat, as if she's debating whether she should scheme up another tactic to trick me or be proud her man is keeping a secret this big from her.

We pull into the parking lot of the Marriage Hall. Close in appearance to churches, which were sold or destroyed and never seen again, the Government established thousands of these buildings nationwide for weddings without God. For the most part, they're identical to this one. Pecan-colored brick walls with a white roof, a steeple with no cross on top. Glass doors with ivory flowers stained on the bottoms and white framing around the edges. White columns barricade the front—more decorative than foundational—and I think of the twelve apostles, men who were pillars of God.

Parking at the front door, I notice the column to the right has a crack running through it, contrasting with the perfect construction of the rest of the building.

Hopping out, I approach Kaitlyn's side and open the door to find her with her arms crossed. Eyes fixed on the ceiling of my truck, she rolls them left to right and back.

"Jamaica?"

"C'mon. Let's go." I tilt my head toward the entrance.

Attention still heavenward, her left brow presses down as her lips twist to the side. "Further south?"

"Let's go, Kaitlyn."

She gawks at me, her lip curled in disgust. "Don't tell me we're going north."

"I told you I'm taking you somewhere you'll love. I know you don't like the cold. Now—"

"So it is somewhere warm." Focusing on the wall ahead, her body sinks as her mind descends deeper into thought. Eyes faded, as if she forgot where we are.

"Kaitlyn?"

She turns to me; the transition to reality seems abrupt for her.

"We're here."

Her expression quizzical, I've lost her again. "Mexico?"

I stay neutral as Lorraine and Yvonne exit their car and wait at the door. They grin at us, the sun shining on their charcoal hair and the white pillars.

"Let's go. Your mom and sister are waiting."

My words stir her out of her dream state as she spots her family, her face lightening as she waves. I'm relieved she's giving up the inquisition—for now—as she returns to the present moment.

Kaitlyn unclasps her seatbelt and I help her down. A usual custom, she wraps her arm around mine.

As I accompany her to her family, she presses her free hand on my arm and leans into me with a smile. "I can't wait to show you what we've picked so far. I need your opinion on some details. I want to make sure you're happy, too."

I bring her to a stop, casting every bit of love on her through my gaze. "Will you be there?"

She stares at me funny. "Of course!"

"Nothing else matters."

Grabbing my shoulder, she lifts herself to her tiptoes and plants a kiss on my cheek before easing down with another luminous smile.

We join Lorraine and Yvonne at the entrance, and I free Kaitlyn to hug her mother, who's smiling at her with outstretched arms. Her excitement is filled with the anticipation of a mother who's been married to her mate for decades and wishes for a lifetime of similar joy for her daughter. Kaitlyn reaches for Yvonne next, and her sister's enthusiasm carries a sense of simplicity. She brightens with my bride's touch. She isn't a hugger except with Kaitlyn; their strong bond is evident in their frequent embraces.

Lorraine knocks on the door as Kaitlyn releases her sister. A groundskeeper unlocks the entrance. An older man, peaceful and calm, opens the door with a warm greeting. Kaitlyn and Lorraine, swept up in excitement, reciprocate with a hurried hello before bolting for the chambers, whispering and giggling shoulder to shoulder next to a quiet Yvonne. I linger in the foyer to give him a more sincere welcoming, though he possesses a tranquility that suggests he isn't offended. In his line of work, he's used to girls being emotional and distracted.

The chandelier illuminates the bridal-white tiled floors, ivory walls, and cream-colored ceiling. In the back of the hall are two archways leading into the main building. My bride calls for me from the left as the greeter leaves through the passageway to my right.

Kaitlyn appears, coming to an abrupt stop with her hair swinging around her shoulders, her hand locking around the frame to halt her momentum. "Come!"

She grabs my arm and directs me through the archway and down the short corridor, a dead end exiting to the right.

We veer around the corner and enter a vast chamber. While the building's outside and entrance are white, the interior is wooden. Two rows of pews contour either side of the aisle. A red rug, bordered with gold, lies on the umber brown path where my bride will walk in four months. It runs up the four steps of the podium, where I'll wait for her. A large white ceramic stand with flowers on top rests at the altar. The vaulted ceiling is so high it's hard to distinguish the wooden pattern in the pine paneling. Four chandeliers hang in the corners, their chains holding them near the center as they brighten the chamber; the dark flooring mutes their light, giving the area a mahogany glow.

Kaitlyn drags me to the left and through a back door. This room is tiny compared to the one where the ceremony will take place; there are racks, stands, two closets, a few chairs, a cheval mirror, and a lighted makeup mirror on a desk with plenty of drawers. Lorraine and Yvonne are inside and become quiet upon our arrival.

"This is the bridal chamber. It's where I'll prepare for you." Kaitlyn glances around it and beams at me. Her eyes carry desire—lightened with love, but edged with fervor. She's always bright when she grins, but I've never seen her this radiant.

Lorraine shoos us away. "Your sister and I are planning your bridal shower. Now get out."

Kaitlyn obeys, towing me behind her. For some reason, she doesn't snoop on them despite how she interrogates me about our honeymoon.

She guides me to the opposite door, stopping to place a hand on the front of my shoulder. "Thank you for paying for our wedding and giving me what I want." Her eyes roll around the open space, imagining how it will look on our big day. "There's no way I could afford this without you."

Pulling her into my embrace, I kiss her hair. "You're welcome. I want to give you all I can."

My bride wraps her tiny fingers around my hand and ushers me forward. Opening the door to the other room, she shifts toward me and then searches the area. It's much like the bridal chamber, though there's no makeup mirror and it's smaller.

"This is your room." She leans her head inside and shoots back with a wrinkled nose. "It kind of smells funny."

I snicker because she's right. The odor is akin to gym socks, but it won't bother me because all I'll be thinking about is how I'm minutes from meeting my bride at the altar for our first kiss.

She escorts me back to the main chamber, walking me down the aisle as she animates how it will be decorated.

"There will be green bows at the end of each pew, lining the aisle. I want to have blue flowers in their centers, since that's your favorite color, but Vonnie's thinking purple. What do you want? Blue or purple?"

Adorned in a faded pink blouse, another gift from someone who doesn't know her well, I contain my laughter as I consider suggesting pink. "Yvonne will have her own wedding. This is yours. What do you want?"

"Blue."

"Then blue it is, but only if it's what you want. I don't care what the colors are, as long as I come out with you as my wife."

She wraps her arms around my torso, pressing herself against my chest. "Blue."

Alone in the chamber, I kiss her tresses and breathe in her perfume, covering her petite frame with my arms as time stands still.

"We can choose a different color for the rug."

"What?" I peer down, caught off guard by her blunt redirection. She wasn't as lost in the moment as I was.

She points beneath our feet. "The red rug leading to the altar. We can choose another color. They have options."

I can't emphasize enough that I don't care about colors. I care about Kaitlyn. "What do you want?"

"Well, the bows are a pastel green." Her hands gesture toward the pew ends, as if she'll magically make them appear. "So I was thinking the rug should be complementing. Still green, but a couple shades lighter, maybe? It will draw attention to the floor and guide the eye to you. Us."

Her head twists and turns, her body following along as she searches around the chamber, envisioning every detail of our wedding day. I memorize every facet of her: the way her shirt hangs over her pants; how her jeans wrinkle around her knees; how her hair slides over her shoulders; how the smallest dimples crease when the corners of her mouth rise; how her brown irises sparkle, even in dim lighting. Kaitlyn and her happiness are the only details I care about. If I can marry her and watch her gush with overwhelming love and joy before our honeymoon, then I've had the wedding I want.

She keeps talking as she climbs the podium, stopping at the stand with flowers on top. I follow her, her motions dancelike as she describes every detail. While I hear the melody of her voice, her comments don't register because I'm captivated by her soul—made more magnificent by our love.

Kaitlyn looks concerned.

"Peter?"

"Yeah?"

"Gold ribbon or silver?"

I'm quiet, hoping I can figure out what we're ribboning.

"You weren't listening, were you?" She seems more sad than upset, and I think she's disappointed in herself. Sometimes she talks about how she thinks she talks too much, and I love her too much to point out the irony.

"I'm sorry, Kaitlyn. I couldn't hear you because I'm stunned by your beauty."

She squints with scrutiny before using my words against me. "Nice try."

I lift her chin with my fingers. "I'm serious. Do you realize how much more beautiful you've grown since we got engaged? How radiant you've become since you started planning our wedding?"

Her face softens.

"Our love is unlocking something powerful deep inside your heart." I whisper in her ear. "I fell in love with you the first second I saw you. God drew me to you, and I couldn't deny you were gorgeous. Then I got to know you and witnessed how beautiful your heart is. And what I saw in you in our first year together dims in comparison to what I see in you now."

I wrap my hands around the curves of her shoulders. Tears stream down her cheeks; she presses at them while sniffling back new ones.

"I'm sorry I wasn't listening." I wipe her tears with the side of my finger. "I heard your voice; I'm just overwhelmed by who you've become. You're the only detail that matters, and you're already beautiful. As long as you're happy with the arrangements, so am I."

Embracing her as she rolls with soft cries, I can't help but tease her. "Besides, I'm busy covering our honeymoon."

"You're not telling me, are you?" She inquires, muffled against my chest.

Rubbing her back, I laugh and kiss her hair. "Not a chance."

Chapter Thirty-One

Peter!

Screens flicker in front of me as I watch my fiancé bolt from his car and chase his newest catch: a man who robbed a woman and her child at knifepoint. He runs past the victims and down an alley, narrowing the gap on the criminal.

Trapped in a dead end, the lanky crook turns on Peter, wielding his dagger.

That's his second mistake of the day.

With no time to pull his stun gun, Peter barrels him to the ground. The blade lies a few feet away, out of the criminal's grasp. He cuffs the felon and lifts him to his feet while another officer consoles the victims.

I don't deploy police, but sometimes while searching for terrorists I catch crimes in progress and report them to available officers. This time Peter responded.

Taking a deep breath, I sit down and regroup. It's been one of those days when I'm catching terrorist after criminal after terrorist. This is part of my calling, but the adjustment is difficult to make, even with Peter's help. He warned me this job would change me, and he was right. I read about evil in the news and dealt with it firsthand when my church family was murdered, but there is a level of depravity in the world that I didn't know existed. It's hardening me. Horrific images keep me awake at night, and sometimes it's a struggle to be around strangers, wondering if they're terrorists. I keep reminding myself that the world is dark because Christians stopped shining Christ's light—and I never want to join them. Jesus saved my life and changed my heart; I want everyone to see Him through me and come to know Him for themselves.

Stress weakening my focus, my gaze wanders over my office. Suffocated in a room with no windows, I'd enjoy having someone to socialize with on occasion without having to visit the cafeteria, but my work demands the strictest privacy and attention. I can have no partners in my office because I have to suspect everyone, including other officials who do the same job.

My five-foot-long desk is buried in notes and paper records. The information is available on my work's SimLink, but physical reminders keep me more organized—a habit I inherited from my father. Surveillance screens plaster the wall above my desk, five feet by four feet of prevention I'm supposed to convert into protection. Feeds flicker in the dim office as I scour the System for terrorists: unusual activities, deviant behaviors, odd financial transactions, connections between known extremists and seemingly harmless civilians. If I can spot an enemy, I can thwart them.

It's taxing to assume everyone's a terrorist, but it's worth it to save lives. There are no more churches to destroy, but terrorists can strike anywhere, anytime. I don't want another person to suffer through what I did. To lose one, five, or dozens of people they know in a fiery flash.

This job becomes considerably stressful when every failure is in the limelight, but the public seldom hears about the plots we overthrow and the countless lives saved. Peter warned me Security is a hard lifestyle for these reasons—as well as the gut-wrenching horrors we see that most civilians don't, like dead bodies, tortured animals, and abused children—so I started somewhat prepared. But knowing and experiencing are two different matters.

On the plus side, at least I can find new ways to help Peter. Over the course of the last two years, I wasn't able to advance his efforts much. Putting our heads together helped us think of new angles, fresh strategies, and possible MOs, but we always crashed into the familiar brick wall of system error messages. My Security credentials are higher than Peter's, but I receive the same result. I keep hoping something will click for me in this job, that my training will come through for us and the girls.

I leave my office, needing to free my mind from the tension.

Locking my door, I jerk with irritation before I'm fully cognizant of the bossy command coming from behind me.

"Hey, you. Come here."

Obnoxious and impatient, the voice doesn't belong to anyone I know. I glance over my shoulder to see who else is in the hallway, because there's no way someone is addressing me with that tone.

There's no one around except for another official. A man with black hair, cloaked in a navy blue Security jacket and matching pants.

My gut instinct is tingling, but I can't avoid him. I know who he is.

His light blue eyes rip through me as I near. He's Damien Harris, the Head of Security. He doesn't allow the public to see his appearance for security reasons, but I remember his picture from orientation.

"I haven't seen you before."

Nausea churns my stomach as I cross my arms; my brash attitude is the only layer of defense I can add to God's protection. "I'm new."

"What's your name?"

His hands stay tucked in the pockets of his windbreaker. Every strand of his raven locks, peppered gray at the temples, is gelled with precision. He reeks of expensive and over-sprayed cologne. Mostly still, his few motions are quick and efficient. Everything about him screams of his controlling nature. Combining his high position with the unnerving cloud of repulsion lingering over him, smothering me in disgust so intense I feel bugs crawling on my skin, I begin wondering if he is the perp Peter and I have been searching for.

"Are you the—"

"Guy in charge."

My cynicism grows with confirmation of his authority. Could he be the perp? But Peter and I checked on him—twice. He had alibis for every occasion.

"What's your name?" He makes no attempt to conceal how annoyed he is with repeating himself.

"Kaitlyn." My shoulders drop with mutual irritation. "Why'd you call me over?"

His expression grows in malevolence. "Kaitlyn who?"

"Reed. What do you want?" A muted scream dies in my throat, but not before tainting my tone.

"I need your help on a case."

"You didn't know who I was. Besides, you work cases? Aren't you busy overseeing the place? I work counter-terrorism, and you've never taken on a case yourself."

He licks his lips with a restrained smile as he undresses me with his eyes.

I can't control him; I can scarcely control my urge to puke. My body belongs to God, and, in a few weeks, it will belong to Peter.

"This one's special."

I sigh with annoyance, but he takes it as a sign I want him to come closer. His hips swaying with his steps, I move back as many paces with an exaggerated look of disgust. "What's the case?"

"I'd like to discuss it over dinner."

Who does this guy think he is?

I flash my ring with a scowl. "No. Let me know if you have a legitimate need." I split for my office, but he stops me.

"You think you can say no to me?"

Spinning on my heels, I sneer at his scorn. "Yeah. 'Cause that's what I'm doing. Leave me alone."

He hisses as I hustle to my office. Walking steadies the shivers trembling down my spine.

Back at my workstation, I lock the door for a semblance of safety. It won't keep out the nation's highest-ranking Security Official, but at least the bolt will make him aware of how unwelcome he is.

I check surveillance and find Peter driving the robber to jail; he's a few minutes from the building. I grab my SimLink and message him: *We need to talk.*

Pulling up Damien's profile in the System, I cross-check him again against the perp's previous itinerary; he still has alibis for every time a girl was taken.

The knock comes. I glance at my door's camera feed and see Peter.

Rising from my seat, I stride to the entrance and press a button. The ingress slides open, and my fiancé's strong jaw softens with a gorgeous smile that I'm too upset to enjoy.

His face falls. "What's wrong?"

Lifting my finger to my lips, I lead him somewhere private.

Chapter Thirty-Two

Kaitlyn
Tuesday, February 8, 2050
1:11 P.M.

Another day passes as I sit in my dark office, the room flickering with intel. It's a beautiful and sunny day on local feeds, even if it is winter. It's nice living in the southeastern pocket of New America: even the coldest time of year is warm compared to the northern half that suffers ice storms, mountains of snow, and sub-zero temperatures. But we pay our dues living where hurricanes strike every year. The Government's buildings are indestructible, built to withstand the severest storms and most ravaging earthquakes—a rare phenomenon for our part of the nation.

No matter how long I do this job, the screens never stop hurting my head. Even with lights on, my skull pounds. Might as well work in darkness and forget how alone I am ten hours a day. Rubbing the corners of my eyes to ease the ache, I pull out the earrings pinching my lobes and stuff them in my pocket. They were a gift from Peter for my last birthday, and I regret having to stash them because they're my favorite: a pair of oval jade pendants bordered with small aquamarines.

I won't feel better until I eat, so I set out for a break.

Not quite to the door, I flinch when it opens sooner than it should.

My muscles stiffen at the sight of the man standing in the doorway, familiar and unwelcome. Black hair, temples streaked with gray. Fairly athletic, though his loose-fitting Security jacket hides his physique.

Damien's blue eyes are darker. I've avoided him since our encounter last week, but, like the first time, his depravity is mesmerizing: He's lethal, fast, and reckless. Every movement, every stare, every breath is like a viper's.

I need Peter. He can protect me from what's about to happen.

"You're coming with me." Damien cocks his head toward the hall, as if I'm a dog who's supposed to blindly obey orders.

Keeping as healthy of a distance as I can, I cross my arms and tilt my head with an attitude. "Do you have a legitimate need this time?"

He's quiet, but his face says he's not leaving without me.

That's what he thinks.

"I'm not going anywhere unless you have an actual Security-based need. I don't care if you are the Head of Security."

He glowers at my rejection and enters my office with a slow stride of authority. I roll a chair between us, but he isn't daunted.

"Do you want to live?" He whispers, leaning over the seat I intended as a barricade. The power of his threat immobilizes me like venom.

"What?"

"Or would you rather I take Peter? I'll have fun with him."

A chill slithers down my back, stealing my breath. "No! I'll go—if you promise to leave Peter alone."

"Go." His hand slides out of his pocket, his finger extending toward the exit as he steps against the wall to make room for my departure. The weight of his commanding glare never leaves me. "No calling for help."

It doesn't slip by me that he neglected to guarantee Peter's safety, but what choice do I have?

Walking past him, I enter the hallway. He closes and locks my door, stepping beside me and setting the pace a foot ahead. He leads me through the halls and into the parking garage. Sunlight peeks through tunneled gaps between the concrete wall and ceiling.

We approach a fancy black car hidden in a dark corner. He opens the passenger door and I duck inside. In the dim light, a cardboard box covered in brown and crimson stains rests on the floorboard. I manage to squeeze my legs between the container and the car's frame as I sit in the softness, not knowing if I'll return. Damien slams the door without regard for my knee that's bruised by the impact.

Though he has alibis for the attacks and a profile in the System—and the perp presumably wouldn't have either—I still think Damien is our guy. Peter's considering him as well, but how can we know for certain when the System might be working for him?

As Damien slides behind the wheel, an undeniable need for Peter consumes me. He'll know what to do. He's strong. He's smart. He deals with bad people every day. He's experienced with handling danger, and he'll find me any second: After what happened with Damien, I gave Peter permission to check on me in the System several times a day. Damien concerns him as well, and we share a hunch that the calamity isn't over. Peter will see what's happening if I'm still in the System; if Damien's the perp and he deleted me, Peter will notice my error messages. Either way, he'll find out soon if he hasn't already. He's probably on a manhunt right now; I just have to buy myself time.

But something inside of me prays he doesn't catch onto my peril; I don't want to think about what might happen if he rebels against Damien and his abundant resources. Part of me wants him to stay safe and far away. Let Damien do what he desires, as long as Peter isn't harmed.

Damien grabs my chin, forcing me out of thought. "Listen close." His fingers crush my jaw until I look at him.

My bones tremble with fright; every breath hurts.

"I see every hiccup and sneeze in this country; I find every secret. I will know if you disobey me in the slightest, and I will kill you and everyone you love—painfully." His jaw is tight, his expression unyielding dominance.

The dome light shines brighter. He lets go and gestures toward my feet. "Open the box."

I'm frozen. I can't blink, can't take my eyes off him. His wickedness is hypnotizing: He fears no one and nothing because he is always the strongest force of evil present.

His eyes widen into a promise of harm if I don't comply. With shaking hands, I bring the box to my lap and remove the lid.

He gives me silence to absorb the details.

> *Melissa Black. 21 years old. Gymnast. Faith in Jesus Christ. Taken May 17, 2043. Stabbed in forehead.*

> *Betsy Martin. 39 years old. Physician intern. Heals for Jesus Christ. Taken January 13, 2043. Stabbed in forehead.*

> *Marie Tinsel. 29 years old. Beautician. Wisdom in Jesus Christ. Taken October 11, 2042. Stabbed in forehead.*

I thumb through the profiles faster, reading only names. Desiree Swanson. Amy Pikes. Valirie Adams. Veronica Steyer. Brittany Griffith. Trinity Lee. Lucy Harvey. Holly White, the pregnant widow. The missing women Peter has searched for. A couple I've hunted for, too. Bringing down the perp has been my highest priority since I started working in Security. We suspected that the perp saw us pursuing him, but we weren't sure why he allowed it. Now I know Peter was right: It's all part of a game.

But if Damien is the one who's been nabbing women, how is he concealing himself in the System while staying in it?

Can the System lie?

My fingers stop at the last page, my chest sputtering.

> *Kaitlyn Reed. 22 years old. Counter-terrorism Security Official. Daughter of Stanley and Lorraine. Sister Yvonne. Engaged to Peter Tryndale, son of James and Dianne. Marrying March 20, 2050. Graduated top of her class, May 14, 2049. Athletic and intelligent. Apostle of Jesus Christ. Taken February 8, 2050.*

He knows I'm a Christian. He's going to stab me in the forehead and kill everyone I love. How can I warn Peter? My parents? Vonnie? I try to keep my breathing level; I won't allow Damien to see my panic.

"Keep going."

I draw the deepest breath I can, fighting the fear tightening my chest, before digging through the next layers in the box: Black hood. Cuffs. Blades. Ropes. Blind folds. Narrow strips of fabric stained with blood.

Another stapled stack of paper, this one much longer. The names of past victims are crossed off and checked. There are also names I don't recognize, uncrossed and unchecked—presumably Damien's future victims.

This is a wish list.

The name on top is written in neat penmanship, standing out against all the other names hurriedly scrawled:

KAITLYN REED

I'm going to die.

Swallowing hard, I lift the packet. My hand muffles the scream that wants to shriek out of me, but—fearing attention will get someone killed—I choke on it. Let it burn like acid in my throat as I turn away.

"Look!"

My gaze returns to pictures of dead women enveloped in blackness, their faces slashed open and blood dried to their wounds. I recognize some of them; Peter and I saw their images in the System before they disappeared. Others were cut so badly they're unidentifiable. All of them have holes in their foreheads.

This reminds me of Deuteronomy six, when God tells the Hebrews to wear His commandments on their foreheads, for His children to dedicate their minds, hearts, and bodies as altars for His worship. It's obvious why Damien put holes in their foreheads: He was attacking the Word living inside of them.

These photographs make the war more real. They were people. They had hopes and dreams. They had more to give to the world.

I have Peter. I have family and friends. Hopes and dreams. I'm not done living: I want to marry Peter and have children. This can't be my time.

Holly White died with blood on her face, her hair stained crimson. Her corpse lies on its side, her shirt raised and tucked beneath her breasts. My eyes fixate on her curved belly, the dead baby inside of her.

My end will be painful.

I jerk and heave, blowing out and sucking in irregular gasps. Certain he notices, I try steadying my air supply. Forget my killer is two feet away.

Breathe, Kaitlyn. Peter's on his way. Stay calm.

Plastic pouches of hair: blond, brown, copper, orange, mahogany, white, black, red.

More small plastic bags, these ones filled with bracelets, earrings, necklaces, wedding bands.

Trophies.

My vision falls to my engagement ring, the strongest tangible token of the love I share with Peter.

Don't take my ring. Don't steal me from Peter.

Every muscle tenses as Damien leans in close enough for me to smell mints mixing with the stench of his breath. His fingers run through my hair, making me shiver with fear.

"I'm the one Peter has been searching for. Now you have to make a choice: Try turning me in and your parents and Yvonne . . . James and Dianne . . . die after you and Peter. Or you can drop it, do what I want, and they'll live—if you keep your mouth shut."

My body quivers as hurried, shallow gasps croak through my throat. Tears build in my ducts, but I hide them to appear strong. He said they'll live, but he made no mention of me. I would give my life for Peter and my family. Compliance is all I have, the only choice that might keep Peter and our families safe.

I stiffen my trembling body and nod my surrender.

He reaches into the center console, his fist rising into view and striking my lap.

Venom rips through my leg, pelvis, torso, cutting off my scream as the sting punches me, the heat burning and bruising all at once. Damien pulls a two-pronged needle out of my thigh.

Dizzy and light-headed, I struggle to breathe.

"What . . . *did you do to me?*"

Two of his evil smiles float in front of me. "Aphrodisiac. A potent one."

Vomit shoots into my mouth. I down the caustic fluid, fooling him into thinking I'm stronger than I am. That I'm as strong as I thought I was until thirty minutes ago.

Jesus, send Peter!

"I gave you the chance to sleep with me willingly. But you and that God of yours." He shakes his head with a sigh.

Panting, my hair falls around my face as I stare at my lap and try to find balance.

"I can't let Peter have all the fun."

"*Mmm. Ugghhh.*" Grasping the seat, my head bobs, following my eyes as they search for something to focus on. Fight to make my vision normal. Fight the headache. Fight the heat scorching my muscles.

"You'll be feeling lots better in a few. Promise." He grabs my hair and twists my face toward his, forces my lips against his. He shoves his tongue in my mouth; the faint trace of mint can't disguise the rancid waste of his saliva.

I push against him, but I have no strength; my hands rest on his chest. He lets go, and my wobbling head can't move away fast enough.

"Don't worry. You'll remember everything." Laughing, he knocks the car into drive.

Pain gone, adrenaline runs hot through my veins. I'm high. Intoxicated. I fight desires racing through my body, but they fade as fear takes over. Damien drugged me and killed his previous victims; I'm the next tack on Peter's map unless he saves me.

I am the woman in the red coat.

Lord, please save me. Help Peter deliver me. Let me feel the safety of his strong arms again. Give me another chance to show him how much I love him.

Chapter Thirty-Three

Fear suffocates me. Through the windshield, I see Damien approaching, his eyes blistering. My door flies open. I lean away, making the shift subtle because resistance might quicken his temper, but it's worth the risk: Every second I buy is a second longer Peter has to locate me. He has to be searching by now.

Damien's hand reaches into the car, then his forearm, elbow, face. The flesh of my arm tears under his grip.

"Remember, you're doing everything I say or you and Peter die." My shoulder pops as his iron claws yank me out.

Unable to predict his movements, I stumble as he jerks me against the back door. My muscles burn under his grasp, but the pain doesn't register; I'm too focused on appearing normal to keep Peter and our families safe. I have to stay strong to defend them. Repulsion floods my veins as his body presses mine into the car frame, my flesh giving way between them. Trembling, I fight to make my abduction seem like an ordinary outing. Nobody needs to know that the man on me is my kidnapper, that he will hurt me and I can't resist. The only person who can end this is on his way.

His lips touch my ear, his tongue slithering along my lobe. Wanting to throw up, I cringe with the filth, but his moan tingles along my skin, awakening the aphrodisiac.

"Peter's life—"

The thought of my fiancé's death terrorizes me.

"Lorraine's, Stanley's, Yvonne's . . . depend on you obeying my every word. No shaking. No crying. No calling out for help. And fix that look on your face."

Lord, make me strong. Keep Peter and our families safe.

I fight the shivers prickling my spine; a deep breath neutralizes my façade.

He pulls me through the parking lot. I stare at a camera mounted on a streetlamp: It's broad daylight; Peter should see me. I hope this hotel didn't hire my father. If Dad catches this, he'll come. He'll die.

As we near the entrance, my free hand sneaks into my pocket and grabs the earrings Peter gave me, dropping one in a corner at the main doors. Peter's the most observant person I know, and he is remarkable with investigations. If he comes, he'll spot it and know I'm here. He'll kick down every door if he has to.

Hotels have surveillance in every hall. He'll find me, unless Damien's deleted me. Whether he can see me or not, Peter has to be on our trail by now.

Damien leads me into the elevator. We ascend to the third floor. The smell of bleach punches the air as we walk out. I drop the other earring, narrowing Peter's quest to one level. Like there's a camera within my mind, I memorize everything in front of me: The way lights appear white inside the sconces, but glow yellow as they bounce off the walls and fall flat on the tan, coarse carpet. The custard-colored walls making the hall feel narrower.

We approach a remote corner of the building; every room we passed was empty. His clasp tightens around my arm as his other thumb pushes against the print reader, unlocking the door. He shoves me into the rearmost room; I stumble headfirst, whirling around as he resets the bolt. Will Peter be able to enter? Or has Damien found a way to rig the hotel's print reader and key chips to keep the police out?

Ducking to the back of the room, I consider jumping out the window, but the fall is three stories and the people I love will die. Peter will die. I swallow hard as I watch traffic passing by on the freeway, jealous of the hundreds who have their freedom. Fighting tears, I realize I'm no longer free. If Peter doesn't stop Damien, part of me will belong to this monster.

Biting my lip, I turn and lock eyes with the demon.

God, where is Peter?

Now under the tyranny of God's enemy, as the Hebrews were thousands of years ago, I remember sharing with Peter the greatest lesson of Israel's Exodus: Our darkest moments are when we witness the mightiest displays of God's power.

I have faith in Jesus; the Lord will do something great through this. I trust in His will, even when I can't understand. Even when I'm scared and I can't shake the horror.

Like now.

The tears don't come to my eyes; their power shudders through my face, quivering my jaw, trembling my arms, stiffening my legs to dead weights. My chest tenses, my gasps quicken, my heart speeding while pins and needles sting my mouth.

"Come here."

My neck tightens as I struggle to swallow. Glimpsing left and right, is there a way out? Damien fades from sight as my concentration narrows on the door, wondering if Peter is on the other side.

The knob doesn't move.

Does God have another rescue planned? Damien's victims are assigned to Peter, but maybe another officer has discovered the missing girls and is also hunting for the offender. Maybe another cop is on their way?

Maybe God has a different plan. He wouldn't allow me to become a slave, would He? I'm His daughter. No matter what, I'll keep trusting Him, even if I leave here broken. Even if I don't leave here alive.

Damien beckons me with his index finger. "Peter?"

I freeze at the sound of my fiancé's name, paralyzed by the thought of his harm—or worse. I stumble toward Damien, stopping five feet away.

"Take off your clothes."

Repugnance blazes through me as I force my shirt over my head and clench it in a fist at my side.

"All of them."

Caving with fright, I release my top. As it collapses on my foot, I take off everything I wear, doing so slowly to buy Peter time, but Damien's grin makes me think he enjoys the tease.

Facing him but refusing to look at him, the only garments I wear are my cross necklace and engagement ring—tokens of the only two men I have given my heart to. The only two entities who have the power to rescue me.

Hand over heart, I clutch my cross. *Abba, Father, all things are possible for You. Remove this cup from me. Yet not what I will, but what You will.*

I memorized the prayer Christ uttered in Gethsemane after my church was dismantled, and now I know why God put it on my heart all those years ago: He wanted me to know how to pray my way through persecution, possibly martyrdom. Christ said these words to His Father the hour He was taken, and Jesus was the truest martyr: He was murdered for believing in me, a perfect Being Who died to redeem a tarnished creation. Gave up His life believing in the love He has for me. Love so strong He wants to spend eternity with me, but dying was the only way our future together could be possible.

Knowing my time is short, I fight the poison pulsing through me, hoping my adrenaline kicks it out of my system. But the venom is strong. Part of me wonders if Damien injected me with a double dose: The pain is gone, but the simplest of motions, like walking, are over-stimulating.

"So you're a Christian?"

A sudden downpour of God's Spirit washes over me and fills me with tranquility, like the calm before the storm, emboldening my tone. "Yes."

"Peter's a Christian, too?"

My hands ball into fists. I'm playing along to shield those I love; if Damien's killing them anyway, why should I?

"I came here so you wouldn't hurt him. You have me. I'm doing what you want. Leave him alone."

"We're just starting here, Kaitlyn. You have a lot to do to earn his life. Does it follow that you're a virgin?"

Defeat swims through my heart, threatening to drown God's serenity. The devil is a thief—here to steal, kill, and destroy. If Damien lets me live, he'll first rob me of everything I've saved for Peter. Ruin what I have spent my life guarding.

Staring at the floor, I nod twice. I want to pray for Adonai's protection, but—overwhelmed—I don't know how. I have minutes, maybe seconds, left until my purity is replaced with shame. Peter doesn't have long to intervene, doesn't have long until he has to fix the next tack on his map. My heart swells as I imagine him in mourning, pushing in another pin with tear-filled eyes, his strong jaw set with anger.

God, I don't want to die.

Will my death be the key he needs to become the Exodus? Maybe losing me will be his motivation to approach the case with a different viewpoint. Perhaps Damien will make a mistake with me. I might be able to leave more clues behind. If any of Damien's victims can disguise evidence that he won't notice but Peter will, it's me.

"What a shame. Beauty. Virginity. Poor Peter will have nothing left once I'm finished."

A boulder rises in my throat; I try gulping it down but can't swallow. I can't breathe. My body will move only its legs, carry me backward, away from Damien. I glance at him, revulsion seizing me as his ecstasy becomes obvious.

Damien brings me to a halt with one word:

"Peter."

I slump in surrender.

He strides toward me, licking his lips with thirst. My chest totters with air, or lack of it. My foot steps back, but, fighting my own body, I lock my muscles. Force deep breaths, like my father taught me to do when I busted my knee as a little girl and became hysterical with pain.

My father. Will I see him again? I pray for him, only to remember my mother training me as a child to pray my way through worry. *My mother.* Will she hold me again? Her onyx hair reminds me of Yvonne's. *Vonnie.* Will we laugh together again? I'll be taken from them unless one person rescues me: *Peter.* Will I marry him? Have babies with him? Our wedding, our children, our future are close to dying with me.

No matter what Damien does, I will always belong to Christ. God promised nothing can separate me from His love. Jesus vowed He is with me always, even to the end of time.

Chapter Thirty-Four

Kaitlyn
Tuesday, February 8, 2050
4:12 P.M.

Blessed are the pure in heart, for they shall see God.

Naked and kneeling on all fours, my back rounds as I vomit. My bile mixes with a puddle of my blood. The slime of desecration saturates every inch of me. My muscles scream in anguish. This was not how my first time was supposed to feel. It was supposed to be with Peter in six weeks on our honeymoon. Not in this hotel room with a pervert, drugged and beaten.

Where is Peter? Is he hurt? Dead? Did Damien delete me? Is the trail too cold? Most of me is glad Peter isn't seeing this, but a fraction of my heart hopes he'll kick down the door and rescue me. It's too late to save my virginity, but he has time to salvage my life.

"In the tub."

Knees aching from the hard floor, I do as he commands with slumped shoulders, a hunched spine, and a hanging head. Porcelain cools my bare feet; I remember the times my shower chilled me before wrapping me in a blanket of warmth. My senses heightened with the drug, it's easy to memorize every wisp of air, every chill of a cold surface, every tickle of hair, the stickiness of sweat, the residual vomit burning my throat, the soreness ripping through my center. I commit every sensation to memory—even feelings I'll want to forget one day, if I survive—because I don't know when I'll stop. Feeling. Breathing. Living. Any second could be my last, and I don't have many left.

Damien warned me earlier I must always face him, so I do. I can't hide my shame; it soaks my skin and bleeds through my pores.

He shoves me by my chin against the tiled wall. My back should feel hurt. But I can only feel the crushing pressure in my jaw.

"I want to kill you, Kaitlyn."

Trembling, my plead for mercy comes out in a squeal. "*Please!*"

"But I also don't want to kill you. At least not yet." A blue handle floats in front of me. His thumb presses a silver circle and a blade darts out, stopping an inch from my eye.

A shriek pounds out of my core, scratching my throat like broken glass. It's hard to keep playing his game. It's hard not to fight, but my howl might've killed Peter. If I hit him, push him, run away, he will torture them. Kill them. Not all of us have to endure this torment. Just me.

His palm smashes my mouth, crashing my skull against the hard wall.

"*Mmm! Mmm!*" My head thrusts side to side, desperate to escape his grasp. My spirit knows this might cost Peter and our families their lives, but the animal in me needs a source of clean air and freedom from the pain accentuated by the venom.

Breathe out the pain, Kaitlyn.

"*Mmmm . . .*"

"Sh-Sh-Shhhh. I'm cutting your face." The dagger's tip drifts closer to my eye. My lids clench together, my ribs tightening as shallow breaths lock my chest.

"And you're keeping my secrets. If you tell anyone anything, I'll kill you. Peter will die—nice and slow, screaming in agony as I wring every drop of blood out of his body. I run all of Security; the walls talk to me. How long have those whores been missing? How long has Peter been searching for them? If they were never found, what makes you think you stand a chance when I decide you're next? If you spill my secrets, I'll spill your blood."

Shivers take control as the cool blade runs against my cheek; attempts at deep breaths turn to gasps.

"Got it?"

I didn't want to beg, didn't want to feel like a dog tethered to a tree with a one-foot chain while his owner kills him one blow at a time, but I hear a whimper and realize the tremors came from my throat. Damien has broken me. He's won.

"Where is your God?"

The words stab my heart as the steel strikes my cheek, and I don't know which hurts more. Blood drizzles down my skin as it rips open over and over. My soul pours out its tears; God's abandonment is the greatest despair. Of this experience. Of my life.

My body shakes, not from the sting of the blade, but with the ache of God's desertion. That I'm not worthy of rescuing.

"God doesn't love you."

"*Mmm!*" *Lie!* I yelp against the palm muffling my voice.

Vibrations of screams blast through my head, neck, and torso. His hand mutes my cries as the knife digs into my cheekbone and slices in a new direction. The blade slashes my gums and scrapes my teeth. I swallow my blood, rancid and metallic, and push it through my lips.

When my eyes aren't gritted shut, I blink away tears and stare at the door, waiting for Peter. God isn't rescuing me, and that hurts badly enough. Where is Peter? Will he come through for me? Does he find me worth saving?

God, why have You deserted me?

Crying, my body braces itself for the next blow, when it starts shaking with the fear of a different threat: Why is Damien laughing?

My lids part, and I force my eyes away from the door—away from my hope of Peter's arrival—and onto the monster who's killing me.

"I wonder what Peter will think of my artwork. How much do you think he loves you, Kaitlyn? Do you think he'll still find you beautiful?"

He steps aside with a malevolent grin.

My reflection gazes back.

Sobs crack my throat; tears come forth as I whimper toward the mirror, blood pasting my feet to the floor. I don't notice my naked body, adorned in the cross of the God Who's silent. I don't notice my yellow tresses patched with crimson. I only notice the blood covering my face. I grab the towel off the rack and soak my blood with it. Leaning close to the mirror, I press the fabric against my wound, peel off the stick as it reopens my cuts. The blood rushes back, but I have enough time to recognize the pattern: Damien carved a crucifix in my cheek. My beauty is gone forever. I can no longer be strong; the beast smiling in the mirror has destroyed me in body, mind, and spirit. Cries are the only words I have, and they lower me to the sink. I pat myself with water. Wash the warmth of my blood down the drain with my beauty.

He asked if Peter will find me beautiful. Does this mean he's alive? Does this mean I'll live, too?

Sorrow sends me to my knees. My jaw clocks against the counter as I fall. I collapse on my side as my teeth come out of my tongue; the familiar taste of my blood squirts out of the pits they created. I hug my knees against my chest and wail.

"*Peter! Peter! Where are y–*" Screaming agony halts my words. My hands run over my scalp and clench into fists, ripping out patches of hair as they come toward my face.

"I can do that for you." Damien, still naked, lifts me by my hair. Brings me to my knees and turns me toward the camera mounted in a corner just below the ceiling.

I love You, Papa. I trust You.

"Tell Peter God's abandoned you. Beg him to save you. Beg him to bring me to God's justice."

Is Peter on the other end of the camera? Does he see me naked, bruised, and covered in blood? My head bows against my taut hair. Remembering that, like my Savior, he loves me for my heart and not my body, I find the will to look at him again.

"Peter . . . I don't know . . . why . . . God's . . . allowing this."

The grip on my scalp tightens; Damien grunts with pleasure as I wince.

My next words race out, robbing him of a chance to stop them. "But I'll never stop trusting Him! Love Jesus! Don't lose yoursel–"

A hard rock cracks my skull, but I don't fall to the ground. The boulder hits me again. Again. Damien holds me in place by my scalp, forcing me to stay on my knees as each strike smashes my body like putty.

My mouth opens for a scream, but I'm stunned into deeper silence with each blow as I surrender to the flashes of black lightning they create.

Shoulders tensed to absorb the impact, they snap when I collide against the floor. My cheek sticks to the ground with warm fluid: My cross is bleeding.

"I doubt your fiancé will see our show, but you're paying for ruining my script." His foot plows my stomach, knocking out my breath.

Bruising bangs through my skull as he pounds my head into the floor.

"There is nothing I won't do to protect my secrets. Understand?"

Eyes clenched, unsure how I'm conscious, my face slides over the smooth surface, slippery with blood and tears.

"When I'm done, what are you going to do?"

I swallow hard; my tongue smacks against the roof of my mouth, finding more blood to spit out.

"Jesus, I praise You."

Damien's voice turns to a demonic growl. "*What are you going to do?*"

A terrified whisper escapes me: "Keep your secrets."

He yanks me by my hair into a sitting position, blood cooling and sticking to my legs.

"For how long?"

"Forever."

"Or?"

"You'll kill me."

"And who else?"

"*Peter!*" I scream his name as more tears fall, mixing with warm blood flowing down my cheek.

He backhands me to my flank. When I open my eyes, I watch the door, my engagement stone fading in my peripheral.

Peter . . .

Chapter Thirty-Five

Peter
Thursday, February 10, 2050
9:30 P.M.

I'm working a confidential case on the West Coast, but SIX WEEKS! I can't wait to marry you, Mr. Tryndale. I'll call you when I get back. We have a few more details to discuss. I love you! P.S. Pirates win!

She sent me this message the night before last, and I keep re-reading it in my excitement. Still concerned about her safety, I've been checking on her, and I won't stop until she's in my arms again. The System confirms she's west, and that's good: She's three-thousand miles away from Damien, and he has time to cool off.

With a smile of contentment, I switch off my SimLink mounted on the dash.

Thank You, God, for joining Kaitlyn and me in marriage soon. Mold me into the best husband I can be for her, Lord. Waiting wasn't easy, but I'm glad we obeyed You. The fact that we waited this long while keeping ourselves pure proves I do love her with my entire being and our love is holy. Thank You for making her beautiful and perfect for me. Help me protect and provide for her.

Driving home from work in the darkness, I daydream about our honeymoon. Relaxing on a sandy beach, sipping fruity drinks as gentle breezes billow through our hair and clothes. Her smile radiating in the daylight. Her soft skin warming against mine in the sun. Spending evenings in our hotel room, sitting in a hot tub, laughing and kissing, maybe drinking champagne. Sleeping next to each other . . .

Six more weeks, Peter.

Purple, holographic borders pop out of my SimLink, distracting me from the road, but the screen is blank. As I lean over to shut it off, Kaitlyn's screams seize me.

"*Mmm! Peter!*"

"*Kaitlyn!*" I shout as I check the System.

"*Peter! Peter!*"

"Are you okay?"

Her SimLink is at her house. She's back.

"*Where are y–*" Kaitlyn's screams turn to piercing wails.

Spinning my truck into oncoming traffic, I narrowly avoid a collision as I scramble toward the freeway. My foot jams the pedal, my surroundings blurring into nothingness. "*I'm coming, Kaitlyn! Talk to me! What's happening?*"

"*Peter!*"

The screen shuts off.

I call Kaitlyn. No answer.

Speeding toward her home, I call again. No answer.

Lord, keep her safe!

My SimLink's history shows no calls; how did her voice come through?

The perp.

He has her. He's hurting her. Like he manipulated technology to delete his victims' profiles and hide their trails, he twisted it to send me the audio.

I race up her driveway, skidding to a stop in front of her tiny house.

Kaitlyn's car is the only vehicle here, but that doesn't mean she's alone. I have to clear the perimeter before going near the door.

Jumping out of my truck, I pull my flashlight out of my belt and my firearm from its holster.

I run around her house, shining light on the trees and lawn, around every obstacle. I hate this part. I'm a sitting duck with no backup. If someone is waiting, the best safety I can hope for is that my flashlight blinds them before I take one to the chest.

It's clear.

Scurrying up her porch, I stash my flashlight and knock. No one answers. I press my thumb against the reader beside her door. Its scanner crosses over my print, but the bolt doesn't unlock like it should. My other thumb gets the same result.

Do I knock on her door as her fiancé or kick it down like a cop?

Holding my gun with both hands, arms extended at a forty-five degree angle, I kick the door.

"*Police! Open this door now!*" I roar louder than I ever have because I know who I'm dealing with.

It doesn't move.

"Kaitlyn, it's me! I know you're in danger. Let me in or you'll need a new door!"

My heel plows into the door, landing next to the knob. Lowers and lifts for another strike, but the bolt clunks just before impact.

Kaitlyn opens the entrance, but I don't let down my guard. If the perp's here, he might've threatened her into lying about his presence.

"Stay there!" My shouts tremor through her home as I direct her to the corner, keeping my gun ready.

I clear her front closet. Pass the empty living room and check the back door. Hurry to her bathroom. Check behind the door and around the shower curtain. Open the closet. Vacant. Open her laundry doors. Hustle to her bedroom. Peek around the bed and slide apart the closet doors. Nobody's here.

Replacing my firearm to its holster, I catch my breath. The sudden calmness hurts my chest, my heart reeling with adrenaline.

The front door is locked when I return, and Kaitlyn is still in the corner—coiled back, only the right side of her face visible. There's no shine in her crestfallen eye as tears stream down her cheek. Her brow yields with shame, a faint bruise covering her bottom lid.

"What happened? Are you okay?"

Making an extreme effort to keep her left side hidden, she won't look at me.

"I'm sorry I scared you, Kaitlyn. I got a call—or something—from you. You were screaming for me, asking where I was. I need answers." I suspect the perp took her, but I can't say the words. I keep hoping there's another explanation. A safer one.

I approach her with an outstretched hand, her anxiety growing as I near. I keep moving toward her, pulled to her like a magnet.

My eyes stay fixed on her, but she stares at the floor.

"Were you attacked?"

She flinches as I reach for her. My brows come together, my jaw setting in the birth pains of rage as I wrap my fingers around her chin, drawing her face toward mine. "What—"

The words stop in my throat. A giant, bloody cross atrophies her left cheek. The blood is dried and her face is clean. The attack wasn't live; it was a recording. My gut sinks as heat rises inside of me. The perp tortured her. I want to rip him apart, but I fight to conceal my wrath. She needs me to be strong.

There's another faded bruise on her neck. Kaitlyn winces as I run my fingers beneath her collar. Grinding my teeth, I slip the shirt down her shoulder—something I would never do before marriage, but the situation is desperate.

Fingertip bruises dapple the meeting of her arm and chest. I replace the fabric and pull down the other side to find similar contusions. Squatting, I grab the bottom of her shirt and bring my eyes to hers, my compassion masking the anger within. "May I?"

She nods, her tears falling faster.

Raising her top, I find purple marks covering her abdomen and disappearing beneath her pants.

I stand and lower her shirt, tilting my gaze toward hers. I rub my fingertips over her tears, tracing the wounds on her cheek as if they're made of glass. She trembles at the feel of my skin on hers, and I struggle to stay calm.

"Are you hurt all over?" I whisper.

Her head quivers, the movement slight.

"When?"

She rushes into my chest, her tears coming faster and soaking my uniform. I wrap my arms around her and kiss the top of her head.

"I'll do anything to protect you. Tell me what happened."

I remember the night I proposed, when I said we had all the time in the world. She warned me that we might not live our dream.

Locked in my embrace, she lifts her eyes to mine and places a finger on my lips. She's shivering with terror; whatever happened is still breaking her.

A rock goes down my throat. It's hard not to demand answers, but Kaitlyn warned me to stay silent.

She leaves my arms and exits the kitchen. Her gait has changed, like every motion causes pain. It's not quite a limp . . . The discomfort is in her center.

We enter her living room and sit on her couch, the white leather giving way beneath our weight.

"Talk to me."

Dazed, eyes fixed on the floor, she shakes her head.

"Kaitlyn."

She ignores me.

"Kaitlyn," I command, my voice firming. Knowing she's frightened by touch, I curb every instinct to stroke her arm. Hold her hand. Hug her.

I've worked with enough victims to know many find it easier to write rather than talk about an attack. I spot a notepad and pens on the end table and grab them.

WHAT HAPPENED? I hand the notepad and a pen to Kaitlyn.

She reads my note, blinks away fresh droplets, and writes her words below mine. *You'll die if you find out, Peter. Let it go.*

I press my pen against the paper. I'M A COP; I CAN PROTECT US. I LOVE YOU NO MATTER WHAT. TELL ME.

I hand it back to her. She skims my words and adds her own:

Everyone I love is in danger, just by knowing me! I couldn't call you because he hears everything; I can't do anything out of the ordinary. The perp found me. He said the walls talk to him. I've hidden every camera, but he can access microphones, too. He might be listening now. Damien Harris.

WHEN?

Tuesday.

WHILE YOU WERE ON THE WEST COAST?

I never left Imperia.

BUT EVERY TIME I CHECKED, THE SYSTEM SHOWED YOU ON THE WEST COAST. I SAW YOU. YOU EVEN SENT ME A MESSAGE ABOUT WORKING A SPECIAL CASE AND SAID YOU'D CALL WHEN YOU RETURNED.

The System can lie.

It's the only explanation. I knew he had power, hacking my SimLink with his location and deleting his victims and assigning them to me. But what kind of resources does this man possess if he displayed illusions of himself and Kaitlyn to provide alibis?

I reflect on how many times I walked past Damien before he talked to Kaitlyn. Yet, as hard as I tried to warn him to keep his distance, I couldn't find him. Since the birth of New America, every Head of Security's residence has been shrouded in secrecy for safety measures, and Damien's office is off the map; it's rumored to be underground, but there was no way I could access it. If only I had found him, Kaitlyn wouldn't have been beaten while crying and screaming for me to save her.

Damien sent that recording because he wants me to suffer. My worst nightmare has become reality: The perp hurt Kaitlyn to punish me. Will he take her again? Will he find me next? What about our families?

I keep asking questions, hoping she knows enough to end this before we die. HOW DO YOU KNOW HE'S THE PERP? I THOUGHT THE GUY WASN'T IN THE SYSTEM? WE CHECKED DAMIEN HARRIS MORE THAN ONCE.

He has some way of hiding himself. He showed me a box full of evidence: Handcuffs. Blades. Ropes. Hoods. Pictures of the missing women. They're dead. Their faces were slashed off, like in your dream. He keeps their jewelry and locks of their hair.

WHY'D HE LET YOU GO?

He knows we're Christians, and he told me he saw you searching for him; maybe he wants you to see me like this. But he'll kill me soon.

The pen stills as she wipes tears into her shoulders.

I swallow, the lump of fear bruising my throat. For the first time since I started hunting this monster, I'm terrified. I have to save her. Protecting her is the noblest duty God has given me. While Damien changed his methods with Kaitlyn because of me, his desire to end her life has to be as heavy as it was with his previous victims. He won't get his hands on her again.

He said we have to make a choice: Try bringing him down, and he kills us, our parents, and Vonnie. Or I could do what he *wanted, we stay quiet and stop pursuing him, and he wouldn't kill everyone. I did what he wanted.*

She pauses in thought, as if she's asking God how to write her next message.

Peter, you've said you can never live without me. You have to. This world needs you; that's why I've done what I can to save you. God is telling me that I'm leaving you, Vonnie, and my parents soon.

You are the person He told me about — the one I love and will save by working in Security. How else would we have met? How else would you have found out Damien's the perp if he hadn't taken and released me? But I could never regret saving you—no matter what it costs me.

Imagining life without her, my heart breaks and my eyes swell with tears.

I am the woman in the red coat. I'm sorry I trivialized the seriousness of your dream. I'm leaving this world soon. I'm scared, but God is giving me comfort and hope. Remember my body is a seed; it was never meant to last forever. Please, promise me you'll find happiness again after I'm gone. Give my sacrifice meaning.

Sacrifice. The torturous tattoo on her cheek, bruises covering her body, agony in her expression, tenderness in her center. Her ominous statement: *I did what he wanted.*

DID HE RAPE YOU?

She reads my note, numbness taking over before she nods a few weak jerks. A calm river of tears streams down her cheek, catching on ridges of her crucifix welt.

I didn't want to betray you. I wanted to fight, but I had to consent or he would've tortured you to death. I won't allow anyone to hurt you, Peter. She drops the pen and shields her face.

Rubbing her shoulder, I imagine what he forced on her while simultaneously blocking it out. I write the only words I can: IT'S NOT YOUR FAULT, AND YOU DIDN'T BETRAY ME. I'M SORRY I DIDN'T SAVE YOU.

I pull her close, kissing her soft hair as the notepad and pens crash to the floor. She feels different in my arms. The attack is changing her, molding her into someone new. She isn't the same Kaitlyn, but nothing can end my love for her; I'll always love her. I'll always find her beautiful. We'll get through this together.

Moisture wells in my eyes, but I hide my weakness. I want to be strong for her.

As I hold her, unable to take away her torment, I absorb a painful truth: No matter how good of a cop I am, I will never be able to protect my bride all the time. Bad guys can get through. One just did. But she's wrong about dying. She survived a horrific attack; it's her fear talking. God won't let someone take her from me weeks before our wedding. He'll help me rescue her. I've searched for the missing women for years, forfeited countless meals and days of rest. I obeyed Him in waiting to marry Kaitlyn. I've done my best for God; He won't let my bride die.

Moans vibrate through my torso. Tiny fists pound my chest as she screams in rage, her wails piercing my heart more than my ears. I hold her petite body tighter. Rock her. Kiss her. Soothe her. There's powerlessness knowing it's all I can do. That I wasn't there to save her. That I failed again and my bride paid the price.

"Kaitlyn," I whisper, releasing her and grabbing the pen and paper. LET'S RUN AWAY AND ELOPE. I HAVE TO STAY WITH YOU AND PROTECT YOU.

It's not how I would choose to start our marriage, but my choice was taken. My only option is to marry her and protect her every hour of every day until this ends, or I might lose her. Damien doesn't let his victims live. Time is running out for my bride.

She's blank and motionless, neither agreeing nor arguing.

IF WE MOVE FAR AWAY AND LIE LOW, HE MIGHT LET US GO. IT'S OUR BEST OPTION TO KEEP EVERYONE ALIVE. WE CAN'T TELL OUR FAMILIES ANYTHING YET. KNOWLEDGE MIGHT GET THEM KILLED.

She skims the message and wipes at tears.

How will we lie low with this scar? She points at her cheek in despair.

Scar. I realize for the first time it's permanent.

I'LL PAY A SURGEON OR WE CAN HIDE. YOU CAN WEAR A SCARF OVER IT UNTIL WE'RE SAFE.

We can't move.

?

You could die with me.

STOP. WE'RE NOT DYING. I have to convince her to fight, that quitting isn't an option. If it's true she'll die, why isn't God telling me?

I am, Peter. And when I do, remember what you said about

how Christ warned us persecution would happen so we'd hold onto our faith. How He's always guiding our paths. I want to hold hands with you and Christ in Paradise. Don't let this cost you your eternity. Never lose your faith.

I'M STAYING AT YOUR SIDE UNTIL THIS IS OVER. NO ONE IS KILLING YOU.

Some matters are beyond your control. Besides, God appointed you to be an Exodus; He called you to save the future victims. What about them? I saw names of girls he hasn't harmed yet, like Deidra Hier and Vicki Ulsef. Who will save them if we run?

The choice is simple, though not easy. I'm putting Kaitlyn first. I thought I could fight this war with her, that together with God's help we'd defeat the monster and rescue the girls. But this is where we're at now. I'm saving her. No matter the cost.

YOU'RE MY BRIDE. DAMIEN SAID WE HAVE TO MAKE A CHOICE; I'M MAKING IT. I'M SAVING YOU.

Perhaps I'm negotiating with the devil, but God called me to be Kaitlyn's guardian. I will let go of every mission, every missing woman, every future victim, to keep my bride safe. I can't save her and hunt Damien. Though there were a dozen slain women and herds of people running through the sea, maybe Kaitlyn is the only child of God He intended for me to rescue.

Block out the memory of the coffin sinking into the sea. It's not Kaitlyn's. It's not mine.

PACK YOUR BAGS. WE LEAVE ASAP. YOU'LL REST SOON.

I won't sleep until our first pit stop tomorrow night. I have to keep vigilant watch. My gun is loaded, and I'll shoot anyone who enters.

Kaitlyn rises to pack, crying all the while. I snap out of the shock and help her as I plan our escape. An unbearable urge consumes me: I want to stash my bride somewhere safe while I hunt Damien and hurt him in every way imaginable before killing him. The only thing I want more is to run away with her and keep her safe at my side. Without me, she's in danger: The second I leave her to slay Damien could be the opportunity he takes to end her life.

I'm taking the uniform I'm wearing and the supplies I stored here. Nothing matters but saving Kaitlyn.

God, please help me save my Eve. I can't be the Exodus and her protector anymore. Forget parting the waters if it means the coffin will sink. She's more important. She's the woman You've given me; You've asked me to protect her with my life, and I will die for her. Please grant us safety as we walk through the shadow of death.

Chapter Thirty-Six

Peter
Thursday, February 10, 2050
10:55 P.M.

We're minutes from leaving this life forever. I should be exhausted, but adrenaline gives me the stamina to keep running. I'm used to long hours; I've spent many occasions searching for the perp and his victims, sometimes lasting days without food or rest.

Nearing collapse, Kaitlyn's knees buckle beneath her weight, her head falls heavy, and her eyes fight to stay open. Her lids are puffy from sleeping too little and crying too much. She'll relax while I drive us to safety.

We'll elope on the West Coast, then decide which country we're moving to and bring over our families after we arrive. If we do this fast, say in less than a few days, we might escape Damien's claws unscathed. Once we're in safety, my bride will work through this. I know she can. Will. God is with us. She'll be okay. In time.

I'm staying in uniform until we're out of the country. It adds power to my authority, grants me privileges without questions. It will keep people from asking about the crucifix on her cheek.

Kaitlyn is ready to leave: She has her jacket and shoes on; her purse and backpack are by the door. She's making sandwiches in the kitchen. I'm in her bedroom, the only space she had to store my belongings. I gather my extra clothes, spare uniform, and the additional arsenal I had stowed in her closet in the event I was called to an emergency while visiting her. I lay them on her mattress, thanking myself for listening to God and becoming a cop. I'm one of the few people in the nation who is permitted to have firearms, let alone these many. Since I've worked my last day as an officer, I'm supposed to surrender them. But we'll be out of reach before Security realizes I'm not coming back. When I'm done packing, I'm ripping out the tracker that the Government puts inside every police officer in case we enter distress. I'll ditch it in my truck, where we've already stashed my body camera and our SimLinks. Then we'll cloak our faces and take public transportation to the airport. It'll be a harder trail for them to follow.

Her windows and blinds are shut. Cameras are hidden. We barely speak. Our disappearing act should catch Damien by surprise and give us a head start.

No one will hurt Kaitlyn again. I'll kill anyone who tries. I'll relinquish every female before and after her—I have to—but I'm not giving up my bride. Anyone who wants to harm her has to get through me first.

A thud breaks my focus.

"*Kaitlyn!*" I shout, running toward the sound.

Limbs and hair splayed, she's lying unconscious on the kitchen floor. Gravity grows stronger, pulling me forward as thunderous bangs strike the entrance. I drive myself toward Kaitlyn, focus on her cheek's dark cross and how it contrasts with her white jacket, but my legs stop moving as my hands creep to my head. I will my feet to carry me a few more steps, making it into the hall. My vision blurs and my weight triples as I collapse.

*****

I open my eyes. Slowly. They fall shut. I recall where I am and what happened. They reopen faster. Dart to where Kaitlyn dropped. She's not there.

She's a few feet over, sitting on the floor ahead of me. A familiar person sits behind her, his long arms and legs straddled around her torso, locking her in his grip. His hand swallows the knife pressed against her throat, her soft flesh bowing beneath the blade. Shaggy, tan hair hangs past his shoulders. He's tall, his torso towering over and around Kaitlyn's. I've seen him a few times, and always with Damien. He, too, had a profile and alibis in the System, and he seemed so vile I never forgot his name: Cyrus Tolbert. Is he the second kidnapper who kept the girl from escaping the car?

I'm not sure how long I've been out, but she's been awake for a while. They've been sitting there. Watching. Waiting.

Dizzy and nauseous—struggling to regain my vision, to focus enough to see only one of everything—I'm helpless as Kaitlyn fights with all of her power to pull the blade off her neck, but she's not strong enough. She writhes in pain as she tries crawling out of his arms, but his grasp is iron. Every part of me fights to help her, but I'm weak and heavy. I reach for her, my hand rising an inch before sinking to the carpet, all of my strength waning with the effort. It's as if I'm trapped beneath a concrete building. The fear in her eyes . . . sweat beading on her forehead . . . rapid, irregular grunts . . . I memorize her in a sense of wooziness, the same way I commit a bad dream to memory.

With a smile never leaving his face and eyes never parting from mine, he presses his mouth against Kaitlyn's ear and whispers. She winces, her blond hair matting against his chest. His lips move again; her eyes widen with horror as they lock on mine, as if she's looking at me for the last time.

"No! Don't hurt Peter!"

Still staring at me, his grin grows wider as he yanks the blade across her throat, ending her shriek as her head slumps to the side and red pours down her neck.

"No!"

Horror snapping me out of the drug, my hand lunges for my holster. It's empty. My vision splits in two as the assassin stands, dropping her petite body as she loses her life. Cheek flush against the floor, her eyes latch onto mine, her soul vanishing in front of me as her killer raises the blade to his nose, inhaling the scent of her blood.

His tongue ascends the knife from its base to its tip, his satiated smile growing as he watches me. He's killing me next. With the precious seconds he's buying me, I fight the poison lingering in my system. Break through the hole in my side pocket and grab the pistol banded to my thigh. He catches on and races at me, knife in hand.

I roll on my back, aim the firearm at his head, and pull the trigger. It's heavier than it's ever been, but I keep pressing until it kicks. The jolt pounds my hand and the bang quakes my body as one bullet goes between his eyes. He crashes a foot away, blood flowing.

Running on all fours, I kneel beside Kaitlyn, lifting her out of her blood and cradling her head. "*I love you, Kaitlyn! Don't leave me!*" Shaking her, I see blood has stained her white jacket: She is the woman in the red coat.

"*Kaitlyn! Please! Don't go! I love you!*" I rub her forehead as she gurgles. Blood pours out of her mouth, deepening the color of her jacket and coating my lap. Surrender her to God as I watch her die, powerless to rescue her. My chest is heavy. I can't blink. Can't breathe. Can't think. Tears flow.

"I love you."

Stunned with grief, I cry and hold her. Peering into her eyes, I think I see a sparkle of life. Maybe she sees me and feels love? I hope so. I want love to be her last emotion. Not fear. Not pain. Glimmers of life dim and vanish as the blood streams out of her throat.

She drifts. Her soul trickles over my skin as she ascends to Christ.

My hand is resting on her neck, covered in warm, sticky fluid. Without realizing it, I had tried to slow her bleeding.

I failed.

Agonizing tears spill down my cheeks. If I was stronger, faster, smarter—she might be alive. If I had neutralized Cyrus before he jerked the blade, I might've saved her. If I had discovered sooner that Damien is the perp, she might not have needed saving. Somewhere in my office was the key I needed to determine he was responsible. If I had spent more time with evidence, this wouldn't have happened. She'd be alive. I'd be hugging her warmth instead of cradling her coldness. Maybe I never should've held her. Maybe loving me is what killed her.

Her face, now frozen in death, was alive with emotion minutes ago. The wrong choices I made that cost us her life are fresh; the reality of her death is hard to grasp. If I could turn back time a few seconds, I might have her back. Not be feeling her warmth seep through my hands like sand through a sieve. I wish this is only a nightmare, that I could wake and see her smiling, cuddle her and feel her delicate arms wrap around me, but her blood is cooling on my skin and arguing against my fantasies.

What if we married in secret and again on our wedding day? It would be so . . . clandestine. Her hands clasp together as she pleads with a broad smile that I'll never witness again.

Wiping my hands on my pants, I lift my fingers and close her eyes. Faded trails of blood stain her lids a light shade of pink.

I'm sorry, Kaitlyn.

"Mexico. I'm taking you to Mexico."

I struggle to think through the mental haze I'm trapped in. I fight to bring out the cop in me. Shut off my feelings, or I won't be able to work through this. I have to wash the blood off my hands and begin my next mission. I don't have long until Damien comes for us all.

I glance at the clock. Quarter past midnight.

Cool air rushes through the front door that Cyrus kicked in. I stifle the shiver running down my spine and return Kaitlyn to the pool of blood, her body still draining fluids. Taking off my boots, I travel to the kitchen sink, avoiding the mess on the floor. As I clean the blood off my boots and hands, I stare through the frame of the broken entrance. The dim light pouring out of Kaitlyn's home shines over a canister of anesthetic gas attached to a hose leading into the kitchen. Cyrus must've fed the line through a crack in her door and used it to knock us out.

After tying on my boots, I head to the porch. Drawing my uniform sleeve over my hand to conceal my prints, I grab the empty container and set it on the floor near the entry, where I find the gasmask that Cyrus used to stay conscious until the air was clean. I put it on in case someone else poisons the home. I close the door as best I can, but the lock is ruined so I don't gain much privacy. My missing gun is beside the wrecked door. He must've placed it here after I blacked out. Was he planning on taking it? I clip it to my hip, keeping it close in case another visitor arrives.

I walk toward the living room, Cyrus' blood splattered over the walls and ceiling. I find the fatal bullet that exited Cyrus' skull and ricocheted off Kaitlyn's ceiling. Rub it on my pants and down my pocket. I snatch the notepad with Kaitlyn's details and stash it with the bullet.

On my way to the restroom, I grip my smaller firearm off the floor and fasten it to the strap on my thigh. I pinch the shell casing between my thumb and forefinger and slide it in my pocket. On the bathroom's hard floors, I strip out of my uniform top and shirt. I pull my utility knife out of my pocket, open it, and rip it through my deltoid. Blood drizzles down my limb, dripping onto my clothes that rest on the white floor.

I yank the blade through my flesh until it clicks against metal. The agony of a knife tearing through my body is nothing compared to the torment of watching my bride die and knowing I failed her. My heart is consumed with an aching torture of guilt making me impervious to pain.

Clutching the handle of my knife, I squeeze the tracker out of my wound, clean it in the sink, and set it on the counter. If Cyrus' SimLink reveals where the girls went, I'll know where to discard it. If it doesn't, I'll have to leave my tracker here. If Damien checks, he might be fooled into believing that I've been left for dead at Kaitlyn's. He may grow suspicious if he expects my corpse somewhere else, but I only need to buy enough time to kill him before he discovers I'm alive.

There's gauze under Kaitlyn's sink; I wrap it around the hole in my arm and clean my knife before replacing it in my pocket. I press on the incision and tape the dressing. I scrub the blood off my skin, making sure I leave none behind; I have to remove all evidence that I was here during the murders. Kaitlyn's house is secluded, but surveillance drones might've spotted me or my truck; I'll have to leave my vehicle behind so Damien doesn't figure out I'm alive. It will be difficult to stay clean once the investigation begins. It'll be obvious a third person was present if I'm not back in time to clean the mess, but I'll tackle this the way I deal with every tough situation: One step at a time. Racing will keep my mind focused on what might happen next instead of what is happening now. I'll start with hiding my trail the best I can. As long as I'm alive, I have time to fix my mistakes.

Slipping on medical gloves, I near Cyrus' body—keeping my gaze off the bare blade, every drop of blood licked off. I'll toss it with his remains when I return.

I rub at his chin until a clear residue peels off. Anti-surveillance gel. It's invisible to the naked eye after it dries, but its properties bend and reflect light rays, forcing surveillance to read images in a scrambled pattern. If anyone viewed him through a camera, his face was blurred. Only Government Officials are supposed to have access to this gel, but criminals buy it on the Black Market; it's a way of wearing a mask without standing out in obvious fashion the way thugs in conventional guises do. Some of the toughest offenders for me to find were wearing this gel. I had to chase them the old-fashioned way: Develop MOs and predict their next strike. Be there in time to catch them in the act. I stashed some at my house and here at Kaitlyn's for emergencies, knowing we would need to disappear if the Government discovered our faith. I'll smear some on before I leave, further fooling Damien into believing I'm dead and his assistant is alive.

His rear pockets are empty. I roll him onto his back, his pants coated in Kaitlyn's blood, and search his front.

Smooth metal brushes against my fingers as I pull out a small chain; it's attached to Kaitlyn's cross pendant. I rummage through his pocket again and find her engagement ring. Tears fill my eyes as I recall kneeling in the park and sliding it on her tiny finger. I felt like the luckiest man in the world because she said yes. I join the ring with the cross and clasp the chain around my neck. I'll wear them for the rest of my life.

Next I find a pouch of her golden hair.

I stow it with the shell casing and keep digging. My hand slips into his other pocket and comes out with an empty syringe. Plunger closed, I pull off the cap to find clear liquid trapped in the needle hub. I recap it and stick it in a pocket. Fish around some more and find a piece of paper: *Jesus didn't save them.*

Too upset to consider the weight of its merit, I stuff it in a pocket with one thought: *them.* Damien played the recording through my SimLink so I'd run to Kaitlyn. Once we were together, his assassin struck. We were both meant to die.

Cyrus' SimLink is on him. I bring out its display, expecting that where he and Damien took the girls is in his frequented locations. It's not, but Damien's address is. I pray God saves me from the urge to torture him; I hope He doesn't let it destroy me if I do.

The SimLink glides down my pocket; I may need it later as evidence of the crimes committed. If I pilfer Cyrus' SimLink, I'll need his tracker, too. Damien might find it suspicious if the two are at different coordinates.

I grab my knife and cut into his arm. There's a tracker on him somewhere; Damien wouldn't release his favorite pet without a leash. I rip through his limb and squeeze it out. Leaving my tracker and SimLink here while stowing Cyrus' tracker and SimLink with me will lead Damien to believe that his assistant is the one visiting him, not me—buying myself more time to end Damien before he kills us.

I pace to the bathroom, rinsing Cyrus' tracker in the sink before cramming it in my pocket. I wash my knife and plant it in my pocket, then I ball the gloves down my hands inside out and throw them on the pile of clothes I left on the floor. I clean the room of blood and stash my uniform top, shirt, and gloves in the trash can liner. I take my tracker to Kaitlyn's front closet and ditch it in her vacuum, a place no one will think to search for a locator beacon.

Returning to the bathroom, I collect the bag of clothes and carry them to Kaitlyn's bedroom, dropping them in a sack on her bed. My extra clothes, clean uniform, and arsenal are waiting on her mattress. I pick everything out of my pockets and dump them on Kaitlyn's nightstand. I pull my pistol out of its holster and set it on the bed as I empty my belt of its equipment. I remove my holster and belt, gasmask, pants, and socks, adding them to the sack with my bloody tops and tossing it in the larger pack. I'll burn my clothes, boots, and other evidence later. Rustling through my arsenal, I pull out my anti-surveillance gel and rub it over my face.

I dress in clean civvies, top my head with a cap, line my hands with leather gloves, and load the items on the nightstand back in my pockets. I spot a vase of marbles on Kaitlyn's dresser and pour them into my clean socks. Moving will be uncomfortable, but the stones will disrupt my walking pattern and make it difficult for gait recognition to ID me.

Adding my guns and jar of gel to my weapons stash, I stick my arsenal in my duffle with my spare uniform and the sack of bloody evidence.

Slinging my pack over my shoulder, I re-enter the kitchen, stooping beside Kaitlyn and inspecting her body. Try to see her as a cop and not as her fiancé, but I don't know how well I can separate the two.

A putrid odor reeks from the jagged halo of blood surrounding her upper body and head, matting her yellow hair into a red, sticky mess. The stench threatens to make me retch. But, like every time I've encountered a dead body, I push it behind me. Floors stained crimson, I stare at her bloody jacket. The woman in the red coat. There were twelve women in my dream, the last one wearing the jacket that turned to blood. Kaitlyn is Damien's twelfth—and hopefully final—victim.

My jaw clenches as I memorize her dead, blood-soaked body; the glassy gaze of her lifeless corpse is forever etched in my mind. I struggle to accept that the only woman I ever wanted to hold and make love to has been taken from me, never to return. Never again will she laugh. Never again will her soft skin touch mine. Never again will her blond hair dance in sunlight as she swings in the park. She'll never be my wife. We'll never make love. Our children and grandchildren died with her. How can God give my life meaning again?

Her finger is naked where the band of my vow of eternal love had rested minutes ago. Her neck is bare where her mother's necklace hung before death. It contrasted with the scar on her cheek, a wound that never would've healed, no matter how long she lived. The irony strikes me that the cross on her neck was a reminder to stay pure, to wait for me, and the crucifix on her face was a relic of the man who stole her purity. She died for Jesus and me; now I'm killing Damien so God can send him to hell with the monster who murdered her.

I'm a different man now. The Peter I was, the Peter I liked, died with Kaitlyn.

As I leave her house, I stick her purse and backpack in my duffle in case they contain evidence. My teeth grind when I see the gas canister, wondering how many mistakes I made. Academy trained me not to rush after an unconscious person until I established the cause of the blackout. If it's a gas leak, it'll knock me out, too. Then I'm useless. As soon as I saw Kaitlyn, I should've escaped out her bedroom window and traced the perimeter. I would've taken out Cyrus before he hurt her.

Kaitlyn changed her bolt's key chip and deactivated her contacts from her print reader after the attack. While we were packing, she gave me a key with a new chip and reactivated my prints in the reader, but it's worthless now; her door is too broken to bolt. I close it the best I can and set the lock anyway, shoving my key in my pocket. It's obvious the door might cave in at any moment, but my efforts might deter someone unintelligent. I can't stay here to guard the scene, and there is no one I can trust to watch it for me. Time is running out: I have to kill Damien fast, and walking will slow me down.

He's about to beg me for death. If he's lucky, I'll give it to him.

214

Chapter Thirty-Seven

Peter
Friday, February 11, 2050
8:00 A.M.

Next month I was supposed to vow to have and to hold Kaitlyn forever. Instead, my final promise to her is to guard those she died protecting.

I hate Damien for this. Once he's dead, I'm hiding his body in his car. Drive it to Kaitlyn's and figure out how to clean this mess. If I survive, I will pause and mourn my bride.

I'm considering shooting to immobilize him, not kill. Torture him until he gives up his own life. Avenge my bride, the wife I'll never hold, the life I'll never live. But vengeance isn't mine. Before temptation takes control, I bow my head over the rifle in my hands.

God, please free me from this. Take control of my emotions so I kill with the right motivations. If murdering him turns me into a monster, Damien wins. If I slay him, I have to do it to protect those who live, not to avenge those who died.

You told me I'd be an Exodus. You gave me that dream. I waited so long to see its fruition, and now it's coming true faster than I can handle. Is this what You have destined for me?

Since becoming an officer, I've known I might have to take a life. But never like this. I'm a murderer, Lord. Before this ends, I'll be one twice over. I'm not sure if what I'm doing is right or wrong, but Damien's above the law: No amount of charges will hold him in prison. Executing him is the only way to ensure the safety and well-being of our families, the future women he'll take, and myself. I think I'm doing what's right, but if I'm sinning, Lord, please forgive me. I don't know how to live according to Your Word in this evil world. I waited years to become the Exodus, and now I see I'm not ready.

Damien's death has to be quick. Painless. I won't debase myself to his level; I won't put somebody—even a monster like him—through agonizing pain for my own sadistic purposes. If I kill him, that's all I can do: Kill. I can't torture him. I can't drag out his misery. Can't become like him.

The filth of my gritty mouth sours my taste buds. My heavy eyes burn with every blink. I ignore all of it. Fight to stay with it. Keep my joints strong and my muscles moving; the race is almost over. Then I can collapse.

Gel on my face, marbles in my boots, and gloves on my hands, I walked to Damien's house and searched his residence from the exterior for anyone who might be inside; I could only rely on the darkness to conceal me from his cameras. I fixed microphone stickers, smaller than one centimeter apiece, to the bottom corner of every window. All sound is transmitted to my earbud. His house is quiet, save for the whir of his fridge. Knowing no one was in the residence, I applied window jelly to every pane on the back end of his home. When a bullet pierces a coated window, the clear gel absorbs the impact and keeps the glass from shattering, making the attack silent and leaving only a tiny hole in the pane. My rifle is soundless, designed for stealth missions. This is my first time using it outside of practice, but other cops have used the same firearm model to take out unsuspecting terrorists without attracting attention.

My vision keeps returning to his garage. It's as large as the rest of his house, with four extra-wide doors—two on each side. What's in there?

Squatted in a tree in his backyard, I scan the horizon through my rifle's scope. There's no movement.

I'm fortunate to have made it this far. Kaitlyn said Damien might have the ability to listen through microphones; I was so caught up when I lost her that I spoke when I should've been dead. He could've spied on us through Cyrus' SimLink. Either he couldn't get a visual because he'd deleted us too quickly, or he wasn't eavesdropping. Maybe God is guarding me. Would He protect me as I take lives?

The marbles are bruising my feet and my knees ache from perching on this wooden arm for hours, but I stay still. I'll endure pain and suffer through hunger and fatigue to ensure Damien dies so no one else does.

He's been gone since I arrived. I watched the sunrise, and I'm growing impatient. Did he maim someone? Is he cutting off a woman's face right now? I wish I could try tracking him, but logging into the System would announce I'm alive and accomplish nothing. All I can do is wonder where he is and who he might've taken.

A black car slows in the morning haze as it nears the front of his house and doesn't reappear on the other side. My earbud relays the hum of a garage door opening.

Damien's home.

My mind races. Did he drive Kaitlyn somewhere when he assaulted her? Was she in that car? How many victims have been inside it?

Eye to my scope, I keep him in my crosshairs as he enters his den from the garage. He's not looking where he's going as he shuts off his SimLink, shoving it in his pocket with a chuckle. Seeing him for the first time since he assaulted Kaitlyn, I'm overwhelmed by the intensity of my hatred. I hate him for being happy. I hate him for what he did with those hands.

Vengeance isn't mine. This is for our families, the future victims, and me.

The trigger is smooth against my glove and pulling it has never been so effortless.

My shoulder absorbs the kick as the bullet shoots through the window and Damien falls on his hardwood floor, blood pouring from the hole in his head.

It's done.

I close my eyes to compose myself. Slaughtering him didn't feel good like I was hoping—or worried—it might. The part of me that misses Kaitlyn wishes I'd made him feel pain first, but the part of me that remembers God is glad I didn't get lost in selfish desires, becoming wicked myself in the process. Today I learned how contagious evil is, and God's power was my only immunity.

Damien's game is over. The ladies of Imperia are safe. Now I have to clean a disaster spanning two houses while hiding from the System that might have an elimination order on me.

Before I can pray about my next step, a woman with red curls emerges from around a corner. She's short. A dark skirt and shirt hugs her athletic frame. I've talked to her before. So has Kaitlyn.

Zaranda.

With her training, she knew how to elude my search of the premises. She also knew how to evade the cameras inside.

I keep my eye on the scope as she studies Damien's corpse with a curious expression, then searches through the window and up the tree for his killer.

For a split second, I wonder if she's on Damien's team. But if she was, then why was she hiding when I searched the place? She was avoiding him, not me.

Is she here to avenge Kaitlyn? It's only been hours since she died. Could Zaranda know?

I lower my weapon as she runs to the side of the house and out the back door, trotting across the yard in high heels, shockingly well-balanced. Kaitlyn was skeptical of Zaranda. Given that she's dead, I doubt her myself.

"Peter!"

My fingers tighten around the gun, readying to aim it at her, but it never leaves my lap. Something tells me she isn't a threat.

"I'm not surprised to see you here."

Unsure if she's friend or foe, I stare down on her.

She cranes her neck, peering up at me. "Were you there?"

Caustic saliva smacks my tongue as it parts from the roof of my mouth. "Where?"

"I know she's dead, Peter. That's why I'm here."

I remain silent, my jaw locked with grief and hesitation.

"Both of you were removed from the System, but I restored you. You can trust me."

Zaranda waits for a response that I don't give.

"She was my best friend. She hadn't been at work and she wasn't returning my calls, which isn't like her. I didn't want to invade her privacy, but I knew something was wrong. So I searched the System and couldn't find her."

Echoing my thoughts, she adds: "He deleted her. He deleted many women."

I strap my rifle to my back, sling the duffel over my shoulder, and shimmy down the tree, the impact stinging my tired ankles as I hit the ground. Approaching her, I stop two feet away. "If you know so much, why'd you wait till she was dead to stop him?" My expression is malicious, though I'm angrier with Damien and Cyrus than with her. The bitterness of my bride's murder is hardening my heart.

"Me? What about you?"

"The only person I trust is dead, and you're at her killer's house. You're answering *my* questions." I tower over her, my fury forcing her to back down. "Why'd you get chummy with Kaitlyn in the middle of the night? You've never been friendly to anyone. You hate Christians, just like Damien. You're high up in Security. How do I know you aren't his inside girl? He'd find a female asset convenient."

I note her fist resting at her hip, bracing for an uppercut. It softens as nostalgia sweeps over her.

"She was nice to me."

Kaitlyn beams in my mind. It calcifies my anger, drowning me in despair.

"No one's been nice unless they wanted something, but she was genuine. Special. She loved me more than anyone has. As we became friends, I came to love her, too. I learned the truth: She loved people because she believed God's love lived inside of her. Her faith was the source of her kindness, and that's why I never reported her or you for being Christians. I'm here to help."

She lifts her SimLink, brings out the holographic screens, and logs into the System. It reports that my tracker and SimLink are at Kaitlyn's, but because my face and gait pattern are disguised, a search for me comes up blank—the result that's displayed when surveillance can't see someone. I'm not listed as wanted as I expected. There's no elimination order, even under Zaranda's high-ranking login. I'm not deleted, either. If what she said is true, then she did restore my profile.

"Do I have your attention?"

My head rises and falls.

"I didn't know what Damien was doing until Kaitlyn died. When I couldn't find her in the System, I went to her house and saw the container of gas and her and Cyrus. I knew he was Damien's assistant, so I broke in here and found evidence. I was waiting to kill him."

She had time I didn't: With her freedom to drive, she could journey to Kaitlyn's, do a mini-investigation, travel to Damien's, search around his residence, and find a secure hiding place. Meanwhile, I had to walk—otherwise my vehicle could've tripped an alarm in the System or somebody on public transit might've recognized me.

"Damien decomposed the girls with lye in a pit on top-secret Government land. He has a box of jewelry, photographs, weapons, and reports. And one recording." She blinks away tears, her voice giving out on the last word.

"I can offer you protection, but you have to be honest with me. Were you there?"

I nod.

"Did Cyrus slit her throat?"

I press my tongue to the roof of my mouth to keep the tears at bay. My lips tighten to stop the trembling.

"Where's the blade?"

"I left it beside him."

She tilts her head with a furrowed brow. "But it was spotless."

My neck tenses, keeping my voice from cracking as my words come out in a whisper. "I know."

Her mouth hangs open, as if she's adding up the facts but having a hard time accepting the conclusion.

"He licked it off."

"You watched him?"

Weak with grief, every breath threatens to tip me over. My head feels like a rock balancing on a blade of grass as the weight of my equipment leans me to the side. "The gas paralyzed me. There was nothing I could do. I barely saved myself."

She balls her fist again. Tighter, this time. And it's not me she wants to strike. She swallows hard and her poise softens. "So you killed him?"

I bow my head.

"Why are your tracker and SimLink showing up at Kaitlyn's?"

"I cut it out and left them there to fool Damien."

Zaranda's lips twist into a knowing pucker. "That's what I thought. When I searched for Cyrus, the System revealed his tracker and SimLink with someone else, but I couldn't see his face because he was wearing gel. After recovering you in the System and seeing your tracker and SimLink were at Kaitlyn's, I figured you were there. That you killed Cyrus and switched your devices with his to buy yourself time to hide. I was going to find you after killing Damien. I didn't think you were going to come for him yourself." She turns to my feet. "Gait recognition couldn't ID you. What's in your boots?"

Ignoring her question, I gesture toward the other end of the home. "What's in the warehouse?"

"Lots of cars." Her eyes shift to the garage, her gaze narrowing in the early morning light. "I'm stripping Damien's ownership and re-entering them as unregistered vehicles. My lab techs will test them for evidence and destroy them."

I fish the syringe out of my pocket and hand it to her. "Could your lab people find out what was in this? It was on Cyrus. I think he injected me with something to keep me out longer than Kaitlyn."

Puzzled, she gapes at the needle in her palm, one eye squinting between her red curls before she lifts her focus to mine. "Why would he care?"

"It's a long story."

"You're in luck. We'll have lots of time once things are sorted." She presses the syringe between her fingers and SimLink. "I'll give you the results. Don't worry about anything. I'll keep you clean in this."

"How will I explain things to my commanders? What if one of them checked on me and saw the error message? Saw Kaitlyn's error message?"

"You both were working undercover assignments for me. No questions permitted."

With the guarantee of protection, my rifle and sacks fall with my burdens. My face slopes heavenward with the relief of safety and the dread of processing my pain.

"C'mon. I'll give you a lift to Kaitlyn's."

Chapter Thirty-Eight

Peter
Friday, February 11, 2050
9:49 A.M.

I failed, Lord. I failed You. Kaitlyn. Her family. Myself. You entrusted Your daughter to my protection, and I didn't save her. She must've had more purposes to fulfill on Earth, but her killers are dead. They'll never touch another person. Perhaps You didn't want me to murder anyone this way, but I have. I'll be a killer forever. I've failed in so many ways, Lord. I'm sorry.

Did Kaitlyn or I make a mistake? There's no way You could've intended for someone to kill her six weeks before our wedding. My existence feels wrong without her.

Zaranda's face is as hard as mine as she drives me to Kaitlyn's, my gear resting on the floorboard. My body is growing heavier with the weight of grief; it's flashing over me like a tidal wave, and I won't escape. I've done all I can. My only recourse is prayer.

You can trust me now.

I'm not sure if God will ignore me after I've taken two lives—one in self-defense and one premeditated, though necessary—but I have to talk to Him. The invincibility that the pain of Kaitlyn's death afforded me is wearing off; the limitations of my broken-hearted humanity are torturing my soul. I'm unsure how to be a God-fearing man in a world that hates the Lord; I doubt my ability to uphold God's values as an officer serving a nation that kills anyone who believes in Him. I stand to protect life, and I've assassinated the two men who stole my bride. With her murder, there is no one to trust in me or for me to trust in. If my heart can sense God's faith in me return, there's a chance I'll believe in myself again.

Trees and dead leaves come and go as we drift through the city; I watch girls taking their morning constitutionals and wonder if they're Christians. They'll never know my bride died for them, that I killed two people to keep them safe. Men stroll down the sidewalk, and I almost smile at the thought that other males around the world won't lose their wives, daughters, or sisters who travel here. That they won't experience me calling them, explaining their loved ones will never come home. A couple is holding hands, laughing together. A pang of resentment sucks at the crater in my heart.

Kaitlyn's house comes into sight, and I want to deny the reality that she'll be dead when I arrive. We pull up the driveway, and I remember every time I drove along it. The dates when I picked her up. The days I visited for wedding planning. The evenings I dropped by for dinner. Last night, when I raced here to save her.

Undercover Security vehicles line the perimeter. Zaranda parks on the edge of the driveway, tree limbs hugging my door. I open the car, stagger out, and close it. Stepping toward the home, a branch trips me and I don't resist the fall. Collapsed on the cold earth, tears gush out of me. I part the trees like a curtain to the last show I ever wanted to watch: The end of my bride. The end of my life.

Two lengthy black vans are parked next to my truck. Kaitlyn's house is a beehive. Security Officials hustle in and out and hover around the perimeter, their voices buzzing with exchanges of information. Two stretchers hauling body bags barge through the busted door and roll toward the vehicles. The shorter one is my bride. I see the outline of her body: her toes pointing upward, the bulge of her trunk, the slope as it descends her face. She's thrust into a van and cloaked behind shut doors.

I'm twenty-six years old and my Eve is gone.

My Kaitlyn was stolen from me. Now she's in Paradise. I weep as I wonder if God will allow me to join her. Stuffing my mouth in the crook of my elbow, I scream as tears saturate my face. I want nothing and no one but my Kaitlyn. She was my gravity. Without her, nothing holds me to this world. I have no reason to live.

Sometimes dreams don't come true.

-TO BE CONTINUED-

To see how God brings beauty out of the tragedy, read <u>Behind Heaven's Veil, Part II: Valiant.</u> Coming soon!

Want to know more about the victims?

www.BehindHeavensVeil.wordpress.com

has free bonus chapters not found in this novel!

The best gift you can give me is an honest review! Please leave your feedback on Amazon or Facebook. Thank you so much!

About the Author:

I have been fascinated with the battle between good and evil since I was in preschool. Saved by a police officer when I was twenty, I went on to graduate from the Alaska State Troopers Citizens Academy, and I have worked with dozens of police officers in two states. Many of these encounters have inspired my writings. (Names and details were changed to protect others.) I hope to encourage others to seek Jesus, the only Person who has captivated me more than the men and women who don the uniform. I live in Alaska with my husband and our two young daughters.

Made in the USA
San Bernardino, CA
25 January 2018